DESTROYING ANGELS

Book 5 of the Harry Stubbs Adventures

by David Hambling

"I turned as soon as I heard the rapid footsteps behind me. Maybe it was just someone hurrying to catch a bus, but the fact this was the first completely uninhabited spot I had passed was probably significant.

Wary, I moved sideways to take a look on the other side of the nearest pillar.

He was a big man, dressed in dark clothing, face covered by a balaclava helmet, hands encased in black leather gloves.

A pulse of terror washed over me like a bucket of icy water. The black outfit and concealed face, even the gloves, meant that no inch of skin was visible. If I had not been thinking of things that looked human but were not, hybrid things, it would not have occurred to me, but I wondered just what I was facing.

Maybe he, or it, just wanted to talk to me. This was not an orthodox way to go about it, but secrecy was second nature to some.

"May I help you?" I asked. "Did you want a word?"

He said nothing, but stepped towards me in the crouched pose of a fighter ready to move in any direction.

Only fools willingly fight an unknown opponent. I would have turned and run, but that seemed risky.

He came forward at speed and threw a strong right at my jaw. I had been watching closely and, anticipating the movement as it was made, was able to dodge left and backwards.

"That's enough of that" I said. "If you have a grievance, speak your piece and I'll listen. Come at me one more time and I'll show you some real boxing."

For RAH — another Harry Stubbs story, as requested

Once out of nature I will not take
My form from any natural thing
But such a form as Grecian goldsmiths make
Of hammered gold and gold enamelling

W. B. Yeats, "Sailing to Byzantium"

Those with Celtic legendry in their heritage—mainly the Scotch-Irish element of New Hampshire, and their kindred who had settled in Vermont on Governor Wentworth's colonial grants—linked them vaguely with the malign fairies and "little people" of the bogs and raths....The Pennacook myths, which were the most consistent and picturesque, taught that the Winged Ones came from the Great Bear in the sky, and had mines in our earthly hills whence they took a kind of stone ... They harmed only those earth-people who got too near them or spied upon them.

H. P. Lovecraft, 'The Whisperer In Darkness"

London, 1928

Chapter 1: Angel of Eternity

Mrs Bridges had been born before the Victorian era, and had survived into modern times. Her contemporaries had been laid to rest long ago. She was far from unscathed; you could see the relentless erosive effect of the years. Her skin was thin and papery, veins showed through at her thin wrists like blue cables. An old-fashioned mob cap covered her hair, but the faint wisps that escaped suggested it had thinned to almost nothing.

As if to make up for her bodily deficiency, everything else about Mrs Bridges was lavish: her black dress, her shoes, the rings and bracelet of black stones, and the cameo at her neck—the only splash of white against the unrelieved ebony. Bailey, who was overseeing the meeting, remained discreetly to one side.

She peered at me so long through a lorgnette that I wondered if she was quite all there. She had been widowed some fifty years previously, never remarried and still wore black. What kind of shock had she been through?

I became uncomfortably aware of my surroundings. The small sitting room must have been her private room as there was only seating for two or three other people. The mantlepiece was crowded with pictures large and small in silver frames. I had no chance to peruse them, but they looked very much like family photographs: men in uniforms, girls at their coming out, wedding pictures, christening photographs. The Bridges family seemed to be legion.

"You're an ugly brute and no mistake," she said, at length and laughed a dry little laugh. At that laugh she became more human and for a moment I could see the woman inside the wizened exterior. "Don't be shocked. I'm in my second childhood now, so I can say what I like. Wouldn't you say he was an ugly brute, Bailey?"

Bailey was a placid, well-fed individual in his middle forties, rather formal in a wing collar. I knew his type from my days in the legal firm. In his official capacity he would be correct in every way, slow and fussy but attentive to legal niceties. And beneath that ponderous polite manner there lurked a keen intelligence. Nothing of financial significance ever gets past men like Bailey.

Mrs Bridges was being honest, giving voice to what many people must have thought when meeting me, but were too diplomatic to say it. Bailey nodded as though agreeing and looked me in the eye.

"I would rather say, madam, that Mr Stubbs' appearance is complementary to his occupation. Entirely consonant with it, in fact."

"Many a heart of gold beats beneath a rough exterior," I said. "Or so I've heard."

"Very good!" said Mrs Bridges, clapping her hands. "Bailey, have you ever seen such broad shoulders?"

"Not in the City, no," he said. "On the rugby pitch, perhaps."

He was being indulgent towards his mistress. Biding his time, and charging it in fifteen-minute increments.

"How wonderful it must be to be able to stride down the street like a battleship in full steam, forcing all the lesser vessels aside," she enthused, moving her shoulders slightly for effect.

I hesitated to correct her. Crowded streets are awkward. Smaller, nippier individuals swerve around and find gaps, whereas I sometimes get forced into the road to get past stalls and knots of loiterers.

"There are undeniable advantages, ma'am," I said.

"Bailey says you're a boxer. I bet you could knock down anyone who disagrees with you. I'd knock Bailey down all the time if I had your fists. He's such a fearful nag."

"Mrs Bridges will have her jokes," said Bailey.

There was the slightest hint of strain behind his bland smile. Mrs Bridges knew exactly how to get under his skin.

"I would knock you down too though," she told him, then to me. "Bailey is supposed to be my man of business, but he really wants to run my business for himself. Do you know how much he pays himself out of my money?"

"Mr Stubbs doesn't want to know that."

I decided that diplomacy would be best. Getting on the wrong side of Bailey would mean being shown to the door in short order.

"Of course not, Mr Bailey," I said. "In fact, it's good of you to be here at all, given that this is not strictly a matter of business."

"Oh, Bailey always wants to know what I'm up to. Always has to make sure I'm not being swindled. You see, practically the only visitors I get these days are people who want to swindle me."

"Mrs Bridges exaggerates," said Bailey. "But sadly, I am obliged to act as a gatekeeper to prevent Mrs Bridges' good nature being exposed to questionable requests for funds under a variety of pretences."

"Of course there are my family," she said. "I've hundreds of relatives now—I have great, great grandchildren if you please. How many of them, Bailey?"

"Seventeen great-great grandchildren, madam."

"They mean nothing to me. Bailey keeps track of their birthdays. My four dear children are all long dead." She glanced at the mantelpiece, seeking out the precious ones in the crowd. "When my descendants visit, it is as though they are coming to see an ancient monument. They seem surprised I can still speak."

"They revere you," said Bailey.

"Pfft, you say that, but they're just waiting for the old dame to ascend to the Pearly Gates. Sizing up the furniture and deciding who gets the plate."

"Madam!" said Bailey, shocked.

She appealed to me.

"It's true. Swindlers want my money; relatives want my money. My other visitors are clergymen—like that bishop of, of, what was it Bailey?"

"The Deacon of Southwark visited Mrs Bridges last Tuesday."

Bailey was back to unruffled efficiency. But he was still watching me like a hawk, alert to any flicker that might suggest a bad conscience.

"Southwark. Even he wants my money. Hinting about the hereafter and storing up treasures in heaven." She raised her eyes skywards. "Tedious! Tedious! Do clergymen pester you for money, Mr Stubbs? Or do you punch them if they try?"

She mimed a jab with one tiny fist.

"I put my sixpence in the plate," I said. In truth my attendance at church is casual and more down to Sally than personal inclination. They do like engaged couples to attend in the run up to a wedding. "I don't get picked out for special attention."

But Mrs Bridges was already moving on, her mind dancing lightly as a butterfly. Or perhaps she had trouble keeping anchored to the here and now.

"Oh, and there are the doctors too. If you count them. What do you think of doctors? They are so terribly young these days. And they all present bills."

Bailey coughed discreetly. "Speaking of business, Mr Stubbs..."

"Which we weren't," said Mrs Bridges. "Bailey, you are so rude! I never get to talk to anyone of Mr Stubbs class, not in my parlour. Allow me to indulge my social curiosity for a minute, at least, won't you?"

"Madam," said Bailey, giving in with a slight inclination of the head.

"I've forgotten what I was going to ask now," she said. "You vex me, Bailey. It's gone right out of my head. Oh, very well, ask him about this business."

Bailey placed half-glasses over his nose and glanced down at a letter he took from a folio. I recognised my own writing.

"You wish to carry out an investigation of the Norwood Benevolent Society for Widows," he said gravely.

"I don't see that has anything to do with me," said Mrs Bridges. "I haven't had anything to do with Society business for years and years. Those awful women make all the decisions."

"Nevertheless ma'am, I understand you are the honorary Chair," I said. "It operates under your name."

"Quite so," agreed Bailey. "Mrs Bridges holds that post for life—whatever designs the others might have. She still chairs their meetings."

He was proud of her position, jealous of it as any courtier over any of the crown's far-flung dominions.

"And because you have nothing to do with the day-to-day running of the Society, there is no suggestion an investigation would be directed at you," I said. "But you do have the authority to agree to such an investigation."

"Over the heads of the Committee," said Bailey. "Against any possible objections. And I can assure you they will object—strenuously."

Mrs Bridges laughed her dry little laugh.

"An investigation—that would shake them up, eh, Bailey?"

"Frankly, Mr Stubbs, you haven't cited any valid grounds for an investigation. The Widows Society is an organisation of utmost financial probity. Any suggestion of irregularity would be—slanderous. And potentially damaging."

"All I have is anonymous information," I said, "A letter that suggests there is wrongdoing."

The letter had been marked simply to 'Harry Stubbs, C/O Lantern Insurance, Norwood, London SE'—the GPO is a marvel though, and it arrived at my office as if it has been fully addressed. It was folded, as though it had been enclosed in another letter before being forwarded to me. And the brief text, all in capitals, had instructed me to 'BURN AFTER READING,' which after noting the postmark (Camberwell) and making a copy I had done.

"English justice does not work by anonymous accusation," said Bailey. "We aren't French, thank heaven."

"Tell him what you told me, Bailey—your exact words. About him being another swindler."

"I don't recall any such phrasing," said Bailey, imperturbably. "I believe I may have said that the case was so thin that I wondered if it was a pretext for something else—gathering information about rich widows, for example. Otherwise, why not go to the police?"

He turned his half-glasses on me accusingly.

"As you say, Mr Bailey, there is no actual evidence at this juncture," I said. "The police would dismiss the matter out of hand. Your own criteria might be rather different, however. You might be interested in the slightest hint of misdeeds and the need to avoid scandal."

"We might," he agreed. "If there were any. All we have is an anonymous letter—sent to someone who is not even affiliated with the Society! And all it alleges is 'wrongdoing' whatever that might mean." His brow furrowed, an expression as false as the smile a few seconds earlier. "Tell me Mr Stubbs, what is your role exactly?"

"In the normal course of events I am a claims investigator for Lantern Insurance," I said, and Bailey already had my business card in his hand as though checking it against my statement. "However, I play an informal role as an investigator for the community at large. People bring their problems to me."

"I see—so you're the Sherlock Holmes of Norwood," he said with a small smile. "Doing all this extra work pro bono out of the goodness of your heart."

"It's not all for free," I said. "And, as you mention it, I could not want a better model than the Great Detective, though I hardly live up to it."

Bailey found this highly amusing. He was not the sort of man who even read detective novels.

"The Great Detective gets an unsigned missive hinting that there are dark deeds afoot. And he speeds to investigate."

"Don't be cruel, Bailey," Mrs Bridges chided. "What do you think he should do with such a letter? Forward it to the Committee so they can ignore it?"

My first responsibility was to protect the identity of the letter writer, who I suspect might be one of the Committee. I was not going to let anyone else see it. It was frustratingly vague...but I had my instructions.

"I represent a completely independent investigative agency," I said. "And one that is not going to share information prematurely with the police, or anyone else. I am thoroughly disinterested, and, if I say it myself, my reputation is founded on honesty."

"If there was any scintilla of criminality in your background you wouldn't be sitting there," said Bailey. "Enquiries were made."

"And perhaps I might be the right man to investigate this delicate matter."

Bailey laughed out loud at that. He may have felt that the case called for someone a bit more polished, more used to genteel society, more suave, who would handle the whole affair with kid gloves—in short, someone more like Bailey himself. But Mrs Bridges thought otherwise.

"Delicate matter! People are always pussyfooting about me as though I'm too tender for the truth. Let me tell you, Mr Hobbs, I'm a tough old bird that has weathered more and harsher winters than you can imagine. I want the truth, however ugly."

Mrs Bridges was fierce. But more than that, she was shrewd. For whatever reason, she knew or suspected there was something worth my investigating.

"Naturally, if anyone in the Society is engaged in anything improper, Mrs Bridges and I would be very interested to hear of it," said Bailey.

"And so I should! So I should!"

"Furthermore," I said. "The investigation will be carried out at no cost to yourselves. If I find nothing, it's not your loss. If I find something…"

"Who is it you want to investigate?" Mrs Bridges asked. "Which one of them is it?"

"All of them equally," I said. "Impartially and fairly."

"Bailey, he won't tell us," said Mrs Bridges.

"Accepting for the sake for argument that your motive is honest, I've no reason to believe you'd find anything. And you would ruffle some feathers."

"Oh, I like the sound of that!"

"Mr Stubbs is counting on it," observed Bailey. "I believe he is by no means as uncomplicated as his appearance might suggest."

This compliment was delivered with an expert backhand.

"Wouldn't be fair, would it," she said. "Exposing an innocent like him to that pack of screeching harpies. You can't punch them, you know—more's the pity!"

Bailey smiled politely.

"Was there anything else, Mr Stubbs?" he asked.

"No, I was just looking for Mrs Bridges' approval on this one simple matter," I said.

"Does it occur to you that you are the victim of a practical joke or simply a malicious hoax? Anyone can write a poison pen letter. And not all our members see eye to eye with the committee."

"This is a source I have come to trust," I said, a half-truth of ever the was one. "Their tipoffs, as we call them, have been reliable. Unfortunately I am not able to share details. Sources must be protected."

"I that case I think the interview is at an end," he said. "You play a good hand Stubbs, but innuendo and unsupported supposition are not sufficient here."

"You hold on to your horses, Mr Augustus Bailey!" commanded Mrs Bridges.

"We've no reason to keep Mr Stubbs any longer," said Bailey. "Unless you wish to ask him about his pugilistic career."

"Perhaps I should remind you that you are my adviser," she said quietly. "You are not officially part of the Society. No man is, and no man has power over it. And that is entirely deliberate on the part of the founders."

"Nevertheless," said Bailey, with a gesture that sought to brush away this inconvenient truth. "Nevertheless, Mr Stubbs has presented no rational grounds for proceeding."

She turned to me, with a rather impish look.

"Perhaps he has something else up his sleeves besides those great thick wrists?"

"As a matter of fact, there is one more thing," I said, preparing to loose my final bolt. "The letter ends with a Latin phrase—Prudentia Semper Triumphat."

"'Wisdom always triumphs'," Bailey translated automatically. "What of it?"

"Do you know where it's from?"

"No…" he said doubtfully, as though wary of being caught out. "Cicero, perhaps?"

"Very good, Mr Stubbs. I liked the way you held that in back until the end. It's the motto of the Society, Bailey."

The words had an immediate chastening effect and I felt the balance of power shifting.

She placed her hand on a book on the table beside her, as though drawing my attention to it, but said nothing. The gold-lettered title was facing me: Grim the Collier.

"I didn't know that, Madam," he said.

"Of course not, it's a secret motto. It is part of a little ritual we have for new committee members."

"Even so," said Bailey, rallying. "That changes nothing. Clearly the phrase is known to many. Many women. Reasonable evidence, grounds for suspicion, that might be worth acting on. And that means bringing in a suitably qualified outside auditor."

The phrase 'suitably qualified' was as barbed as it could be.

Mrs Bridges though had made up her mind, and Bailey was just annoying her.

"If a member of staff is making anonymous accusations, then it is a serious matter. Mr Stubbs will cause pointless annoyance to the ladies, and they'll resent me for it, you say. Well, I say, go ahead then—investigate them to your heart's content. You'll need to mind they don't peck your eyes out, but the more ruffled their feathers are, the better I'll like it. Teach them to mind their Ps and Qs."

"Madam," objected Bailey. "This kind of sniping is just...."

He trailed off, wisely, before saying anything which he might regret.

"Petty?" She challenged him to disagree. Bailey looked pained. "Childish, were you going to say? Well, I am a child, and I can behave as pettishly as I like."

There must have been times when Catherine the Great stamped her little foot, and her courtiers scraped and drew back and hesitated to contradict her. It was not a question of the right or wrong course of action, but one of who really held power, and whether she was only allowed to do the things that he approved of.

"Perhaps you can proceed within set limits," Bailey said. "And on the strict understanding that you are in no wise Mrs Bridges' agent."

Bailey was fast a calculator. He already had his plan of action.

"Strictly understood, Mr Bailey," I said.

"Oh good," she said. "And you'll report back to me?"

"If there is anything to report—" said Bailey.

"No, no, you must report back to me anyway. I want to know everything you find. Even if you don't find anything criminal. I want to know what those witches are up to."

"I shall make a full report," I said.

"Wonderful! Bailey, make a diary note now—make an appointment."

"I will arrange a date for the meeting with Mr Stubbs in due course."

"Now—I want to see you write it down."

Bailey obediently lifted a quilted tome from a side table, and, taking a gold fountain pen from an inner pocket, made a lengthy note in swooping, elegant handwriting.

As he did so, she placed her hand on Grim the Collier again and, looking me in the eye, tapped it twice.

"Thank you very much, madam," I said.

"I do so hope I can remember whatever it was I was going to ask you by next time," she said.

I had not seen Bailey touch a bell. Maybe he had a secret hand signal. But however he had been summoned, the butler appeared at my elbow to escort me out.

Against all expectation, Mrs Bridges has given me the go-ahead to investigate the Society of Widows. The group was as respectable as any other organisation of its type, with the sole mission of managing the substantial investments of a number of women who had been left husbandless.

The Society was something of a closed book to outsiders, yielding its mysteries only to widowed women. Mrs Bridges' description of the committee members as witches had been merely a figure of speech. But I suspected it might be more true than she could have imagined.

As I walked down the path to the gate, I heard two of the maids talking at an upper window, oblivious to how their voices carried in the evening air.

"It's him," said one of them. "I told you so."

"Well I never," said the other. "That's Harry Stubbs alright. What's she want with him?"

Chapter 2: An Unexpected Assistant

As I mentioned in my interview with Mrs Bridges, much of my time was occupied with generally unpaid and often trivial investigations for local people. They wanted me to look into what they regarded as mysterious happenings: apparent hauntings, supposed curses, allegedly mysterious disappearances, and generally things that went bump in the night. I have been through quite a catalogue of these, and am now an expert on this class of foibles and misapprehensions.

I can, for example, tell you that if you hear a hammering noise every night, the first thing to check is the plumbing.

My real work, which was sporadic, were those missions assigned me by the enigmatic Miss de Vere. She was a glamourous American lady, who represented an organisation referred to by the initials TDS. This could be characterised as a secret society involved in the occult though in truth I knew very little about it. Even what the letters stood for was an open question. My researchers have turned up any number of aliases used over the years—Templars of the Sacred Darkness, Tenebrae Dominium Sacrum, the Twilight Dominion Sisterhood, Tempus Dei Silentium, Temple of the Dark Seer—and I have come to doubt whether any of them is the original. My suspicion is that the answer changes with the tides and TDS has always stood for whatever they want it to.

According to Miss de Vere, our world is like an overripe apple, spinning though an endless void, on which various spores, germs and other agents of decay descend from space. These are other-worldly beings seeking, as Darwinian law demands, to colonise a new world. To earthlings, these visitors from the heavens might be seen as angels, demons or other supernatural beings. Whatever aspect they wear, TDS seeks to exterminate them and keep our planet free from alien influences.

My job, for better or for worse, is destroying such angels. A fallen angel is, after all, nothing more nor less than a demon.

Dr Blake. who I came to know in the aftermath of his experience in the Dulwich Horror, has probably done as much research into this area as anyone. If he is correct, then TDS may have been carrying out its mission for thousands of years, a fact which on its own boggles the mind. But he also suspects the modern version is a new group which has taken on the old name to puff itself up; the truth is lost in layers of haze.

Whether TDS, or the others like them which Blake hints at, are genuinely defending wider humanity or simply serving their own selfish interests, neither he nor I can say. Their aims seem to be broadly benign, though their methods are extreme. What I do know is that they wield considerable covert as well as occult power. Crossing them is inadvisable.

Miss de Vere strongly supported the mission to investigate the Widows Society. I had received a telegram to pursue the case using 'ALL MEANS POSSIBLE'. I had never received such an emphatic instruction before.

Fictions portrays the private investigator as a lone wolf with only hip flask for company, a man very much on his own in a largely hostile world. He has no colleagues as such, the police with whom he interacts treat him with suspicion, and the criminal fraternity see him as a threat. Perhaps the odd barman or taxi-driver will exchange banter with him and help with the occasional clue, but that is as far as friendship goes. As for the fairer sex, he is invariably unmarried and any relations with glamourous and dangerous females will be as short-lived as they are intense.

My experience has been rather different. Sitting alone in my office I might look like a one-man operation, but I am on friendly terms with the women in the china-packing concern which occupies the rest of the floor. I need never drink a cup of tea on my own if I do not want to, and in fact I rarely even make my own tea. Kitty, the manager next door, is always keen to hear as much about my cases as I can share, and offer observations on human nature.

My relationship with Kitty is purely one of cordial friendship. Unlike the stereotypical fellow, I have an actual fiancée, Sally, and not only do I have a strong romantic attachment to her, but she is also a practical support. In my last major case, in which I was imprisoned in a psychiatric establishment, I would never have made it through without her help. Like Kitty, she is also perceptive when it comes to the human side of things.

Perhaps more importantly for the business of investigation I have built up a network of friends, associates and helpers of various sorts, all with their special skills and knowledge. When it is a question of occult matter or ancient books, as it often is, I can turn to Captain Cross. If it is anything relating to what our press like to term 'the underworld', what Elsie Granger can't tell me is not worth knowing. Mr Hoade at the library is the man to consult about anything relating to local history, and if anything needs deciphering, decoding or unravelling, Miss Frey has a knack for it. Dr. Blake has a deep and scholarly grasp of many things, especially when it comes to the further shores of science. And so on.

The more challenging the case, the more resources you need to deal with it. Even Sherlock Holmes, who Mr Bailey had uncharitably invoked, had help.

When I started out investigating I was a pawn, Mrs Crawford's pawn in the Shackelton case. Now though I am a player in my own right, with my own board of pieces to deploy. The skill is knowing which to call on and when and where.

This modest network is not on a par with the great machine which my patron Arthur Renville can call on in his business. If a cargo of damaged barrels of herrings judged to be of no resale value is to be handled, he can locate a fifteen-hundred weight truck, round up a dozen strapping but discreet labourers to load and unload it, and find a source for new barrels, a few hundred gallons of fresh vinegar and a chap who knows how to re-pickle and a place to do it, all in less time than it take most people to do their grocery shopping.

I am in a sense still a pawn, or perhaps a knight, on Arthur's chessboard, and he brings me into play whenever anything peculiar arises in the parish that he believes needs my expertise to resolve.

So it was that I looked up from a rather dull book of mythology at the sound of an exchange next door—a male voice talking to the women who packed china tea-sets for dispatch.

I caught Kitty's voice in particular: "It's the door on the corner there. Just let yourself in, dear."

Kitty is an effective gatekeeper and an inquisitive one, and it is rare for her to let anyone through without quizzing them on what their business might be, and she usually insists on escorting them herself. I surmised that this must be someone who was known to her, and, from her tone, for whom she had some sympathy.

As a mental exercise I tried to imagine who it would be before he turned the door handle, but drew a complete blank. I could not think of any intersection of people that both she and I knew and with whom she would be casually friendly.

There came a half-knock on the door which was half-opened by a young man whom I instantly recognised. Arthur Renville Junior, eldest son of my mentor.

"D'you mind if I come in?" he asked, boldness battling with timidity. "Mr Stubbs?"

"Make yourself at home, lad," I said.

Young Arthur had recently started at public school, and was home for the holidays. He had exchanged child's garb for that of a man, a new tweed jacket with a tie in blue and green stripes. He threw himself into the chair opposite me, slouching in a pose borrowed from the silver screen. These days every man was Ronald Colman. His new shoes were scuffed and his trouser knees stained from climbing about somewhere he should not have been. The transformation from street urchin to gentleman was by no means complete.

"I'm looking for a job," he said, in a serious, thirteen-year-old voice.

"Is that so?"

"I'm at leisure for a few weeks and the inactivity is driving me mad," he said. His accent, formerly pure South London, had shifted more out into the Home Counties, but was mobile. He was not quite sure who he was supposed to be when he was with me, but seemed to be striving for worldly maturity. "I thought I could give you a hand."

I resisted the temptation to laugh, as that would have been most unkind and the boy meant well.

"And what sort of opening would you be looking for, Master Renville?"

"Just—anything," he said, his tone suddenly pleading. "Aw, please Mr Stubbs, it's just so boring kicking around here."

I was not unsympathetic. Arthur had decided that his son was going to be a gentleman, and had packed him off to an establishment which would knock off his sharp corners and smooth down the rough edges. That was bound to be a painful process for the young man. It would be difficult for him to fit back in with his former associates here, after months apart. Many of them would have taken up apprenticeships and other occupations. To the others he would be an outsider, a toff, a public-school boy.

I knew what it felt like to be an outsider. But my sympathy had its limits. I did not want the little blighter hanging around my neck like an albatross all summer, and there was an obvious way of curbing him.

"Anything between us would have to be with your father's written permission," I said.

"If I get a note from Father, will you take me?" he asked, eager as a puppy.

"I don't know as how you'd find it as entertaining as you think," I said. "My work is a deal more boring than folk imagine. It's not all about kicking down doors and getting into fights— neither of which activity, I might add, you would be ideally suited for. Nor do I meet ghosts and goblins on a regular basis. It's more bookwork and interviewing witnesses and suchlike."

"I can do that. And I think I can handle myself pretty well in a scrap," he said, jutting his jaw out. "I've been in a few."

I considered the possibility that Arthur really would consent for his son to assist me. It was exceedingly unlikely, especially if Mrs Renville got wind of it. But the boy was the apple of their eye, and young people's powers of pestering are considerable.

"I suppose you have some education in ancient languages," I said, rummaging through a drawer. "That might come in useful."

"Latin and Greek," he said. "I won the prize for Latin Composition last term."

"Very impressive," I said, pleased at this confirmation. "Perhaps you could carry out a spot of translation."

I opened a drawer, fished out the old book wrapped in tissue paper and slid it across the desk. This unprepossessing volume was the most valuable thing I owned. He looked at it as though suspecting a trick.

"Vita et Peregrinationes Magni Paracelsi," he read from the title. "The Life and Travels of the Great—Paracelsus?"

"A tome acquired for me at no small expense," I said. The payment to Captain Cross has been in kind rather than pecuniary, but it had been significant. "Printed in the year 1499."

Young Arthur leafed through the Travels suspiciously, trying to make out the antique typeface. It was one of those scripts you had to figure out one letter at a time.

"What's the point of it?" he asked with a little too much whine.

"The point, Master Renville, is that this is the only account extant which describes Paracelsus' journeys and which might have a bearing on certain antiquities very pertinent to my work."

Exactly how Cross had obtained this work is another story. It is a shadowy book, not included in catalogues, dismissed by many as an eighteenth-century fake, but Cross swears it is legitimate. I have long harboured a particular interest in Paracelsus. He has a habit of cropping up in my cases, his works providing vital clues in a way that seems uncanny. And he seemed to have some connection with this area.

I had hoped, from what I gathered of the contents, that the book might tell me more than I could glean from the rambling contents of other works. I thought it might speak in plain terms of the alchemists' encounters with beings from other worlds. So I had been disappointed to find that it was in Latin.

"Is there no translation?" I'd asked.

Cross had shaken his head doubtfully.

"Everyone who's interested in Paracelsus reads Latin. Well, almost everyone."

"I'm sure it won't be difficult to find someone," I said.

A few names had sprung to mind, like my friend Dr Blake. But translating a whole book is a tall order, and nobody owed me that big a favour. I had resolved to hold on to the book until the opportunity presented, and some sufficiently educated person fell into my debt.

That had been some months ago. And now...

"Who's Paracelsus?" he asked.

"If you were to read the book, you would discover that, and plenty more," I said.

"But it's worse than Latin homework. There's pages and pages of it."

"Should you be looking for an opening in this enterprise, the only vacancy I have is for someone able to carry out translation from Latin," I said. "Perhaps you might consider this as a sort of entrance test before you can graduate to other tasks."

"I've already got enough homework for the whole summer holiday," he said.

"Investigation is apt to be arduous, tedious and interminable," I said. "If you want to be an Investigator you'll have to knuckle down to it. Or find another job."

For a moment I thought he might start crying, but young Arthur bucked up, sticking his chin out again.

"You know, I think I'll take a look at it," he said, back to his Ronald Coleman voice. "But I'll need some materials— dictionary, a Latin Grammar, et cetera."

I suspect he would already have most of what he needed, but I was willing to indulge him.

"Naturally," I said. "Mr Hoade at the public library will be very helpful with lending you anything you lack. I'll let you have a card to show him to prove your bona fides. But I will have to ask you to leave the Travels here."

I was not about to entrust a priceless antique book to a schoolboy, even Arthur Renville's son.

"I quite understand," he said politely. Then, shifting tone again. "Does that mean I can work here?"

"If you can get that letter from your father," I said. "And this is strictly a probationary arrangement, contingent on an acceptable level of performance of your duties and other factors."

I had not thought of what these were. But I was determined that if he was going to make a nuisance of himself he would be dropped like a hot brick, whatever his parentage.

"Aw, thanks Mr Stubbs!" he said, and was on his feet and out the door in a flash—an attempt to forestall, I suspected, any change of mind on my behalf.

Perhaps I should have refused him straight off the bat. There were countless ways that the boy could cause trouble and complications, and the responsibility of taking care of him weighed heavy lest anything should happen. On the other hand, Arthur might well be grateful for me finding occupation for the lad and keeping him happy.

And the lad might be useful. Another pawn to my chess set. Also, I did hope to get that book translated.

I leafed through the incomprehensible text, trying to get some hint of what it contained. Sadly there were no pictures to guide me. Print had not reached that level back in those early days.

Paracelsus had travelled all over what had been the known world, in search of esoteric knowledge. While his contemporaries confined themselves to libraries and endless rehashings of medieval authorities, Paracelsus went in search of the true founts of wisdom. He had a healthy disrespect for the scholars who were then the leading lights of medicine, and preferred to talk to bone-setters, midwives, village herbalists and the like, people who had an actual practical knowledge of what they were talking about—whereas most university doctors never saw an actual patient, which they saw as beneath them.

Paracelsus is never an easy read. He spins off in odd directions, he rants for pages at a time about the stupidity and ignorance of his age, and he speculates at length, trying to make sense of the few facts available to him. Not for Paracelsus the medical encyclopaedias of our age with neat diagrams and colour plates; he must scrape together odd bits of knowledge however he could, and it is painful to see a man struggle so.

His wanderings took him across what we would now call Germany, and Russia and Scandinavia, and also, intriguingly, to the British Isles. A great fat man with a huge capacity for drink who carried an executioner's sword, he had the most overbearing manner—like many, he was never wrong about anything—but who was kindness itself to his patients and would talk to the lowest beggar as easily as to a prince.

He travelled to Egypt, and saw wonders and horrors which he did not dare describe. Perhaps the plunder of some forgotten Egyptian vault gave him the foundations of his knowledge. Or perhaps he just felt his travels needed a bit of colour. Travelers these days say that Egypt is hot, dusty and poor, and the grandeur of the pharaohs had vanished well before Julius Ceasar set foot in the place.

As to what Paracelsus found in England, we have no hint. He was greatly interesting in mining, and it is believed that he may have visited the tin mines which were then such a big industry in Cornwall. But I believed there were other stops on his itinerary.

Mr Robert Browning composed his epic poem, Paracelsus in Dulwich Woods, after meetings with the Gypsies there. Paracelsus always spoke about the need to talk to Gypsies and other country folk as repositories of wisdom which never reached the scholarly world. In my adventures I had continually stumbled over hints of secret knowledge in these parts.

Item: Ernest Shackelton's strange fascination with the Antarctic and what lay beneath the ice came from a boyhood in Norwood.

Item: Madame Blavatsky's circle started dabbling with the occult art of palingenesis (a topic also explored by Paracelsus) after she moved to Norwood

Item: The Gypsies knew of the strange forces associated with the mineral springs at Beulah Spa and the underground forces that drove them, another subject dear to the heart of Paracelsus.

Item: Rober Browning's epic verse play Paracelsus, composed while wander the woodland in Dulwich

Item: The Whatelys, supposedly of Romany stock, their supposed possession of a copy of the Necronomicon—genuine or otherwise—and occult workings therefrom, also hinted at by Paracelsus.

...and so on.

My suspicion was that the Swiss physician had passed this way and his notes would tell me far more than I would ever find out myself. And now I had found my translator.

I am aware that this makes me sound like one those eccentrics, the ones who take up so much of my time by putting two and two together then getting five. And I was aware that hunches and forebodings are unreliable guides. But Paracelsus' writings about his journey did indeed shed light on the situation. But as to whether it was such a good thing for Master Renville, was another matter.

Chapter 3: The Recording Angel

Mrs Barbara Kennedy was not the sort who suffered fools gladly. And she seemed uncertain whether I fell into that category.

Mrs Kennedy was a handsome woman in her middle years, her clothing dark but not entirely black, with a jewelled brooch at her throat of subdued, dark emeralds. The effect was serious rather than sombre. An equally soberly-dressed young woman, who I now understood to be Mrs Kennedy's secretary, had admitted me into the house and guided me to this study, before taking her place behind a desk. I had seen two other women, presumably clerks, also in black. It hardly took my detective skills, such as they are, to appreciate that the Widows Society employed entirely its own kind.

I have visited premises where a commercial enterprise was run from a house before, but that was a matter of a back room given over to business. In this case the entire house seemed to have been converted, but without losing its decidedly domestic character. This was clearly a living room with bay windows, braid curtains and decorative knickknack, but with desks instead of sofas and armchairs.

"Just what is it you wish to investigate, Mr Stubbs?" Mrs Kennedy asked, looking at me over her glasses, after I had introduced myself.

I had not been offered a seat, nor was one even set out. Mrs Kennedy made no pretence of setting aside her paperwork as she talked to me.

"I understand you oversee the Society's financial affairs," I said.

"You understand correctly. And our books are audited every year."

Shelves of black bound volumes lined walls, which represented the full transactions of the Society back to the year dot. Mrs Kennedy had been the first member of the committee to respond, but evidently her consent was from a desire to deal with me promptly rather than to help. The interview would be a short one.

My debt-collector's nose picked up the scent of lucre all around. Good Axminister underfoot, and the decorative items included antique vases, the bronze bust of what I took to be a Greek goddess, and some oil paintings of nautical scenes that looked like originals.

Even the embroidery sampler on the wall behind Mrs Kennedy was in a respectable gilt frame. Rather than the usual 'Home Sweet Home' or other platitude it read "Go to the ant, thou sluggard; consider her ways, and be wise: Which having no guide, overseer, or ruler, Provideth her meat in the summer, and gathereth her food in the harvest. Proverbs 6:6-8"

I had met people with too much affinity for insects. In this case though I suspected it was the female gender which was seen as worth imitating. Words for widows to live by, I supposed.

"If you wish to look at the books, or to have an independent auditor do so, that can be arranged." She gave me a wintery smile. "But I would be very, very surprised if they were to find anything amiss."

"As it happens I have perused the summary in the public records," I said. "And I admit I found them somewhat perplexing. Your financial affairs are not entirely straightforward."

Her smile only grew.

"The profit and loss figures are easy enough to interpret," she said, with the implication that even I should be able to understand them. "As for the rest of it, we prefer to maintain a certain degree of—opacity. A lady keeps her secrets veiled when she is surrounded by men who have designs on her fortune."

As she spoke she signed a document in front of her and held it up.

"Beaumont, send this by First Class post at once."

The assistant came over wordlessly, received the letter with a slight curtsey and went back to her own desk.

"My concern is that concealed in that dense thicket of transactions there might be lurking something which you do not suspect," I said.

The Society worked through a whole spider's web of interconnected companies. Many of them were likely no more than shells, legal fictions, all owning shares in each other and carrying out transactions which were mainly sleight of hand. Getting to the bottom of it was far beyond my meagre skills.

"The auditors would have noted any such thing," she said, "That being, you know, their job. Like any other benevolent society in the land, we keep a close eye on our finances. We know what is happening even if others do not. The only unusual aspect is that our Society happens to be run for women by women." She steepled her fingers. "I am always tempted to paraphrase Jane Austen: 'It is a truth universally acknowledged that every widow in possession of a fortune must be in want of a man to manage it for her.'."

A more confident or less wise person than I might have made a patronising or ingratiating remark.

"The Society has always shown a healthy profit under your management," I said.

The Society appeared to have been quietly making money since its inception. It has weathered the financial storms that had sunk many another venture. If Mrs Kennedy had been a gentleman, I might have looked at what clubs she attended and who her friends were with financial connections.

"We have good financial advisors and our investments have performed satisfactorily," said Mrs Kennedy. "Which further undermines any suggestion that there is embezzlement. It was embezzlement that you were interested in, I take it?"

She slit an envelope with a wooden letter opener with more emphasis than necessary. It stood to reason that, as she was the Society's financial mastermind, she must be aware of, if not responsible for any irregularity.

My anonymous letter had not suggested the malfeasance was financial, so it was interesting that was Mrs Kennedy's assumption. Clearly, she felt she was the obvious suspect and resented it.

"Not as such," I said.

"'Not as such'? Well, Mr Stubbs, here are the public accounts for last year." She hefted a volume which she must have had ready for my visit. "Everything you could wish to find is in there. You may borrow it."

I took it up quickly. Getting this had been one of the main objects of my visit. Was this a success, or did it mean that there was nothing to see here? Or, having made my acquaintance, had Mrs Kennedy decided that I lacked the skill to unearth whatever secrets were hidden inside?

Many a criminal has fallen because they overestimated their ability to outwit the police. Mrs Kennedy did seem like a woman very secure in her own abilities, and if she was not openly disdainful of me, I did not feel that I stood very high in her estimation.

I moved on to my next goal.

"I suppose that brings me to the subject of Mr Parrish," I said. "A gentleman who devoted considerable effort to investigating the Society. Until his untimely death."

She looked at me over her glasses again, and her grey-blue eyes were flinty.

"Are you making an insinuation?"

"I'm here to investigate, not insinuate," I said. "Perhaps there is something you can tell me about the matter."

Mrs Kennedy pursed her lips. She could have thrown me out there and then and been perfectly within her rights. Even if I had been obstreperous about it, the telephone in front of her gave her a direct line to the police station if I needed to be forcibly ejected. But I was expecting a more thoughtful response, and I was not disappointed.

"Beaumont," she said. "Will you leave us, please?"

"I'll take this to the post," said Beaumont, letter in hand, getting her coat from the stand.

"I trust her with everything," said Mrs Kennedy. "But I don't think she needs to hear your innuendos."

"I'm not about to say anything unsuitable for Miss

Beaumont's ears," I said, not liking to see her sent out.

"It's Mrs Beaumont," said Mrs Kennedy. "All our employees are widows."

"Of course. As I say, my job is one of investigation," I said. "So perhaps you can tell me what happened with Mr Parrish."

"Nothing happened," she said. "This man Parrish wrote to me asking questions. Eventually I agreed to meet him just to impress on him that no information about the Society's financial or other affairs would be forthcoming, but it only made him more eager. When I refused to communicate any further, I believe he bothered other members of the Society and our employees. And then he died. That's all there is to it."

"He died," I repeated.

"People die before their time every day, there's nothing mysterious about it. My late husband, God rest his soul, was thirty-four when pneumonia carried him away. Mr Parrish died of an accident, I believe, which is common enough, especially in persons with unhealthy habits. I'm sure you can find the death certificate in the public records."

I had already been to the public records, not to mention the newspaper accounts which I had scanned in the archives in the West Norwood Library, which described Parrish's plunge from a third-floor window with rather more breathless excitement. There were hints of suicide, although the police had not seen anything suspicious in it.

"Parrish had some rather complicated theories about the Society."

Mrs Kennedy opened her mouth but saw something over my shoulder and stopped speaking. Before I could turn, a woman came in with a vase of fresh flowers. She placed this on a windowsill, then rearranged a few blooms.

"Thank you, Mrs Sanders," said Mrs Kennedy, and watched the door close behind her before going on. "I did not know him. But in my uneducated opinion, Mr Parrish suffered from a form of paranoia or obsessive mania. I can't say whether that contributed to his demise, but his letters betray a mind that has wandered far from the usual byways. He had some very choice language for us! 'Black Widows' indeed."

Not the least of Parrish's allegations was that to become member of the Widows Society, a woman had to murder her husband. This was easily disproven. He had spent a great deal of time looking for suspicious deaths before becoming one himself, an irony not lost on commentators.

Parrish was an eccentric, and there was no suggestion that he had actually been murdered, but the sudden death of a man who believes he is being hounded by sinister forces was worthy of wry remark. One newspaper took the line that Parrish should have paid more attention to his safety than his obsession, one suggested that his death was a final act of attention-seeking to try and prove to the world that he was right. The third took no strong line, but instead highlighted the mystery of the thing, the usual unanswered questions about drink, drugs and female acquaintances and that all possibilities remained open.

I suppose journalists have to write stories that will sell newspapers.

"Indeed," I said. "But it did cause some speculation."

"You think I murdered him to hide some dark secret," she said. "Or maybe I had Beaumont do it?"

"There isn't a scrap of hard evidence for murder," I said. "But it is within the bounds of possibility that Parrish's death was not accidental, and that it was connected, however indirectly, with his obsession with the Society. "

"Well now you've dressed it up in polite language and it looks more seemly. But it's still a slanderous accusation of murder."

Was I reading too much into how strongly she objected? Or was hers a perfectly normal reaction to an outrageous accusation? I have been in this business so long I cannot remember what the normal reaction of an innocent person should be.

"Nobody is accusing you," I pointed out. "But—you don't seem very inquisitive that perhaps someone was trying to protect you from a man who was dogging you. You told the police he had threatened to break in here by force and compel you to tell him what he wanted to know."

"Yes, and I have the letters to prove it," she said.

"And you don't think that someone might have been worried

for you, either as a friend or because you are the Society's proverbial goose laying its golden eggs?"

"No, of course not," she said, but she stopped short there. Perhaps the possibility had never occurred to her. Confident in her own innocence, she might always have simply accepted the story that Parrish died accidentally without ever thinking there might have been more to it. "But it was an accident. And who would do a thing like that?"

"My investigation has only just started," I said. "I don't know if Parrish's death is even pertinent. But if on reflection you happen to recall anything that might help, I'd be much obliged if you would let me know."

I had not had a chance to give her my business card, so I placed it on her desk.

"My card," I said. "Thank you for talking to me, Mrs Kennedy, I won't take up any more of your valuable time. I can let myself out."

She mainly seemed relieved to see me pick up my bowler, and I murmured something polite as I stepped out. But when I took a wrong turn as I stepped into the corridor her voice followed like an arrow.

"The other way, Mr Stubbs!"

I tipped my hat and with an embarrassed smile went in the right direction. My brief diversion had enabled me to snatch a glimpse of something more that intrigued me on the way in: a former dining room with a massive safe against one wall, the sort of thing that would be at home in a bank vault. The massive door was open, and one section of the safe was piled high with bars of gold like the ones you see in pictures of the Bank of England's vaults. There must be a king's ransom there, and one of the more important kings at that.

There was also a smaller safe against the other wall, open and empty. Why have two safes?

Moments later I was back on the street, where Arthur Junior was waiting patiently.

"Were the inquiries satisfactory, Mr Stubbs?" he asked.

"Moderately satisfactory only," I said. "Mrs Kennedy seems like an efficient money-manager, and as jealous of her territory as you might expect, but essentially co-operative. But we do have some accounting records to examine."

"I see," he said seriously.

She had not given me any of the bluster or dissimulation that you often get with male business managers. I believe she had achieved and maintained her position on merit. Rather than simply being dragged along by her financial advisors, she handled them as a skilled driver handles a team of spirited horses, and somehow got them all to pull in the same direction.

Arthur suddenly jostled my elbow, and when I looked at him he nodded towards the woman coming down the street towards us with slow, faltering steps. She was in full Victorian widows' weeds, draped all in black, down to the hat and thick veil.

"A widow," I said, when she had gone. "On the street where the Widows Society operates. Not extraordinary."

"She's a suspicious character, why's she hiding her face?"

"It is customary," I said. "Both to shield the world from the sight of her grief, and as a mark of respect for the dead."

"Looks suspicious," he said, glancing back at her.

To the suspicious eye, everything looks suspicious. If veiled widows were going to be suspects, young Arthur was going to have a long list to deal with in this case.

Mrs Beaumont, younger and unveiled, passed on her way back from the post box. My attempt to catch her eye was futile. She looked straight past me, perhaps worried I might try to engage her in conversation. No loyal secretary would talk behind her employer's back.

"An employee," I said to Arthur in an undertone once we had passed, and he looked back at her too.

"D'you think she knows anything?"

He asked this as though he thought we might whisk her up and take her back to the office for interrogation, tie her to a chair and question her until she cracked. Life would be so much easier if that schoolboy vision were possible, but in this investigation my powers were virtually non-existent. Even if I had been a Scotland Yard detective I doubted whether Mrs Beaumont would have anything germane to tell us. Even in the darkest of murder mysteries most of the players are merely baffled bystanders.

"At the moment, we don't even know what there is to know," I said. "But you'll be pleased to hear that Mrs Kennedy is prickly about our suspicious death."

That cheered him up at once.

"Did they kill him?"

At present that hardly seemed likely. Obscurely though, I did not want to disappoint the boy.

"I don't know. But I do aim to find out."

Chapter 4: Grim the Collier

By the time Mr Hoade found me I was thoroughly lost. I had strayed far from the path and had wandered down so many side turnings that I doubted I would even recognize the right way. His appearance was like the keeper of the Maze in Crystal Palace Park who threads his way in to rescue those who have been lost for longer than they find entertaining.

I was in the reading room of Upper Norwood Library, and I was lost in a literary labyrinth rather than a literal one. But I was heartily glad to see my rescuer. Hoade would set me on the right path.

"You seem to be amassing a collection, Stubbs," he remarked with a librarian's dry humour at the semicircle of open books piled two deep around me.

"I'm trying to find the right book," I said. "But I'm not sure it is even in here. Perhaps you could...?"

"I'd be glad to offer professional services," he said, drawing up a seat next to me.

Mr Hoade was the Assistant Head Librarian, and had been a great help to me in the past. I would even call him a friend. But I realized that in this case there might be an element of danger.

"This is in connection with a current case," I said.

"Of course." He inclined his head.

"Knowing about it might be dangerous."

His brow furrowed. Hoade spend his days filing, cataloguing and extracting information. Books were to him as bricks to the bricklayer or loaves to the baker. Telling him that there was danger lurking somewhere was as unlikely as there being a tiger hiding behind the shelves.

"A lead was passed to me in a surreptitious manner," I said.

"Indicating that the person who did so believed it was too much of a risk to share the information openly. That being the case, I feel I should exercise due caution in sharing with anyone else."

"You can't tell me why you can't tell me," said Hoade, half-amused. "It's like something from an espionage novel. But even in that case if the hero, say, needs a message translated from a foreign language, so long as the translator does not know who the message is to or from, perhaps they can be given the task? And they won't necessarily be strangled just as they are about to reveal the vital information?"

He was joking, but I was uncomfortably aware of the similarity of the situation he described with something which had happened in Upper Norwood Library during the Roslyn D'Onston affair. A man had been killed while in the act of divulging vital evidence to me. Which was why I now frequented this library instead.

"I'm not sure," I said.

"You are as mysterious as young Renville," he said. "I trust he really is working for you."

I had given the boy a business card and written on the back that the holder, A Renville, was acting as an assistant by way of identification.

"Absolutely," I said. "And I am glad that he is observing basic security precautions."

"He comes with a list of questions and won't even let me read them," he said. "Zealous young chap, you seem to be keeping him busy."

"He keeps himself busy," I said.

"But about this business of yours—tell you what, Stubbs," he said, eager the break the deadlock. "You say as much as you can, without giving away the vital details, and I'll help you as far as I can, and if we start to get on to dangerous territory and can't meet in the middle we'll stop there."

I do not think he believed in the danger—more fool him, as it turned out—but I do think the lure of adventure and excitement were too strong for Mr Hoade to resist. I do not say that the life of a librarian is drab, but to him I believe I was a colourful character whose life was full of exciting escapades, and he enjoyed a little vicarious taste of that.

It was not merely self-interest and the hopeful sight of the maze-keeper that persuaded me to confide in him. If I had the right to risk my life, then Mr Hoade did too.

"It starts here," I said, sliding a slip of paper to him.

"'Grim the Collier of Croydon'," he read, and gave me a quizzical look.

"It's the title of a book," I said. I showed him the book, which was in fact a play of that title, which had led to several other books. None of which had made a great deal of sense. "I just need to know what it has to do with the case."

The book has been on the table in Mrs Bridge's drawing room, as though she had been reading it earlier in the day. It had been striking because it was the only thing out of place. Mrs Bridges was surrounded by flunkeys, and everything was taken away as soon as she put it down. The daily newspapers were all neatly folded and arranged on a side table, next to some weekly magazines. The old lady was still sharp enough, and interested enough, to keep reading about the goings on in the world.

In my business you do encounter old people who may be suffering, as they say, some depletion of their marble collection. More than one has come to my office to seek my services with regard to a poltergeist of intrusive spirit which moves things about at night, hides things, or replaces them with identical copies. It is no use telling such people that the problem lies with their memory. I listen attentively, take notes (which impresses clients as well as forcing you to listen to them), and make some sympathetic utterances. When they run out of steam, I explain that I would certainly intervene if there was a danger to life and limb, but that in my experience these spirits are merely pranksters.

Such people are grateful to be listened to, and often reveal, by their gaps as much as by what they say, the deficits in their mental functions. I had not observed any of this with Mrs Bridges. She did not once struggle for a word, repeat herself, or become vague. In fact, I suspected she was considerably more acute than she wished to appear. She was as sharp as anyone, and if she had drawn my attention to that particular book it was intentional and rational.

Hoade was one of my pawns, or perhaps one of my foot soldiers. I his superior officer, so to speak, his wellbeing was my responsibility. And I was only too aware of how the occult can be a flypaper for inquiring minds like his. Not in the way that crosswords, which Hoade was addicted to, were. Once some people come into contact with it they get stuck, and then they get stuck more firmly, and then they are totally enveloped by it—and die as a result. My survival thus far is perhaps because I do not have the right kind of enquiring mind, due partly to lack of intellect and partly due to deficiencies in my education. Discovering the truth about the mysteries of the universe only drives you mad if you understand the blooming things.

Mr Hoade though was just the sort to be at risk, being both scholarly and inquisitive. One of those people who, if he found a box marked WARNING DO NOT OPEN would open it just out of curiosity. I saw too much death and destruction in the war to be tempted that way myself, too many men who found something interesting and had it blow up in their face.

Towards the end of the war, when we were advancing through villages which had been occupied by the Germans, we were warned to treat everything as a booby trap. It was a wise caution. All sort of innocent-looking items, from code books to packets of cigarettes had been set up with wires and contacts which would blow whoever picked them up to kingdom come.

I could see Hoade getting drawn into the occult, going deeper and deeper. Even in the cosy confines of a suburban library there was danger.

Miss Frey was another one whom I was keeping an eye on. Her aptitude for ciphers, and the ease with which she mastered occult formulae, verged on the alarming. If she would ever take it upon herself to become a witch, and if she found the right books, there was no doubt that she would be able to understand and wield arcane powers faster than ninety-nine per cent of the acolytes in the psychic research brigade.

"I can certainly tell you a bit about old Grim," said Hoade, sitting back in his chair. "He's a local celebrity, actually. Norwood isn't much for folklore, he's about the nearest we have to a folk-hero."

"But 'of Croydon', not Norwood?"

"Norwood overlaps Croydon, so we can count him as one of our own," said Hoade, brushing my objection aside. "He was an inhabitant of the original Great North Wood which once covered this very spot."

"Fair enough. Can't say I'd ever heard of him."

"This was back in the sixteenth century." He looked at the wall as though picturing the scene. "Norwood was all forest, and the only people living here were outlaws, hermits and the charcoal burners who provided the fuel for the metropolis. They would cut down one of the oaks, pile up earth around it, and start a slow fire inside the mound to turn the wood into charcoal. Charcoal was the coal of the day, so Grim, who was chief of the charcoal burners, was a called a collier."

"I see," I said, light dawning. I knew nothing about charcoal or where it came from, so this was all new to me. I had assumed that Grim the Collier was a coal miner, which made no sense at all.

"Now it seems the local bishop was none too happy about all the fires burning in the forest, as the smoke drifted over his episcopal palace, and got into a dispute with Grim over it which went to law. Grim argued that while he made the smoke, it was the Good Lord who wafted it in His bishop's direction and nothing to do with Grim. He won the case and became a hero."

"Really?"

"Oh yes," he said.

It is rare enough for a common workingman to be taken to court by My Lord Bishop and come out the winner, a victory I might say very much against the odds. I bet Grim was the talk of every pub for miles.

"But that's not in the play," I said, "or in any of the related works."

"No, it's in the local history section. By the time of the play, Grim was a sort of stock comic character like John Bull—a down-to-earth chap who represents the common man. Not too bright, but salt of the earth, and always gets the better of his betters, if you see what I mean."

This all seemed quite safe and, to be frank, irrelevant.

"But as your interest is on the supernatural side, perhaps the play will interest you, since it has Grim meeting a demon from Hell. It's a slapstick comedy for the popular stage, so don't expect too much by way of occult lore. But the theme does fit in with your interests."

I weighed the book in my hand. I did not feel like reading through all that olde-worlde language if it was going to be all obscure jokes that were topical three centuries ago.

"What sort of year is this all taking place," I asked. "Is this the same time as the Gypsies were here?"

The question occurred to me because on a number of previous occasions, not least the Stafford case, Gypsy lore had proved to have a kernel of truth to it.

"Nobody knows exactly when the Gypsies arrived, but they were stablished in the 1660s, when Pepys recorded visiting them in his diary. And the historical Grim won his case in court in the 1650s, so thereabouts." said Hoade. "The play was some time after."

"What about the 1430s?" I asked. That would have been when Paracelsus paid his visit.

"Quite likely. The family name is older. Grim comes from a word meaning a mask, which also gives us grimy—a mask of dirt. It takes a few generations for something like that to be established."

"So it was a family name for people who'd been charcoal-burning for a while."

"There was a lot of play made of the fact that they were black from soot, just as the Devil was supposed to be. They were a people apart. Maybe some of them did have darker skin. Maybe some charcoal burners were Gypsies, or some Gypsies were charcoal burners, or the two communities intermingled."

Clearly this possibility was irksome to him. Such mixing made it difficult to keep things clear, distinct and classified.

"That might just be all I need to know," I said.

"If there's anything more you want to find out about the history of charcoal burners in Croydon, or Grim the Collier, you are in the right place," said Hoade. "Our collection on local history and folklore is second to none. In fact, if you went to the British Library asking about Norwood, your inquiry would probably end up being referred back here."

"I will have to give this some thought," I said, closing the books one by one, preparatory to replacing them on their shelves. "I wouldn't want to waste your time."

"Oh, don't worry about that," he said. "I suppose you will be involved in some fieldwork. Maybe you'll be able to add a chapter to the story of Grim the Collier."

"I very much doubt that," I said. "I rather doubt he's in the picture, I think he's more there as a clue."

"That there is devilry afoot?"

He asked it with a smile, but it was too close for comfort, so I just nodded and offered him my hand.

"Thank you, Mr Hoade, your assistance had saved me a lot of trouble as always."

"My pleasure, Stubbs."

Mrs Bridges had not given me any information openly because, for all her money and position, she was scared. It was possible that my life was already in danger, and that would extend to anyone seen to associate too closely with me. I knew also that Miss de Vere took a dim view of information being shared outside of those whom she considered suitable.

Mr Hoade could add two and two together faster than anyone, and he had an inquiring mind and, by his own account, the best possible source of information.

"I hope you won't waste time looking into this further, will you?" I said.

"Of course not," he said. But his poker face was not as effective as he might have thought, and I detected mischief.

Grim the Collier had been associated with devils, which was one thing. He was a local, and maybe connected with the Gypsies, who were also reputed to be diabolists. And the Gypsies had left, or rather been driven out, at just about the start of the last century, sometime around 1800 or so. That was well before Mrs Bridges' time. But it was just about exactly when the Widows Society had been founded.

Chapter 5: The Ministering Angel

I was hanging about at a street corner on Norwood High Street at eight in the evening. Night had settled in, and people hurried past me under the streetlight. Once I might have felt uncomfortably conspicuous, but tonight I did not care who looked at me.

I was smartly dressed for a night out, in a good suit, a shirt with the latest style collar and a striped knit tie. Like a thousand other men, I was waiting for a woman to show up at a rendezvous, and I caught more looks of sympathy than suspicion.

After my experience with Mrs Kennedy I had not expected to secure any more interviews. When you are invited to be a cat set among the pigeons, you cannot expect the pigeons to be good sports about it. Mrs Kennedy's businesslike approach had been to talk to me as a way of being able to tick off the matter as concluded—after all, she had also talked to the unfortunate Mr Parrish. The others might not see any point and would put me off indefinitely.

So I had been surprised at the prompt and polite reply from Mrs Smith, though slightly bemused about the circumstances proposed for our meeting.

I was entertaining myself with classifying the passers-by and considering how I would describe them in an official report. Two messenger-boys in unform but with collars undone and chewing gum, signifying that they were no longer on duty, conversing loudly. A man pushing a handcart loaded with empty bottles. A couple in their Friday night best bound for the picture theatre, arguing about whose fault it was they would be late for the performance.

The mention of the time was the cue for St Luke's Church clock to start tolling the hour, and before it had finished ringing eight a pair of headlights drew up just feet away. I could not make out the car from the glare, but the thrumming engine bespoke a limousine rather than some little flivver.

I had not been expecting this. I wondered for a fleeting moment whether I was going to be 'taken for a ride' as they say in America, and what I was going to do about it. Then a uniformed chauffeur hopped out, threw a suspicious glance at me and opened the back door with a little flourish.

Mrs Smith, nee Farmer, had been an actress in her previous life. She was young and on the stage in 1917 when she had married Major Smith. Perhaps his family would not normally have allowed it, but many hasty alliances were made in wartime and the match was, in one sense, a success for the family. When Major Smith severely injured leading an assault near Amiens a year later, he was already the father of a son. He died of his injury within a year, but saw the family line continued. Mrs Smith was a respectable widow before she was twenty.

A decade later, she could still make an entrance. If she had been playing the part of widow, you might have thought her costume was over-done: rich raven-black satins and velvets, from head to foot, and black fur trim on her coat, as well as a black onyx bracelet emphasising the slenderness of one wrist. The black perfectly set off her pale complexion and delicate features.

A maid, whose outfit was only slightly less monochrome but a good deal less opulent, followed her out of the car, carrying her mistress's hat. It looked as though Mrs Smith was set for a night out at the opera.

"Mr Stubbs," she said, with the faintest of smiles. "Delightful to meet you. If I may say so, your request was rather opportune."

"Pleased to meet you," I said. "Though I'm curious why that should be so."

The chauffeur stood midway between us, facing me. A driver is sometimes the de facto bodyguard for an unaccompanied lady, and sometimes the actual official bodyguard. Knit tie or not, from his look I had failed some vital test. I was too focused on her to pay him much attention, but I registered a solid figure, definitely a heavyweight and in good physical condition, spotless uniform.

Should one take a lady's hand in these circumstances? As a hireling rather than a social acquaintance, and under the hostile gaze of the chauffeur, I settled for a polite bow.

"I happen to have need of someone with experience of the boxing world and you turn up at just the right moment. Almost enough for one to believe in kismet."

Her manner was bright, but she spoke to me as though through a pane of glass. As though she was speaking for the benefit of the maid and chauffeur as much as for me.

"There's a van," I said.

A delivery van had pulled up behind the limousine and the driver did not look like a patient sort. He was already leaning out the window to gawp at the group of us and looked ready to deliver a choice remark.

"We're moving, mate," the chauffeur snapped at the van driver, before he could be accused of any dereliction of duty. Touching his cap to Mrs Smith, he quickly climbed back in and maneuvered his vehicle out.

The van driver raised a hand in half-ironic thanks, looking up and down Mrs Smith before he followed. Before the war, they say, men would have rushed to open a carriage door for a lady...but people talk a lot of rubbish about the golden age before the war.

"Excuse me," said Mrs Smith, and she stooped so her maid could put her hat in place. It came with a dark veil which obscured her features. "There. I am incognito. Recognisable or not, Mrs Smith is not officially present. Do not speak my name!"

"If you say not," I said. I could not tell if she was joking.

"Am I fit to be seen?" she asked her maid, and pirouetted a full three hundred and sixty degrees.

"Yes, Madam," said the maid.

"Very good, then. Now, you go get yourself a cup of tea, and meet us here in one hour." She carelessly fished coins from a sequinned purse. "There's a corner house somewhere near here. And don't go talking to any strange men."

"Thank you, Madam," said the maid, with a curtsy.

"Tea shop's down that way and first right, Miss," I supplied, pointing towards the Lyons on Knight's Hill.

Mrs Smith tugged at my sleeve.

"Take my arm," she instructed.

I complied, ruefully thinking how inevitable it was that someone was bound to mark Harry Stubbs with a beautiful, veiled woman on his arm, a woman who was certainly not his betrothed Sally. Word would get about.

Most men are susceptible to the slightest flattery by attractive women. Early on in life I learned that I am no Ronald Colman or Errol Flynn; others who are less brutish never learn this lesson. They look in the mirror and think they are the handsomest thing on two legs, and believe everything a woman tells them. I soon became cynical, as every time a pretty girl talked to me rather than some other man it was because she wanted something—usually she wished me to beat him some man who had offended her, or occasionally just to make him jealous. My attitude softened later, but I like to think I am not so easily swayed as some. Mrs Smith's undeniably striking looks did not make me any less suspicious of her.

I was still curious to know where we were going. My first guess, that it was a dinner engagement at one of the few decent restaurants hereabouts, was obviously wide of the mark, as one hour would barely be enough to sit down and get what the smart set call hors d'oeuvres. (I had researched the matter just in case).

She directed me toward the old fire station, and I immediately made the connection. The building had been more or less unoccupied since the war, and served a number of purposes, including as a place for public talks and union meetings and amateur theatrical productions, not to mention on occasion the storage of materiel for enterprises co-ordinated by Mr Renville. But it was also known as the venue for unlicensed boxing matches. The metropolitan police were content to turn a blind eye so long as there was no disorderly conduct.

I had heard of these bouts, and talked to a friend at the gym who had been there.

"It's a ruddy circus, Harry," he said in disgust. "Might as well have dancing bears and prancing ponies."

"No fighters I've heard of?" I asked, wondering what calibre of matches were carried out.

"Nobody anyone has heard of," he said. "Or ever will. Just the spectacle or two men hitting each other. Money, that's all about it."

"A lot of blood?" I asked, as that is what the low crowd always like to see.

"Nah," he said, after a moment's thought. "Not really a lot."

He had been rather vague on quite what had been so unsatisfying about the occasion, but it seemed I might be about to get the opportunity to see for myself.

"You wish me to accompany you to a boxing match?" I said.

"Yes of course," she said, taking a firmer hold of my arm. I was suddenly aware of her perfume: something subtle, understated, but persistent. Expensive, I guessed. "Don't be so tentative, I'm not made of glass. And I can keep up with you, even in these shoes."

"I gather then that this is something you had wanted to do before my communication," I said, recalling her words about kismet.

"Yes. Marks, my chauffeur, was funny about accompanying me—he did not want me to go—and I don't know anyone, well, suitable for this sort of thing. But you're just the perfect man."

That was a new description for Harry Stubbs.

"You've not been to a boxing match before?" I queried.

"Never, obviously. Is that my car? It would be just like Marks to circle round and check you weren't kidnapping me...no, but I have a personal interest in this particular boxing—what's the term—boxing league?"

"What sort of interest?"

"I own it," she said, with a small laugh. "Or at least, the Society does."

"It seems odd that someone with no knowledge of the noble art should want to risk money on it," I said. "And odder that someone of your obvious means should invest in anything which might be questionable."

Perhaps she did not know that the bouts were technically illegal, even if she did know the entire field of boxing was crawling with criminals. But surely if Mrs Smith had any financial advisors at all they would not have let her within a mile of such a venture.

"For an investigator, you are easily fooled by appearances," she said. "Cars and chauffeurs can be hired by the hour, you know—so can dresses. I may not be what I seem."

"I have familiarised myself with the public records," I said carefully. "I do not believe you are the sort of person who hires dresses."

"Ha-ha! I was forgetting you're a licensed snooper as well as a renowned boxer. That'll teach me."

We were fast approaching the old fire station. Suspecting there might be less scope for conversation inside, I pressed my point.

"The Society is a very worthy organisation, but if my information if correct, somebody inside it is misbehaving," I said. "Have you come across anything amiss, anything that does not seem right?"

"Ask me later," she said. "I might tell you something."

The front door to the old fire station was shut and locked, but a steady trickle of men meandered down the side alley alongside the old fire station, showing the way plainly enough.

The widow in her finery attracted plenty of looks. They could not see her face, but they could tell she was young and beautiful and mysterious. And beside my hulking form she attracted even more attention.

Inevitably at this sort of gathering, I was recognised immediately. Nobody would call me renowned, but in these parts anyone who followed the fight game knew me, being the nearest thing to a local champion. They might call me a has-been, though never to my face. At least I was a once-was.

I received a couple of "hellos" before we had even reached the door, tips of the cap and nods of polite recognition.

"Show them this," Mrs Smith murmured, passing me a card as we approached the side door. I caught the words SPECIAL INVITATION.

Two doormen were working the entrance, collecting entry money. As soon as one of them caught sight of the card he leaned inside and shouted.

"'Ere Mickey! Got a 'Special' coming through."

The doormen stood aside most respectfully as Mrs Smith and I came through, arm in arm. A smiling man in a shiny suit hurried up to take the invite off me while bowing to my companion.

"So pleased to see you! And—why, it's Harry Stubbs, I believe?" He stuck out a hand, looking as delighted as if I had been his long-lost brother. "Michael Powers, call me Mickey, everyone does."

I did not recognise Mickey Powers specifically, but I knew his type. You meet plenty of questionable characters in the boxing racket, promoters and agents and publicity men with both hands in the till and no concern for the battered, sweaty men who bring the money in. I knew their smell, and this Powers absolutely reeked.

These are men with no sporting prowess themselves, but who do very well out of the boxing business. So many boxers end up damaged, worn out and washed up by the time they're in their mid-thirties. If I had continued in that line, I might have been one of them. But the fast talking, over-friendly individuals who hover around them, always offering unmissable opportunities, men who never take a punch themselves, you will not see them begging for coppers or slouched in a pub mumbling about the old days.

I enfolded his proffered hand with my own and squeezed just enough to let him know what I could do.

"Pleased to meet you," I said. "You the one running this here show?"

"Doing my best," he said, with a big fake smile, leading us towards a back stair. "This way to your box, Sir and Madam."

The so called 'boxes' were simply a wide balcony partitioned off into sections with movable screens. Below us was the auditorium and the boxing ring, and across the way was another balcony. Our host directed us to two wooden chairs either side of a card table.

"Best seats in the house, Mr Stubbs, Madam," he said. "You'll enjoy a fine view from here."

This was a blatant lie; the best seats for any boxing match are ringside. There were a couple of rows of chairs down there, with men standing behind them further back. But it was a small place and we would see everything from here.

The ring itself looked to be legitimate, set on a raised platform and the regulation sixteen feet square, the minimum size as you would expect in a smaller venue. It seemed well constructed, the corner posts solid, the canvas clean, with little wear on the ropes. That was a good sign. Promoters who are just going through the motions of legitimacy in order to present a gory spectacle usually skimp on such matters.

"Very good, Mr Powers," said Mrs Smith, speaking to him the first time, so that he seemed to swell with pride and delight.

"And, if I may say so, you have chosen an excellent guide to introduce you to the noble art," he said, looking from her veiled face to me and back. "Mr Stubbs knows the sport inside and out. And here we are—"

One of the doormen appeared behind him with a tray bearing two tall, slender glasses which he placed on the table.

"—some bubbly to celebrate the occasion, with the very best compliments of the house."

"Thank you," I said.

"Sadly I have to leave you and attend to matters," he said. "Please enjoy the show."

Having delivered his master stroke, Powers bowed and backed out.

Mrs Smith did not give him another look, but settled herself elegantly on her chair. Having first checked to see where the exits were, I joined her. It is always well to know how to leave in a hurry from any strange situation. This one was far from comfortable.

The sections of balcony either side of us were occupied, one by a trio of young men who I would say were city clerks on a spree. On the other side were two older gentlemen, both of whom were holding folded papers and looked ready to take notes. Experienced fightgoers, in other words. I did not make eye contact with either group, which would have been a breach of etiquette. The point of boxes was that your neighbours could not importune you.

Opposite us on the other balcony were two couples enjoying an evening out, another party of clerks, and a severe gentleman on his own in horn-rimmed spectacles.

I was not expecting any particular trouble. But even the best regulated fights can turn into scenes of disorder, and unregulated fights, where there are less controls on gambling and where disputes about refereeing decisions can quickly flare up, are considerably more volatile.

The general public is aware only of the top tier of the sport, in the form of the high-profile fights that have made fighters like Jack Dempsey household names, and in some cases rich men, where there managers and promoters are kept honest. But that is merely the most refined form of the sport: the sort of boxing attended by men in evening dress, the spiritual heirs to the actual Marquess of Queensbury and other noble patrons of pugilism.

There is a whole world below that, populated by legions of fighters who never have a chance of appearing in front of a big crowd. Some of these are legitimate sporting activities which feed into the big money league, where promising talent gets to show itself off. The world that I once inhabited, lured by dreams of glory.

But others are rougher and readier, closer to the traditional working-class roots of the game. I'm not talking about the sort of bare-knuckle bouts that take place outside pubs, with details of the match spread by word of mouth, but the semi-respectable bouts, some of them between former big names, and exhibition bouts, a few rungs higher than fairground sideshows but not so very different. These are staged more for the sake of the box office draw than any purse or prize, and can range from genuine sport to sheer brutality with a good deal of rigged activity and downright cheating. The aim as usual is to deceive honest punters into betting on the wrong man.

This venue hosted matches of the latter type.

Below us, the auditorium was filling fast. It would be a

capacity crowd, and a rowdy one, amplified by the small space. There was no alcohol on sale, just packets of peanuts, but I doubt there was a man down there who had not already imbibed a couple of pints or had a hip flask handy.

"Have you been here before?" Mrs Smith asked.

"Last time I came here they were putting on Gilbert and Sullivan," I said. "It's not Drury Lane, but it was an honest production."

"You don't think this is an honest production?"

"We'll see."

Mrs Smith unfolded a black fan and used it to conceal her face as she threw her veil aside to take a sip of the supposed champagne.

"That's simply awful," she said, making a face. "And lukewarm."

The preliminaries for the first bout were getting under way, and whatever I had to say was lost in the cheer of the crowd. The lights abruptly dimmed, leaving just the boxing ring brilliantly illuminated. The fight was on and the crowd roared their enthusiasm.

Powers was standing out in the middle of the ring, all lit up, and with a big megaphone in his hands. At his signal the ringside official rang the bell once, and noise of the crowd instantly turned to an expectant hush.

Smiling—now he really was enjoying himself—Powers raised the megaphone to his lips.

"Ladies and gentlemen!" he started, in that showman's drawl that rendered the phrase as "lay-deez an' gennell-menn."

"Welcome to this evening's spectacular, in which I can promise you—promise you—fights the like of which you have never seen before and never will again! Gladiatorial combat of the twentieth century, contents of strength, skill and above all—fortitude!"

The crowd roared its approval, anticipating blood.

Chapter 6: The Fight

The front man's job is to whip up the audience into a frenzy of excitement, or at least raise the temperature above lukewarm. The roar of the crowd behind makes a big difference when you're in the ring, and a cold, silent audience always makes you wonder what they're looking at. But Powers's hyperbole took an unexpected turn.

"We live in an age of wonders, when medical science is uncovering the secrets of the human body and making the impossible, possible! These men are all heroes, injured in the service of their country, shattered, crippled, barely alive—but thanks to a new regime of physical improvement they are not just fit but superhuman."

Mrs Smith watched rapt from behind her fan.

"These are no ordinary boxers, but athletes of preternatural physical character! None of them is allowed to fight ordinary opponents, by law, for fear of killing them! What you are about to witness is a match of Olympians!"

So, that was the pitch.

"In the blue corner, weighing sixteen stone and eight pounds, we have Private Patrick Brady."

The name meant nothing to me, and there was no mention of his record of fights and wins, which was unusual in boxing.

"Formerly of the North Staffordshire Regiment, the Prince of Wales's own."

Mrs Smith took a pair of golden opera glasses from her bag and put them to her eye to inspect the fighters.

The man in blue trunks was a musclebound character: his arms and legs and chest were so heavily layered with muscles he seemed to have been inflated with an air pump. His left shoulder was a mass of surgical scars and there was more scarring down one leg. There was also an inverted V-shaped scar running down either side from the bridge of his nose, almost like the tracks of teardrops. His head looked tiny, and it swivelled about like the turret of a destroyer, looking this way and that.

"And in the red corner former, at fifteen stone ten pounds, Guardsman Thomas Applemore, formerly of the Grenadier Guards, mentioned in dispatches on two occasions for his personal bravery in the face of the enemy."

The one in red trunks was another odd specimen. He was taller and his bodily development was not quite as pronounced, but he had the same pronounced surgical scars all the way down his back, and again the inverted V stamped on his face.

The two of them paraded around the ring, holding up their arms and making defiant gestures. They made three slow circuits, because this was the business of the night: giving the punters a chance to have a good look at them and see what they thought before placing bets. There was a regular churn of activity down there with slips of paper being passed to and fro. I immediately identified a man in tartan waistcoat as a bookmaker, and another on the other side of the room who was scarcely less conspicuous.

"Looks like a pair of Frankenstein's monsters with all those stiches and things," I said. "Do you think that's all real, or is it makeup?"

"It's real. And some people do call the doctor who looks after him 'Frankenstein,'" said Mrs Smith. "But I don't think he can assemble men from spare parts—not yet."

Powers made a bow in our direction, and withdrew, climbing out through the ropes as the referee climbed in and signalled to the boxers.

The fighters touched gloves, the bell rang and we were off.

Even on such an occasion as this, when I had no expectation, my blood was still rising. I cheered with the crowd as the first blows were exchanged. All detachment fled and I was caught up with the excitement of the fight.

This is what it is all about, two men coming to blows, and

what makes a fight for the spectators is the commitment the boxers bring to it, whether they are just putting on a show or going for it hell-for-leather. Of course looks can be deceptive, especially for the uninitiated. Many fine boxers have been booed for what appears to be a reluctance to get in and mix it, but this is deliberate drawing out the opponent to observe them, or in some cases a tactic to wear them down before making a move.

There were no such tactics at play here. Both fighters went at it with the utmost conviction, as though there was a purse of a hundred guineas at stake. A flurry of blows was exchanged in the first few seconds, and then another, before the fight began to settle down and I could make sense of it.

My immediate verdict was to confirm what my friend had said. This was a circus, and neither of these men showed any of the hallmarks of an experienced fighter. Their footwork was patchy, their punches no more than average.

The blue trunks, the muscle man, punched as though he hated his opponent, and hit with such force that you could hear it. Red was more astute though, much better defensively, coming in with fierce jabs on the frequent occasions when his opponent's guard was out of place.

They circled each other, moved apart, then together, each trying to put the other off-balance at just the right moment so they could attack. Blue trunks scored a straight right in the jaw that staggered his opponent and the crowd cheered loudly.

"Go on, knock his block off!" shouted someone.

"What's happening?" asked Mrs Smith. "Who is winning?"

"It could go either way," I said. "Blue has the strength, there's no doubt about that. But Red has the reach on him, and if, I'm not mistaken, a superior tactical skill."

They closed again suddenly, both delivering and receiving punches until the scarred man in the red trunks dodged sideways and away. They maneuvered for a few seconds and then together again.

I watched breathlessly for several more exchanges which all seemed to come off pretty evenly. Blue Trunks kept aiming knockout blows which he never could land effectively, all were blocked or only partially made contact. Red was less ambitious, only going for the odd big punch and mainly chipping, chipping away and dancing clumsily backwards before the other man could get him lined up for another piledriver shot.

Most fights are won by inches, not by knockout blows. The steady infliction of fatigue and damage, or the steady accumulation of slightly more points than the other in the eyes of the judges, are what wins the vast majority of fights.

Both men had blood on their faces already—and then the bell went for the first round. My watch showed that statutory three minutes had passed. There was no short-changing here.

"Will you kindly tell me what's going on?" Mrs Smith asked, a little impatient.

I ran through some of the points with her, while trying to see how the two were doing in the break. Each had a corner man who applied a sponge and offered a bottle of water, but there were no trainers in evidence.

"There won't be any future heavyweight champions of the world coming out of this venue," I concluded. "Nor anything superhuman. You could see fighters as good and better at any boxing gymnasium up and down the country. But they know how to whip a crowd, and the fighters..." I trailed off, trying to put my finger on what it was that had kept me on the edge of my seat. "They're well-matched for one thing, so you don't notice the weakness on either side. And they're giving it their all, which is what any audience loves to see."

"The house seems to be enjoying it," she said.

There were shouted conversations and arms waving above the hubbub below. This was when bets were doubled or hedged, odds adjusted, everyone now having formed their own opinion of the fighters. The man in the tartan waistcoat was laughing and smiling and handing out slips of paper left and right.

Powers was off on one side talking to a group of men while keeping an eye on the ring where the action was about to recommence.

Now that I had more idea what do look for, I was able to keep an eye out for the two boxer's different foibles. Neither of them had much of an actual fighting style; they were unfinished articles, with plenty of potential which was yet to be realised.

Red Trunks had the makings of a decent out-boxer, that is, one who fights at a distance. But he would need to learn some decent footwork. The muscled man would be more of what we call a 'slugger.'

Before the end of the second round I could list half a dozen points for them to address in their training, all basic skills that should have been acquired long before they reached this stage. This was an amateur fight in all but name, but the weight and conviction of the punches were all that mattered as far as the crowd was concerned.

Towards the end of the second Blue Trunks did score, a straight left to the chin that staggered his opponent back to the ropes. He was not quick enough on the follow up though, and the taller man had his guard up and managed to fend him off while backing away until the bell went a few seconds later.

Now the crowd were really getting excited, and their yells reached a crescendo as the third round started. Now Blue was on the attack, always pushing forward, while his opponent tried to sidle away, taunting him with long-range shots, or went in for a clinch when the two got close.

This was a more skilful display, but it went down badly. Cheers for Blue were mixed with jeers towards Red.

Halfway through the round, Red seemed to regain some of his bounce. He threw himself at the more heavily muscled boxer, landing some decent blows and opening a cut under the man's heavy brow.

After that things become more interesting. It was not exactly a classic contest between different fighting styles, but there was enough of a genuine match in there to keep me watching. I would have put Red ahead on points, but then Blue caught him—exactly the same straight left to the jaw as before. This time, though, he was weakened and though he stopped the next two punches, the third—yet another straight left—caught him on the temple and down he went.

The crowd roared and the referee was there on the count, waving his arm with each beat.

"A-one! A-two! A-three!"

It was not a clean knockout. Red was still moving even as he fell over, but woozy and disorientated. He did not seem to have any idea where he was or what was happening.

"A-four! A-five! A-six..."

The crowd was shouting for him to get up—or at least half of it was—and he seemed to come to himself all at once.

"A-seven, a-eight—"

Red got his arms and legs under his body and was right back on feet, snapping into a fighting stance. The referee gave him a long look, then signalled for the fight to continue.

Blue was on the attack again, but this time the defence stayed firmly in place and he made no progress until the bell went and we roared approval.

The noise was considerable, and Mrs Smith indicated to me that we should leave. It seemed she was not especially enjoying the spectacle, or at any rate she had seen enough for her purposes. Whatever those were.

We made our way down the narrow staircase, through the deserted foyer littered with peanut shells, orange peel and discarded wrapping papers and back out to the street.

"So what did you think of it?" she asked. "Please be honest."

"Well," I said. "Not as shabby a performance as I was expecting. That was not real boxing, not the actual sporting type. It was more for the entertainment of the crowd and to give the betting fraternity something to take wagers on. But not the grubby blood sport that these things sometimes are."

"Interesting," she said. "And the men—how did they seem to you, physically?"

I recalled Powers's spiel about disabled warriors brought miraculously back to fighting form. I recalled also that the late Major Smith had come home paralysed by shrapnel in his spine, and died of pneumonia after a few months.

"In terms of health, strength and fitness I would say they were both more than adequate. I have no idea whether they were actually maimed as Mr Powers suggested though. And in terms of correct training, to fight well and to avoid injury, I would say they were lacking both, and that is likely to lead to calamity in the long run."

Like racehorses, boxers do the work and take the risk

without having much of a stake themselves. And that is even at the better end of the sport. A boxer can only fight so many times. Pushing men to fight more than they should, and putting them up against unsuitable opponents, and not stopping fights when they should be stopped, is a good way for them to end up with brain injury. Not that anyone else cares.

"Thank you," she said. "That was all I wanted to know."

"And what I would like to know is whether you can share any suspicions about misdeeds in the Society," I said.

"I hoped that the display would relieve your doubts about us." She seemed entirely serious, and entirely convinced herself. "You know about the Society's good works—schools, orphanages, hospitals—but now you can see how much more we are doing. We can cure the sick and advance medicine. We are doing things that nobody else can!"

She had lost her husband. But she thought she might help prevent others dying the same way.

"That was circus," I said. "Not a medical demonstration."

"But Mr Stubbs!" she protested. "Isn't it a spectacular way to prove it works, those poor disabled men up and fighting again?"

You can take the woman out of showbusiness, but you can never take the showbusiness out of the woman. Clearly the whole thing appealed to her flair for the dramatic, though doubters like me know how much deception there is behind the scenes.

Mrs Smith did not believe there was anything wrong with their support for what we had just witnessed. But anything involving a doctor who had attracted the nickname 'Frankenstein' was enough to arouse suspicion. I suspected I might have discovered the trigger for the anonymous denunciation. Whether there was anything truly sinister behind it was another matter.

A sound behind us attracted my attention.

"One moment, please, Mrs Smith."

I stopped under a streetlight and turned around to face the two men who had followed us out of the fire station, fifteen paces behind, pausing long enough to let them know I was aware of them. They slowed abruptly and pretended to take an interest in an empty doorway. I could not make out much except dark clothes, and caps pulled down. Neither of them looked exactly Herculean.

"What is it?"

"Just some street jackals," I said. "Looking for pickings. Hold your handbag in front of you with both hands."

We walked on and she started to ask something, but I was distracted by the sound of running feet. The two thieves were bolder, more foolish, or more desperate than usual. One of them rushed at me, brandishing a cosh, the other was going for Mrs Smith.

I pulled her behind me and gave the man who was running at her an almighty shove in the chest, I saw him stagger away. The other one swung at me, clumsily, and did not make contact. He was trying to keep his distance. The first hung back, unsure, unable to get at Mrs Smith without coming into range of my fists. The element of surprise had been well and truly lost.

The one with the cosh made a couple more swishes at the empty air between us while I got the measure of him, and as I stepped forward, fists balled, he bolted, followed by his companion.

I watched them go, their shadows disappearing after the third streetlight along with the sound of their running feet.

Mrs Smith was trying to speak, but all that came out was "Wha-wha-wha…"

"Just purse snatchers," I said. "Unfortunately, if you are in a place like that in expensive clothes, there are certain people on the lookout for likely marks."

"My goodness," she said, recovering a little and putting a hand to her breast. "My goodness me."

"I should have warned you," I said. "But no harm done, I hope."

"Nothing like that has ever happened to me before. It's just…never happened before."

She was dazed, and for a moment I was worried she might faint. I took her arm again.

"Let's get you back to your maid and your car. The Lyons Corner House is just a short way down this street."

"My goodness," she kept saying, and then laughed out loud and put her hand over mouth. "I beg your pardon."

"Shock affects people in different ways," I said. "I've seen them all. I'm very sorry you had to go through such a distressing experience. But there's no harm done."

"Lucky I was with you," she said, holding tighter to my arm. "But you won't tell Marks about this, will you? He'll be furious."

"I won't."

There was little chance of resuming the conversation about the Society. But I had already decided that Mrs Smith was not the source of my anonymous letter and had no notion that the Society might be doing anything wrong.

But for my part, I had more than a few questions about the spectacle we had witnessed and just what was behind it. Not so much the extensive surgical scarring, more about the desperate ferocity of the fighters. Maybe someone with no experience of the fight game would not have noticed anything amiss. But I meant to do some investigating.

Chapter 7: An Evening of Wireless

I had arranged to spend the evening with my two fellow lodgers. Ours is a congenial little community: our landlady prefers long-term residents, and the three of us have been there a few years, all respectable single men.

"As respectable as we need to be, at any rate," says Thompson, with a wink, "while maintaining our self-respect as virile single men."

Thompson was a smart fellow with a neat moustache, whose dark hair was always combed with the sharpest of partings, and whose patent-leather shoes shine like mirrors. He worked in life insurance, and every week he reaped a harvest of new policies, the getting of which came with stories of greater or lesser plausibility.

Barnes was an older gentleman with silver hair, who called anyone under forty 'young man.' He wore a wedding band but never mentioned a wife or children. With his income he could surely have afforded a place of his own, but he seemed to prefer the communal life of a lodging house.

Barnes had all the skills of a good bookkeeper, and had pursued that occupation until he found the boys out in the field were making more than him. For the last fifteen years he had earned a good living as agent for a building society. His talent with numbers stood him in good stead—he could tell you what seven and a half per cent of fifteen pounds was, or calculate weekly payments as easily as though he had the numbers written down in front of him.

Moreover, he still did a certain amount of investigation of others' books. I knew for a fact that he had helped Arthur Renville in this capacity when questions had arisen over whether a business was on the up-and-up or shady dealings were involved. Barnes had a nose for sniffing out funny business hidden in ledgers, so he was just the man I needed.

We were on the most cordial of terms, and when I asked for his help in a matter involving accounts, it was though I had asked him to assist with a crossword puzzle.

"Wheel it out, young Stubbs," he said. "I'll give it a once over."

When Thompson heard Barnes and I were set to spend the evening together, he said we should hold the party in his room, and he would provide some musical entertainment.

You never know quite what to expect from Thompson, because he always has that glint in his eye. He is inclined to a little light rule-breaking—smoking cigars out of the window in his room, organising card games for shilling stakes—simply because he wants to feel he is an independent man, not under the thumb of a woman. Or at least, not yet.

"You haven't taken up the harmonica, have you?" asked Barnes, facetiously.

We both knew it would be his new wireless set.

"Have you got that working properly then?" I asked.

"Have I ever," said Thompson. "I'll tune in to a top-notch concert and you can have a musical accompaniment to your cogitations."

This arrangement would allow Thompson to show off his new toy, without Barnes and me being obliged to sit through the interminable tuning process and pretend to take in interest in kilocycles, and whatever else was involved.

Thompson seemed more than happy about having even a semi-attentive audience, and we agreed a time. This was the first time I would get to hear the new wireless set, though I had caught the occasional hiss and whistle when I was passing his room. Two men had brought it round in a van one afternoon, an item the size of a tea chest wrapped in sheets for protection, and carried it up to his room.

The landlady had watched suspiciously, sceptical of Thompson's claim that it was simply an addition to the furniture.

"There's nothing in the tenancy agreement about wireless sets," he observed.

"Musical instruments are prohibited," she shot back at him. "They are a nuisance to other residents. If that thing is going to make horrible noises all evening, it can go right back where it came from!"

Thompson had been spending weeks mastering the thing. Mainly, he listened through an apparatus that looked like a pair of earmuffs so as not to trouble the rest of us, but occasionally he wired up the loudspeaker, just to test it out. Or, more likely, see how loud he could make it before the landlady came knocking on the door, though in fact it was barely audible outside his room.

That evening, Barnes and I dropped round to Thompson's room. I was bearing a collection of ledgers under one arm, and a paper bag with half a dozen bottles of beer. Drinking was permitted, strictly in moderation.

"Greetings," said Thompson. He had arranged his table in the middle of the room and borrowed an extra chair, so we sat round three sides while the radio occupied the fourth place.

"So, this is the apparatus," said Barnes, looking the oaken cabinet up and down.

"Merely the outer shell, old man," Thompson told him, opening a hatch to show a mass of wires. "All sorts of gubbins in there—condensers and vacuum tubes—to do the work. Though the actual working principle is quite simple."

"A crystal tuned to vibrate in sympathy with radio waves," said Barnes, showing he was not quite a neophyte.

Thompson looked a bit put out about not getting to explain it, but anyone with an interest in scientific matters must have read about it by then. Our surroundings are filled with invisible waves, similar to light but at much longer wavelengths, and these can be used to transmit sound or other information. The art was advancing fast. Thompson's neat little cabinet was far more compact than the radio set which carried orders to my artillery battery in the war.

That was only used when we had just moved; as soon as we were established they laid down a field telephone line. Radio in those days was not reliable, not compared to modern sets.

"Now you're here, I'll get it warmed up," said Thompson.

In the meantime, I passed Barnes the ledger.

"These are the accounts for the Widows Society," I said. "This one is the summary and it all goes back twenty years, so if there's any recent jiggery-pokery I assume it will show up."

"Not necessarily," said Barnes, placing wire-rimmed spectacles on his nose. "There might be some stealthy undermining of the Society's assets going on. Selling off the old manor a few bricks at a time, from the inside so nobody notices—until it collapses. But if there's anything more recent it'll show."

I did not know the exact dates, but it was possible Mrs Kennedy had been running their finances for more than twenty years. She was more than clever enough to make sure that I did not have any material that would incriminate her, but the exercise still seemed worthwhile.

Thompson fiddled with some knobs, and after a while an amber light came on. Presently, as the set warmed up, the loudspeaker started to emit a quiet hiss, like bacon frying in the distance, which grew steadily louder.

"That means it's working," said Thompson. "I'll turn this down and see if I can tune in to the airwaves."

He made an adjustment and stuck a device like a baby's dummy on a wire into his ear. It looked highly professional, and less peculiar than the earphones, which made him look as though he was hunting for submarines.

"The bottom line is all in apple-pie order," said Barnes. "Which is as you'd expect. No fraudster would make it that obvious. The question is whether there is a discrepancy hiding somewhere between this bottom line here and these ledgers here."

"Sounds like finding a needle in a haystack," I said.

"Depends how clever they've been and how much they've taken. If it's just sixpence missing from the till, I'd be here until doomsday adding up and comparing. But larger amounts will always show up somewhere. Even if they have a complete second set of books for the real business, they have to make these balance somehow."

Meanwhile, Thompson was making faces as he turned the

dials and listened to the result on his earpiece. I gathered that some evenings the reception was better than others. On a bad night, there was nothing to be heard but 'static'.

"I'll start at the summaries, then go down to subtotals, and down from there until I find something or I get fed up," Barnes said. "Don't you go forgetting about those bottles."

I opened a beer and distributed three glasses. We clinked, and they continued about their assigned tasks, Barnes jotting numbers in a notebook as he did so.

Thompson was studying a copy of Wireless Week with a list of radio frequencies and programs.

"I think I've got 2LO," he announced. "They're pretty reliable. Let's see if we can catch the news at the top of the hour now..."

He flicked a switch and turned the volume control for the speaker. A gentle whooshing sound like waves breaking on a beach surrounded us. Thompson made a tiny adjustment and a voice suddenly filled the room.

" ...O' clock. This is 2LO. London calling, London calling," said the announcer. "We are broadcasting this radio program from the BBC studio at Savoy Hill, London."

"Glad to hear it," said Barnes. Neither of us would have been so very bothered if the radio had not worked, but it would have been a mortification for Thompson if his new toy had been a damp squib when he tried to show it off.

The reproduction was good, the words easily intelligible. It sounded as though the announcer was speaking through a ball of cotton wool, but the human speech was clear and distinct, with just a hint of frying bacon in the background.

"Well done," said Barnes. "Got it first time."

"And now the news headlines. Serious strikes in Serbia. Efforts are being made by the government to induce the employers to meet with workers on a friendly footing. Workers have downed tools in several major industrial centres, and rioting is reported in two locations, but the police are said to have the situation in hand."

"The latest from Serbia," said Thompson, "straight from the horse's mouth."

"Plucky waterman saves life at Chiswick. This morning, at a quarter past ten, shouts were heard from the Embankment close to Ponder's Row, Chiswick. James Bates, a waterman, whose attention was called to the cries by a bystander, jumped into the water and rescued Susie, the five-year-old daughter of Mr. and Mrs. Holmes of Sunbury Place, Chiswick..."

"There you are," Thompson said. "The news delivered to you—at the speed of light."

We made appreciative noises, although I suspect Barnes had the same reservations I did. Both of those news stories had been in the afternoon papers. All the radio really did was read the stories for you in an educated accent. Or rather, just the gist of the story; everything was covered in a few lines when in the paper it might have had half a column.

"And now, the headlines again, for those taking notes," said the announcer, and proceeded to go through the same stories once more but at slower speed, with long pauses between sentences.

Barnes and I exchanged a look, but Thompson was already working on re-tuning the set. After some bursts of crackling and a whistle like a railway train, the noise faded out and was replaced by the music of a hundred violins.

The effect was more like standing outside a concert hall than being in one, but it was still delightful to know we were hearing an orchestra playing hundreds of miles away.

"Beethoven?" asked Thompson.

"Handel," said Barnes.

Whoever the composer was, and whoever the invisible musicians were, they were doing a grand job. Thompson conducted the orchestra with a toasting fork while Barnes continued to rustle pages and take down figures.

At times the sound would grow fainter and Thompson would make an adjustment to keep it tuned. I would have found this irritating, but I think he enjoyed having an active role in the experience, and pretending that operating the machine required some sort of abstruse technical expertise.

"Nothing to report so far," said Barnes, making a note.

We drank and listened to the distant musicians, and I savoured the fact that I was listening to the future. Sally and I would certainly have a radio set in our living room one day. With this sort of entertainment on tap, you hardly needed to leave the house. I imagined a cosy little scene with her and me, and her little boy, and maybe another little one in a crib, and a nice coal fire burning in the corner.

It was not that I disliked my current lodgings, or found evenings at the pub or with Barnes and Thompson tiresome, but it struck me then that I was ready to settle down to a life of comfortable domesticity in a place I could call my own.

The music faded. Thompson began to fiddle with the dials again.

"It's not the radio," Barnes told him. "That's the end of the movement. It'll start up again in a minute."

"If it's the end of their piece, why isn't the audience applauding?"

"It's not music hall, you Philistine," said Barnes. "At proper concerts nobody applauds until the end."

"Well, you're an education to us all, Professor Barnes!"

Sure enough, the music did start up again, and we settled down to listen to it. The reproduction was not as good as a gramophone record, but you need to make allowances when you are getting something for free. At least we were; I assumed Thompson had paid his radio licence, though knowing him there was some doubt about it.

"There's a lot of lucre in that Widows Society," said Thompson, looking over one of the ledgers. "I wish there were that many zeroes in my order book."

"And I thought we were having a national financial crisis," I said, "again."

"There's always one of those," said Thompson. "But whatever happens there are still plenty of rich people with piles of cash. Piles of it! If you could see how much money some people have, you'd join the Communist Pary tomorrow."

"I doubt that," I said, and we laughed.

"Anyone with any sense is working out how to skim a

bit off," he said. "There are these huge fortunes everywhere. Landowners, industrialists, banks, investment funds, government departments, tycoons, old aristocrats, war profiteers...people like you and me work all hours trying to make enough money and we think we're rich if we land a few quid extra. That's nothing to them. They're in a different world. The crumbs off their table would be a fortune to us."

"Which is why they keep thieving fingers away from their table," remarked Barnes without looking up.

"That's essentially why the Widows Society was founded," I said. "So that women who had inherited money but did not know how to manage it would not be preyed upon by unscrupulous men."

"That's me," said Thompson. "Show me a rich widow and I'll have a go at preying on her. Especially a young one who's been missing the carnal joys of male companionship."

"Lucky your Sally has you to protect her, Stubbs," said Barnes, "or she wouldn't be safe from this one."

"She's a young widow," I admitted, "but she's hardly rich."

"She works at the pickle factory," said Thompson, giving me a nudge. "You can get all the chutney and pickled onions you can eat! That's riches."

"You old romantic," said Barnes.

"I'm not saying I would set out to marry money," said Thompson, looking into his beer glass, "but a fortune does make you look at a woman differently, don't you think?"

"Marry for money and you'll get what you deserve," said Barnes from his notebook.

"That's telling you," I said.

"There are easier ways of making it," Thompson said. "Like taking a spade to one of those money mountains. There are banking families you know—the Rothschilds, the Barings, the Barclays, people like that—that spend ten thousand pounds on a blooming painting. More money than they know what to do with."

The music swelled and swayed around us. We might not be the rich, but we three were certainly among the luckier ones. All of us had a good meal in our bellies, decent clothes on our

backs and a sound roof over our head, and there were plenty of
people out there who could not say the same. But I did not want
to sound pious, and besides, I was enjoying the orchestra.

"You know, Stubbs, I think this Widows Society may be
above board," said Barnes, closing a ledger. "When there is
funny business going on, there is obfuscation and smoke
screens. Everything here is laid out as clearly as you could want,
strictly by the book and all balancing to the penny every time."

"That can't be right," said Thompson. "Someone somewhere
must be making something from it."

Barnes scoffed, and passed over his notebook showing the
totals year on year.

"New investments, divestments, income, expenses and
net value by year," he said. "Took it all down in two minutes.
You show me where there's scope to skim anything out of that,
clever clogs."

The music had ended, and now we were treated to a talk on
pig farming in Suffolk, which came through clearly, although
the speaker sounded as though he was standing at the end of
a tunnel. He explained the details of fodder per acre versus
pigs per acre, and the number of bushels of feed required over
a certain period. I have no head for numbers and lost track of
what he was saying almost at once.

"Are you interested in pig farming?" I asked.

"Not particularly," Barnes said.

"Can you re-tune it to another station?"

"In a minute," said Thompson. He put down the notebook
and went to his bookshelf, where he picked out a well-thumbed
copy of The Investors Guide.

"He's on the trail," said Barnes.

We listened to a deal more discussion on pig breeds, and
rates of reproduction and growth while Thompson wrote down
numbers, much to Barnes's bemusement. I did not know what
to make of any of it.

"Your Widows Society is making a lot of money," said
Thompson, with the air of one who had just won an argument.

"Money makes money," Barnes said. "The accounts show
that clear enough."

"But every year—1920, 1921, 1922. Beating the market every time when you add it up."

Barnes scanned the rows of numbers and nodded.

"Is that surprising?" I asked.

"Clearly you've never been an investor on the Stock market, Stubbs," said Thompson. "Look how much higher they are than the national Stock Index, every blooming year."

"They're doing well," Barnes said.

"Was her husband's name Midas? Because this Mrs. Kennedy has the touch. And that gold makes me wonder…the old 'mineral assets' trick?"

"You don't think?" said Barnes. "I never checked for that."

"It's a game a fellow in accounting told me about," said Thompson, while Barnes started going through the ledger, leafing through from year to year and jotting down two numbers each time. "The organisation buys gold from itself and treats it like depreciating asset, when in fact it's gaining value."

"You're right," said Barnes. "There's something here smells of Billingsgate. Mineral assets indeed, depreciating at ten per cent per annum."

Thompson took a swig of beer and looked at me accusingly, as though I was consorting with criminals.

"So what does it mean?" I asked.

"They're making even more money than we thought, and hiding it," said Barnes. "They must have a pretty big stock of gold somewhere, though."

I told them about the safe and the stack of bullion, and they both nodded.

"One bar is four hundred Troy ounces," said Barnes. "At four pounds five shillings per ounce, that's seventeen hundred pounds per ingot."

"Blimey," said Thompson. "I think I'll join. I'll put on a wig and a hat with a veil, and nobody would know the difference. Old Widow Thompson, just lead me to the gold."

"But how, how can they be making so much money?" I asked.

"Maybe it's a conspiracy of widows," said Barnes, half-serious. "Inside information. Companies all employ women these days, doing the typing, and widows have to go out to work. When they type up a secret company report, maybe they send a copy to Mrs Kennedy."

The discovery did put Parrish into perspective. Perhaps he had seen or guessed the true magnitude of the Society's success, which led to his pursuit of Mrs Kennedy—and his fall.

"Let those that have ears, hear," said the radio announcer.

We all looked up then, startled. The last we noticed, the radio was telling us about pig farming, but the voice had changed. It was much louder for one thing, louder than anything that had come from the speaker previously.

It did not speak in the well-educated tones of the other radio announcers, but in a strange, sexless voice that might have come from a machine.

"Let those that have understanding use it, for the time of trials is upon us, and a fire will be unleashed on the land."

"Religious program," said Thompson, reaching for Wireless Week.

"He's very loud," I said.

"That which was cast down shall be raised up, and those that were cast down will be exalted. Those that are on high shall be humbled and crushed to the earth, and the staff and the rod shall be in the hands of those who bowed to them."

"He's mixing his gospels," said Barnes. "Or he's not using the King James Version."

"Let those that have eyes see the truth. That which was hidden will be revealed; all things will be revealed and all secrets will be known."

Thompson was looking at the dials.

"I can't tell what the station is," he said, "but he must have quite a transmitter. 2LO is broadcasting a hundred watts, and I'm getting at least ten times the signal from this one."

"Does that mean he's very close by?" I asked.

"There aren't any transmitters near here," said Thompson. "I don't know what he's doing on this wavelength."

"Watch for the signs that you may know when the time is. The sword and the flame shall conquer..."

It carried on in that vein; the announcer did not even pause for breath, his speech just unrolled endlessly.

"So now we can get religious maniacs in our bedrooms, rather than having them harangue us on the streets," said Barnes. "That's very modern and convenient."

"I wonder what he's on about," I said. "Sounds like a religious revolutionary."

"A revolutionary with a very powerful radio set," said Thompson.

"The rising of the sun will guide you. Let those who have understanding apply it; let those who have wisdom ponder. The new is coming and the old will be swept away."

"Very repetitive," said Thompson. It seemed like he was so impressed with the quality of the sound transmission that he was not paying much attention to the words.

"I don't care for it," said Barnes. "Stubbs?"

I shook my head.

"I'm trying to tune to something else," said Thompson. "But he seems to be broadcasting across the whole bandwidth. Ah no, that's where he stops."

The voice was cut off mid-sentence and replaced by gentle hissing.

"Get us another station," urged Barnes.

Thompson turned the dial and flicked switches. All we heard were snatches of the eerie preacher interspersed with the hiss.

"It's not allowed," said Thompson irritably. "I expect they'll take his licence away pretty sharpish, confiscate his set and get him off the air. The GPO have radio direction finding equipment to locate rogue transmitters."

Until they did though, the options were to listen to his ramblings or turn off entirely. Which, reluctantly, Thompson did.

"So the entertainment of the future is going to keep getting interrupted by intruders," Barnes concluded. "There is something to be said for the old-fashioned reading of a book."

"There's an address to write to," said Thompson. "I'll have him taken off the air."

"Could he hear us?" I asked, suddenly suspicious.

"No, of course not."

"Now that would be alarming," said Barnes.

It was not quite the evening Thompson had intended, but at least we had been able to hear his radio in action. And I had made a valuable discovery. Maybe there was nothing technically illegal in the Society hiding their accumulation of gold, but it was certainly suspicious.

That rogue broadcast bothered me, though it is not my place to go investigating every strange thing in the borough. Or maybe it is. It occurred to me that the broadcast might be something more than it seemed and I thought I knew how to find out.

Chapter 8: A Visit to the Cemetery

Sally straightened my tie, which was already straight, then checked her face again in a little folding mirror. She was not usually so agitated.

"You look wonderful," I told her. My protective instinct was aroused.

"And you look wonderful, too," she said, taking my arm.

"Beauty is in the eye of the beholder," I said, chuckling. I was smart enough, in my new suit, polished shoes and dark blue tie, but I was still afraid my prospective brother-in-law would get a shock when he saw me.

"Why do we have to meet him here, of all places?"

"Because," she said, determinedly leading me to the gates of West Norwood Cemetery. "Because I mean to meet this head on. I don't want a spectre hovering over the feast."

We were meeting Lucas, currently the legal guardian of Sally's four-year old son. He held a post in the church, not a parish vicar exactly, but similar rank, and Sally was somewhat in awe of him. Sally had been, for a time, a fallen woman, and the boy had been taken away. Now she was back on her feet, and our imminent wedding would make her a decent married woman, with a home of her own for the boy to come back to. I could not see any spectres in the case, but I did not press the matter.

It is a well-known phenomenon that relationships mature through a number of stages. In the case of Sally and myself, the easiness of our early days has given way to a more complicated interplay. Mainly, this manifests itself over the question of what to do of an evening. As a rule, I have to keep making suggestions—go to the pictures? A walk in the park? Visit a cafe?—until I hit on one she approves of. Sometimes this can go on for a while. If she would just tell me what she actually wanted to do, the entire process would be greatly abbreviated. But, I now understand, the point is that it has to be my suggestion, rather than hers. Being the man, I have to be in charge...after a fashion.

We are both adapting.

It struck me as a little ominous though, that Sally's sister had sent her husband rather than coming in person.

"What was she like growing up?" I asked.

"Just about normal, I suppose," said Sally. "Sometimes we fought, sometimes she looked after me. She got religious at fourteen; I didn't."

We walked up the hill hand in hand, past the rows of grand tombs, family mausoleums and enormous headstones and the occasional obelisk. On a sunny day like this, the place had a sort of sombre splendour. A cemetery in sunshine is a strange place. I recalled being there at midnight when it looked very different.

"You're none the worse for that," I said.

"And here he is," she said, as a tall man in a dark suit raised an arm in salute.

He did not raise it high, but just enough to make a dignified greeting. Lucas was tall and angular, pale and serious looking. He was a less forbidding character than the patriarch I had been expecting.

"Hello Lucas," she said, kissing him on the cheek.

"Hello Sally," he said, looking pleased. "You're looking well. And—Mr Stubbs?"

"I'd be honoured if you'd call me Harry," I said, shaking hands.

"Lucas," he said, no less happy than when greeting Sally. His grip was decently firm. "I'm so pleased to meet you at last, having heard so much about you from Sally. She does sing your praises."

Sally blushed a little.

"Florrie sends her love," he added. "And your boy is looking forward to seeing you again."

"He is?"

She actually sounded uncertain.

"Of course he is," said Lucas. I had already decided he was the better sort of vicar, one with a real warmth about him. "He's always got on well with us, but, you know, there is no substitute for a mother's love."

There was no sense in opening a discussion about the three years Sally and her son had been kept apart. It was not as though my being in Sally's life changed her nature, but in the eyes of the world having a husband made all the difference—even one without a 'proper' job.

"And this," said Sally to me, indicating the headstone, "is the resting place of my former husband."

The arrangement of the cemetery is not exactly haphazard. It is more like the seating at an entertainment, where all the good places go to the ones with money, and everybody else fills up the gaps in between.

Suddenly, the location made sense. This was the grave of the famous Freddie, whose untimely death had sent Sally's life into a spiral of decline, eventually leading her to prostitution, an occupation she had been pursuing when we met during the Roslyn D'Onston case.

I knew Freddie had been a housepainter and had drowned in the Croydon Canal while walking home drunk one night, at a time when he had been struggling to make a living. I did not need to be told that the combination of no work and spending money on drink, rather than food, was a sign of a man in serious trouble.

"So, that's him," I said, stupidly.

"The father of your son," said Lucas to Sally. "If it wasn't a school day, of course I'd have brought him—and Florrie."

Sally has been allowed to take the boy out for increasing lengths of time, and it seemed she had passed some sort of test. She was too choked to reply, but Lucas went on, smoothing over the gap.

"The young man is doing very well. He breakfasted this morning on toast and soft-boiled egg without making the slightest mess, and cleared up his things afterwards."

"Is that unusual?" I asked.

He raised his eyebrows in amusement.

"He has better table manners than his cousins," said Lucas. I had gathered that Lucas and Florrie had two daughters and a son of their own, the eldest a year older than Sally's boy. "And he's such a cheerful little soul. We shall miss having him about the place."

"We'll look after him," I said.

"I know you will! And there will be plenty of visits, of course—and children's parties, and church outings, walks and everything. The gang of them will stay thick as thieves."

Lucas was not at all the man I had been expecting. He was all affability, and I could not recognise Sally's depiction of him as a sanctimonious, disapproving clergyman.

Sally was looking down thoughtfully at her husband's grave—her first husband's grave, I should say. Lucas took me by the arm with a clergyman's tact.

"We should leave Sally on her own a minute," he said. "She used to come here often and stay for hours, but I don't think that will continue. There's another man she needs to look after now; the baton has been passed. But she needs to take her leave of Freddie properly, before she stops being a widow and starts being a wife again."

Of course Sally was a widow, but I had never thought of her that way. I groped for something to say. I had some trepidation about having a conversation with Lucas on my own. I had literally nothing in common with him apart from Sally, and the Sally I knew was a long way from the one he had known.

"A widow knows the ways of men," said Lucas, regarding me. "Sally is a different woman to the one that married Frederick. Alas, he drank more than was good for himself—or her, or their boy. And he had some very, well, 'artistic' notions about what was decent, which caused trouble with the family."

I could tell he blamed Freddie for everything that had happened since. Perhaps, as the man was dead, Lucas had forgiven him. I was not anxious to dwell on the subject.

"You don't live far away," I said.

"No, just the other side of Dulwich," he said. "Barely three miles as the crow flies. I suppose you heard about what the press called 'The Dulwich Horror?'"

Of course I had heard of the Dulwich Horror. Everyone had. While I had not been directly involved, I had met some of the people who had been—one of whom, my photographer friend Tom, had been killed in the event. I doubted whether respectable people like Lucas paid much attention to the newspaper accounts of those tragic deaths, but I would not disavow my friends.

"Certainly," I said. "In fact, Dr. Blake, who was one of the survivors, is an acquaintance of mine."

I had decided to be as honest as practical with Lucas, given he was going to be family.

"Oh, really?" he said, sounding impressed. "How remarkable. A very resilient fellow. But tell me, do you know...?"

He was off at once, asking a whole string of questions about the case, which I did my best to field. My knowledge of those events is second hand and very imperfect, even though I knew some of those involved, but Lucas listened to me as though I was an oracle. I mentioned that Dr Blake had helped me with some of my cases.

"Has he really! Some of your more, well, unusual types of case rather than the quotidian insurance business I expect, yes?"

Sally had told him little, but if he had made any sort of enquiries about me at all he would know I had a reputation as a ghost-breaker and investigator of haunted houses. Rumour, always adding a few dabs of colour to the truth, had me marked down as a vampire-hunter to boot. At least this was a topic I could talk about.

"Dr Blake is very knowledgeable in metaphysics and all kinds of scholarly stuff that goes way over my head."

"Fascinating," he said. "So, in your line...do you ever see things? Or do you just witness the aftermath, so to speak?"

This was a sudden and serious question to spring on a man without at least loosening his tongue with a few pints. His curiosity was fierce.

"Certainly I see things," I told him. "And hear, smell and touch them too, sometimes. But I don't expect anyone else to believe me, and I don't argue with doubters. No reason why anyone should believe anything they haven't seen for themselves, and I don't blame them. That is, I mean…"

In my nervousness I had forgotten I was addressing a man of the cloth. I was trying, in my sluggish way, to work out how to back-pedal, but he had not taken umbrage.

"You are a lucky man," he said. "In my line, as you would say, we subsist on faith alone. 'A wicked and adulterous generation looks for a sign, but none will be given it,' saith the apostle."

"I've seen signs," I said, "but none of them was very welcoming."

"We are promised signs and wonders if our faith is strong enough, but…you know there are times when I almost envy the Roman church, with its moving statues and trinkets that weep blood."

He spoke wistfully, but might not have been so happy to see some of the things I had. I felt emboldened to speak up.

"Why, right in this cemetery I witnessed things that belong in storybooks, and solid as anything…and got some cracked ribs into the bargain."

I put a hand to my back. That night I had been flung against a gravestone with such force I thought my spine might have been broken. Recalling it brought a sympathetic twinge to the affected area.

"My word," said Lucas. "But, of course, you prevailed?"

"I did, or else I shouldn't be here now," I said. "I can show you the exact spot where it happened, so long as you promise not to spread it about."

If the gravestone had not toppled over with the impact, I would have been smashed against it like a swatted fly. I guiltily noticed it was still recumbent, every time I passed.

"Well, well, well," said Lucas, lost in thought. He looked up at me. "I have so many questions—so many—but there will be other opportunities. We should get back to Sally before she gets maudlin."

I was distracted by the sight of a woman in black walking among the gravestones, suddenly reminding me of the Widows Society, and the sinister 'Dr Frankenstein'. A young woman, with the blackest of hair and the palest complexion, seemingly lost in thought. That reminded me of something.

"One thing," I asked. "I was wondering if you had ever encountered the Widows Society?"

"Well, of course," he said. "They are good people: charitable to a fault, and always so helpful to other women who have been bereaved." He paused to glance round at me acutely. "You are not just asking out of idle curiosity...perhaps you have heard some rumours about them: seances, mysterious rites, that sort of thing?"

Of course, I had not heard anything like that, but then I am not so attuned to the churchgoing community as Lucas.

"I would like to say it was malicious nonsense," he continued, "but in truth, I have heard similar allegations too many times from too many mouths. My personal—you might say pious— belief is that, like the Masons, the Widows Society have antique secret rituals which are not necessarily at odds with our faith."

"That's interesting," I said.

"But, as I say, they are very free with their charity," he concluded, "which makes it easier for the bishop to wink at any reports of irregularity."

For a vicar he sounded like a thoroughgoing cynic. I decided I was going to like Lucas.

Sally wiped tears away when she saw us coming, and then Lucas was talking enthusiastically about Sally's little boy and what games and sports he liked. After that, we had to talk about our plans for the wedding, and the details of the house Sally and I would move into.

"Now, let me see you two standing together," said Lucas, stepping back and inspecting us. "You make a fine couple," he pronounced, beaming.

"Beauty and the beast," I said.

"Far from it," he said. "More like 'the brave and the fair.'"

"Glad to hear you approve," said Sally. "I suppose we'll go ahead with it then."

"Ha-ha!" Lucas looked at his pocket watch. "I'm sorry, I have to leave you. But it is reassuring to know Sally will be in good hands."

We shook hands again.

"He certainly took to you," said Sally, as we walked to the

gates. "I can't remember seeing him so chipper."

"He thinks I'm some sort of hero," I said.

Lucas must struggle against evil on a daily basis, but it was so vague and intangible it was impossible for him to really pin down. That I had not only seen the tangible form of supernatural forces but fought them—battled demons, he might have said— must make me enviable, or even admirable.

"I was expecting him to be sniffy and purse his lips, but I think he'd have loaned you a hundred pounds on the spot had you asked."

"That's one half of the family squared," I said.

Sally's side was the most important. If Lucas had made difficulties, Sally would not get custody of her little boy. On my side, the worst we faced was ostracism.

I had never actually lied to my Ma and Pa about Sally, but you might say I had been economical with the truth. One thing they certainly did not know was that she had been working on the streets when I first met her. She was not just a woman with a past, but, to their way of thinking, with the blackest sort of past.

A man called Collins had, under the guise of taking her under his protection, persuaded her by stages that she should repay him by making money in the oldest way known to man. By that stage, she was so indebted to him she could see no other way.

Collins had long since left these precincts for Manchester. Rumour said he had been caught cheating at cards and found dead in an alley. They say he had been stabbed a dozen times and had the ace of spades stuffed into his mouth.

Now, she had a letter from the convent explaining what a reformed character she was. She had not touched a drop of booze since she entered the convent, and there was a letter from the doctor, too. confirming she was clear of any infectious diseases. She was morally and medically clean, but that is not enough for some.

"It'll be alright," said Sally. "They're good people, your Ma and Pa. They couldn't be nicer to me."

"I'm sure you're right," I said, but I recalled how Ma had made cutting remarks, in the past, about girls who were no better than they ought to be, and glamourous movie stars seen out walking with men who were not their husbands.

"Goodness," she said, sympathetic but still amused by my discomfort. "And I used to think you were fearless. You'll face all sorts of monsters but you're still afraid of your old Ma."

"Only a little bit," I said. But the gravestones reminded me of how much more there was still to fear out there.

Chapter 9: Dr Vengler's Warehouse

Young Arthur was delighted to hear he was going undercover, but I had to bring his exalted idea of what this meant down a few pegs. He thought he could disguise himself as a wandering sailor or an itinerant brush salesman, or something equally unlikely for a thirteen-year-old.

"Here's some clothes that ought to fit, more or less," I said, taking out the shopping bag Sally had stocked from a second-hand shop.

He held up the rumpled jacket with obvious displeasure.

"What am I supposed to be?" he asked.

"You're supposed to be what you would've been if you hadn't been so lucky with your birth," I said. "A young man in need of money."

It was an obvious enough disguise. There were plenty of boys going about looking for errands which would earn them a bit of spare change: running messages, keeping watch, delivering food or drink and carrying out other tasks to free up older and better-paid workers.

"All you need to do is knock on the door and ask if there's anything they need doing," I said.

"But what if they say yes?"

"Then you do it and earn yourself a tanner," I said. "If you're lucky. The main thing is, though, remember you're a spy. See everything, observe everything, note everything. Got it?"

"A spy?" That was more like it.

"You'll have to make up a new name for yourself," I said, "in case they ask. Create a life story, one that's credible but that they can't check."

"I could be Pierre from France, or Belgium," he said, adopting an accent. "Je parle Francais, but my English ees very goot."

"Or you could be from Peckham," I said. "Just talk normal and keep the lid on that boarding school voice."

"Righty-ho then, Mister Stubbs," he said in stage Cockney.

The lad was enthusiastic, and wanted to be helpful, but children can be something of a trial. My previous experience had been with teaching them to box, and that was so very much simpler. You never had any trouble with pupils in that classroom. Not after the first incident was dealt with.

As we went I asked how he was getting on with his translations of Paracelsus' journey.

"It sounded like you were just getting to the interesting bit. He had just embarked at Calais," I prompted.

"That's right. And he was sailing to a place he called Folcanstan, which is actually Folkestone."

"And how do you know that?" I asked without breaking stride.

It was an honest question rather than an attempt to catch the boy out, but he answered as though he were speaking in court.

"I checked it with Mr Hoade, the librarian, who has a dictionary of Latin place names. You said I should ask him about anything difficult."

"Quite right," I said. "Good work. So, did he get to 'Folcanstan'?"

Arthur had out a clutch of folded papers, which he arranged as he walked until he found the right one.

"He had to wait several days for the right winds, but when they changed and the tide was right, it took less than a day. Most of the passengers were very sick on the way."

"That's about par for the course," I said, remembering my crossing on a troopship. There might have been a few hardy souls who did not lose their breakfast over the side, but I certainly was not one of them.

"Except for Paracelsus of course. He had a cure for seasickness, a drink called herbal bitters. He invented it. Is that the same as a pint of bitter?"

"Not exactly," I said. "Bitters is a flavouring. You just add a dash or two to cocktails."

I am hardly a cocktail drinker myself. They are all the rage among the smart set in the West End, but the only mixed drink you can get around here is half and half.

"Oh," he said indifferent. "Anyway, he got to Folkestone and found a guide, a man who he calls a 'wandering priest,' who can translate for him because they both speak Latin."

I imagined the guide as a Friar Tuck figure, a man able to match the heavy-drinking alchemist bumper for bumper.

"They went Northwards to Meddestane, which is what they called Maidstone, and Paracelsus got into an argument with some other priests and they had to leave. Then they got to Croindene, which is Croydon, and everyone told them not to go into the wood because it was too dangerous, and his guide said it was too dangerous, and Paracelsus said he was going anyway, and he did go, and his guide got embarrassed for being made to look like a coward and went with him."

"Did they say why it was dangerous?"

"It was full of outlaws and dishonest men," said Arthur. "In those days, if someone was a criminal, they would declare him an outlaw. That meant he was outside the protection of the law, so anyone could just take his money or his horse, or kill him, and nobody would do anything. So the outlaws had to go and hide in the woods because that was the only place they were safe."

"Was Mr Hoade advising you on this?" I asked.

"Yes, he helped. And almost as soon as they went into the wood they were ambushed by ten outlaws with weapons drawn."

When he did not continue, I looked to see why he had stopped and he just grinned.

"That's as far as I got," he said. "It's a bit slow, but it's a good story."

I was pleased he was getting into it.

"Now, we're pretty much where you start work," I said. "You remember what you have to do?"

He repeated his instructions back verbatim. He was no slouch when he was paying attention. I sent him on a couple of test runs first, not telling him that these were places with no connection to the case. After he reported back on what he saw with decent accuracy, and without making any trouble with the householders, I decided to let him loose on the real goal.

A few casual inquiries at the gym and the pub suggested the boxers were based in a disused warehouse under the tutelage of a man called Dr. Vengler, the one some of them called 'Frankenstein.' I meant to have some conversation with him, but nobody knew exactly where he was.

But there are only so many disused warehouses about, and the simple if time-consuming expedient of looking for properties leased or rented by the Widows Society turned up an obvious candidate. We walked to a bus shelter conveniently close to our target where I waited. He was back in five minutes.

"The warehouse is all locked up," he reported. "But I can hear people inside."

"Calm down a bit," I said, "and elucidate a bit more. Put some flesh in the bones. What does the place look like?"

"Well, it's er, a warehouse," he said. "It's all locked and shuttered. Locked from the inside, though, not padlocks on the outside. There are some smashed-up planks lying about outside. I knocked and I knocked—there's no bell or anything, or a sign—but nobody came."

"Better," I said. "And the activity?"

"There was nothing to look through, but when I put my ear to it, I could hear men running about, and voices. It sounded like PE class!"

This seemed more than plausible, and helped confirm the notion that this was in fact the place where Dr Vengler's boxing operation was based.

"And the warehouses on either side?"

"One of them's open and they've got window frames laid out on the ground on newspaper," he said. "Painting them. They told me to clear off out before I even opened my mouth."

He sounded slightly offended. People did not generally talk to him like that. Maybe he would learn a little something about what ordinary people go through, and maybe that would be no bad thing.

"They were saving you the trouble of offering your

services," I said. A place like that would have all the labour it needed, and not want any boys coming in to spill paint or steal things.

"Yeah, well," he said. "The other one has a watchman who just laughed at me. I could go around the back."

"Don't do that." The last thing I wanted was for the boy to get a beating for trespass or suspected burglary or anything. "I'll take it from here. You wait here for me."

I passed the warehouse with open doors, giving no more than a glance to the workmen there, and proceeded past the place I believed to be occupied by Vengler to the next one, which had a big nameplate outside and a door knocker for deliveries.

"Hallo," said a man looking at me through an open hatch in the door before I could approach. He was a curious fellow with bulbous eyes, no chin and a rather vacant smile. It was unusual to see a young, able-bodied man in such a lowly occupation; usually that sort of job went to greybeards and maimed veterans. I wondered whether he was quite the full shilling.

"Sorry to trouble you," I said, proffering my card. "My name's Harry Stubbs, Lantern Insurance. It's about your next-door neighbours; they don't seem to be answering the door."

"I don't read," he said, taking the card. "But thanks all the same. I'm Timmy. You're a boxer, like them next door?"

"I've been known to indulge in the pugilistic art," I said.

"You look better than them though," Timmy said, looking me up and down. "You haven't got all those scars, unless there's some under your clothes. They don't like you looking at them... Are you joining up with the doctor's circus?"

"Are they taking on new men?"

He squinted with concentration for a moment.

"I don't know," he concluded. "Do you know him? The doctor, I mean?"

"I don't."

"Um." He sucked his teeth, frowned and scratched his scalp. "He's very strict! He's a good man though. I do jobs for him." He tapped the side of his nose knowingly. "On the quiet."

"What sort of jobs?"

"It's on the quiet!" he said, suddenly agitated. "That means I can't tell you, or I'd get in trouble."

"Forgive me," I said. "I do apologise."

"It's all very hush-hush over there," he said, lowering his voice. "They never use the front door. He never lets them out, but he comes and goes sometimes, him and a few others. Go round the back door, that's where they all go. But they don't like you looking straight at them. Careful or r they'll clout you one."

"The back...?"

"There's an alleyway on this side," Timmy said. "With a gate, but it isn't locked. But don't gawp at them. The doctor doesn't mind, but those men...they've got hard fists. I suppose you have, too."

"I suppose I have," I agreed.

His mind was working, and you could see his expression change every time something new occurred to him.

"You, you watch yourself now," he said. "The doctor, he's good to me, sort of, but don't get on his wrong side. And those men—he doesn't let them out."

"Very interesting," I said. "Thank you, Timmy."

I tipped my hat and passed him sixpence for his trouble which he took with delight.

I assumed an air of confidence as I walked down to the alley to the yard behind the warehouses. The whole area was in a run-down and dilapidated state. Not too many businesses were thriving, and none of them was exactly bustling with comings and goings. You more had the sense of trade in hibernation, waiting for better times. Peeling paint, faded signs and weathered woodwork were the order of the day.

I have found that the more furtive you behave, the less people are inclined to trust your good intentions. Though in this case it would not have made any difference, as the individual I encountered would not have trusted the Archbishop of Canterbury in full regalia.

He was a solid, square-jawed fellow with a good deal of muscle on him, in a singlet and shorts which showed off not only his build but criss-cross patterns of stitches. Seen up close and in good light, the scarring was even more arresting than it had appeared at the show.

The man in the alley was engaged in cleaning clothes in two tubs, one full of soapy water, the other clean, and hanging them up on a wooden rack.

"Begging your pardon," I said, suppressing a smile at the sight of this monster doing laundry.

"Who are you?" he demanded, a fellow Londoner none too friendly, straightening up. He was the same height as me, though my hat gave me a slight advantage. His head was bare with an army crop. The V-shaped scar down both sides of his nose was even more livid seen close up.

"My name is Harry Stubbs," I said, proffering a card. "Of Lantern Insurance, though I'm here today on personal business."

He knocked the card out of my hand and it fluttered to the ground.

"Now clear off out," he said, gesturing with a thumb. "Stubbs."

"I haven't told you my business."

"Out," he repeated, with the same gesture.

"That's uncalled-for," I said. "I only wish—"

He took a step forward with a raised fist.

I can take a hint as well as any man. Something lay behind this hostility, and any further attempts at conversation were unlikely to be fruitful. While most raised fists are mere bodily rhetoric, this one looked like it had a practical intent.

Under other circumstances I might have bid him a good day and returned at a later time, in the hope of encountering someone less obstreperous. But I felt that if I wanted to make real progress here a more robust response was called for. I could not let one bad-tempered underling bar my way.

"I have business here," I said, "only it's not with you. So, if you don't mind—"

He came forward and, without ceremony, threw a punch at my face. Having seem him coming, I blocked without any great difficulty while stepping back. I had lost my hat, but he would know I was a trained fighter and no pushover. In half a second we were squared up in fighting stances. We shuffled and circled left and right as he tried to push me back and I responded by sidling around him.

"I'm not going away," I told him. "If you try and hurt me, I'll hurt you worse."

For reply, he came in with a more determined attack, a series of punches low and high. I blocked most and dodged others. That called for some sort of response, and in our next exchange of blows my jab caught him on the cheek.

I was pulling my punches. Bare-knuckle is a brutal business and you can easily damage yourself or your adversary. My aim was to establish my credentials, and make this person aware that I needed to be taken seriously.

He was hitting hard though. The anticipation of pain makes it difficult to punch a hard object, whether it is a brick wall or an opponent's chin, with the same level of force you would apply to a punch bag. Extensive training, great emotion, often aided by drink, or complete madness are what give bare-knuckle fighters the ability to strike out without hesitation. This one seemed to be naturally combative.

I was not prepared for his response, which was to step up his attacks. A lesser fighter might have been in trouble. I found myself backing away under the onslaught, ducking and blocking for all I was worth, concentrating on defence. When a blow landed on my chest, it was like being struck with a hammer. I knew at once it was going to leave a bruise with four knuckle-spots of deeper colour.

But for all his power and aggression he was sloppy, and pressed as I was, as soon as I saw an opening I could not resist the impulse to deliver a second jab and giving him a matching bruise on his other cheek, even as I was retreating.

I was half expecting him to go berserk at that—which would have given me a good opportunity to end the fight at once—but instead it slowed him down, as though suddenly appreciating that he might be up against a better man.

I caught motion to one side in the corner of my eye, but could not risk turning my head or looking away—always keep your eyes on the other man.

"Stop it! What are you doing?"

An older man with a cane marched up behind my opponent. He had a marked German accent. Hearing him, my opponent turned and lowered his fists.

"I asked you, what are you doing?" the old man demanded, rapping his cane on the ground for emphasis.

"He was trying to get in," mumbled the boxer, abashed.

Hands grabbed me from both sides. Two men had come up behind while I was distracted, and as I half turned I saw more. I was surrounded by the whole crew, five or six of them, all muscle and anxious scowls, disfigured by V-scars, like the matching shirts of a sports team. Like my original assailant, most of them looked ready for a ruck.

If I was going to fight my way out, this would be the time for it, but a split-second's calculation indicated that was not the way.

"Excuse me sir," said the man with the cane, addressing me as politely as though I were not being physically restrained. "Who might you be?"

He was a fellow with greying hair and horn-rimmed glasses, in an old-fashioned check suit. I realised it was the disapproving man who had sat opposite us at the fight.

"Harry Stubbs," I said.

He looked at me a moment before smiling.

"Ah, the English heavyweight—of course," he said. "I saw you at the fire station last week, with a certain mysterious lady."

"I'm sure I should know your name," I said, "but our host did not make introductions."

"Dr Vengler, Mr Stubbs," he said. "Lately of Geneva. Now, please might I ask you to take your shirt off?"

The hands holding me loosed their grip. I knew better than to run for it. Protestation would be equally useless. Without a word I removed my jacket, tie, shirt and vest.

"Hmm," he said. "Turn around slowly, if you please."

I sensed him approach, and I realised that he was looking up at my left ear, a piece of which had been sliced off during the Shackleton affair.

"I think something unusual happened to your ear, Mr Stubbs," he said. "Tell me what happened here?"

Most people assumed it had been lost in a fight, but maybe to the practised eye it was obvious that it had not been bitten off, or even cut with a blade.

"I couldn't rightly say," I said evasively. "Something unusual."

There was a distinct mutter from the boxers, as though someone had just answered back to an officer and was about to cop some trouble, but Vengler just smiled.

"As a letter of introduction, your ear will get you through the door, Mr Stubbs," he said. "You may put your clothes back on. But, it is very important that you please understand this: if you raise a hand against me, these men will make you regret it most extremely. Yes?"

"Nothing could be further from my mind," I said, donning my vest.

"Then we can have an interview. Now, everyone—please return to your assigned activities until you are further instructed. At once!"

He rapped his cane again so sharply I almost jumped, and the men responded with military obedience, dispersing at a jog.

My assailant returned to his washing without meeting my eye, pretending not to be cowed. Re-dressed, I picked up my bowler and, as an afterthought, my business card. Those things cost money.

"I do not encourage visitors," said the doctor, leading me into the warehouse. "But there must always be exceptions."

"I thought I might be in trouble when your man squared up to me," I said, by way of conversation.

Vengler made a clicking noise with his tongue.

"No! You would have defeated him quite quickly, I think," said Vengler. "He is good, but he is not a match for an experienced fighter in good condition, such as yourself. "

The smell inside the warehouse was comfortingly familiar, the smell of a thousand gymnasiums: sweat, liniment and rubber-soled shoes.

A row of windows beneath the roof was supplemented by powerful electric lights. It was kitted out as a boxing gym, with wall bars, a row of punching bags down one wall, and a couple of padded areas for floor work, as well as a full-size ring with a proper sprung floor. Two men were lifting weights, next to a rack of dumbbells.

Elsewhere, mattresses and bedding were neatly stacked against one wall, and I noticed boxes of tinned goods and other supplies, and a curtained off area that looked like washroom facilities. It seemed the whole boxing crew was camped here permanently.

"This is what you came to see," he said. "Although I think perhaps you have already had all the demonstration you need?"

"After the show at the fire station, I knew they could box," I said.

"Rehabilitation," said Vengler. "There are too many broken men in the world and I am seeking to mend them."

"If you're turning men who can't walk into boxers like that one, you're not far short of a miracle worker," I said. "I don't think you're doing it all with weights."

We watched the men doing arm curls with dumbbells—left arm, right arm, left arm, right arm.

"The human body is straightforward and responds in predictable ways," said Vengler. "Anyone can build his strength from nothing up to the level of a Hercules with the necessary hours of work. This simple truth has made Mr Charles Atlas a rich man!" He chuckled to himself. "Discipline is the key—as you know yourself."

His observation was perfectly correct. We have the greatest admiration for unstudied success, for the man who can casually pick up a cricket bat and score a century, but real sporting achievement is founded on hard grind. Plenty of men have the talent to be a runner, or swimmer, or boxer of the first water, but very few have the necessary willpower to hone that talent to the necessary edge. Many and many were the times I swore that my training regime was too much, and that I would throw in the towel on the whole boxing lark. The early mornings, the long runs, the restriction on what you are allowed to eat—and more particularly what you are allowed to drink, and when.

"Exercise is not enough to get you back on your feet when you can't walk," I said.

"A miracle of science," said Vengler, opening the door to an inner room, a cube of sheet plywood in one corner of the warehouse. This would once have been the manager's office, and like the rest of the place it showed little sign of being modified for its new role. The desk and chairs looked left over from the previous occupants, and the filing cabinets and cupboards had the makeshift look of second-hand furniture, easily bought and quickly discarded.

One side of the room was a dispensary with racks of mysterious bottles and jars, all neatly labelled, and what looked like first aid supplies. In the corner was the wooden cabinet of a radio set, similar to the one owned by my friend. It made me think of German spies in the war, receiving secret orders over the airwaves.

"Mrs Smith accepts your fantastical claims, at face value," I said, taking the indicated seat. "I thought I ought to find out more."

"But you are not here on Mrs Smith's account," he said, sitting opposite me. He took a cigarette from a silver case stamped with a wolf's head, offering me one as well.

"I am not," I said, waving a hand to decline. I would tie myself up in knots if I tried to lie, and the truth would serve me just as well. "I am here on behalf of other interests, independent of the Widows Society which I happen to be investigating."

He blew a long jet of smoke.

"That is excellent news," he said. "The Widows Society are good patrons, but it is not good to rely on a single source of support."

"Is that why you have the boxing show as a side venture?"

"I like the show. It is good for the men." He gave a fierce smile. "The circus maximus is an ancient and honourable institution. The gladiatorial arena—you must know the joy of victory, Mr Stubbs! The ultimate proof of man's physical and mental fitness. A more thorough researcher would have them fight to the death like gladiators, to truly recreate the Darwinian struggle for survival, no?"

"But your real interest is in medical research?" I prompted.

"Yes, of course." He tapped ash from his cigarette. "The

claims made at the show are true. Reality concealed by the mask of fiction. Six months ago, the man you fought was a physical wreck, incapable even of walking due to spinal damage. Now look at him."

"Very impressive," I said.

As we spoke I could feel his eyes moving over me, inspecting my damaged ear, my flattened nose. It was like the touch of an insect's antenna: not painful, but an alien, unwelcome intrusion.

"You are, of course, sceptical. I am a nerve specialist." He raised a finger to forestall any interruption. "Not one of these 'talking cure' men who treats rich ladies: a real nerve specialist, a surgeon expert in repairing nerve damage. James was a paraplegic who could not use his legs before I operated." He laughed. "You may raise your eyebrows, but it is all true."

"I don't know a thing about it," I said. "But what I heard was that nerves don't heal."

"What you heard is the accepted view of the medical establishment," he said, "which happens to be inaccurate. I would say 'outdated', but the truth has been known for a very long time."

His look was a challenge. Vengler wanted to know who he was dealing with, what I knew. At this stage I was prepared to show some credentials.

"Paracelsus always said the aim of alchemy was to create medicines, not gold," I ventured. "He claimed that with the art of palingenesis he could restore tissue even if it had been reduced to ash. I have seen the results of that process with my own eyes."

"I see," he said, nodding slowly. "Interesting. I am merely a surgeon, but our history goes back further than most Europeans realise. The transplanting of skin and cartilage, which my colleagues are so excited to apply to victims of the latest war, are not new techniques. They have been known for thousands of years."

"Thousands?" I queried.

"These things are documented in Asia, to those who can be troubled to read them." He waved a hand. "The ancients knew if a man had lost skin from his face, for example, or had his nose cut off, it would be possible to repair the damage with tissue taken from elsewhere on the body—or from another body. Here, we call this the 'Italian method,' but it was stolen. Central America, China, Sumeria...their techniques survived, here and there. The British have lately retrieved some from India, which is why your English surgeons have also taken up the idea."

"Like Paracelsus, you are reviving the secrets of the ancients."

"I can claim very little of the credit for discovery," he said. "My steps have been guided." He looked up at me, and his gaze was steely. "But I have been able to apply surgical techniques for regeneration which have been lost for centuries, and I have made them work. Full palingenesis from the dead is for wizards, but as a humble surgeon I am content to restore the living."

"Quite an achievement," I said, and I meant it—while at the same time thinking that I would not wish to have anything to do with him. I doubted whether Vengler would be bothered if a patient died so long as he learned something interesting.

"They do not understand," he said, gesturing towards the door, and the sound of several pairs of feet running up and down the length of the building. "They only care about themselves. If I was to release them, they would leave at once, and go back to being...dock workers, or delivery van drivers or whatever. You understand, they are all volunteers. They are aware of the risks, and of the conditions I demand, before I make the first scalpel cut. But then they are mine!"

"You do leave a signature on your work," I said.

"Yes. That is not carelessness, or lack of skill!" His voice rose suddenly, in emphasis rather than anger. If he had been holding his cane he would have rapped the floor. "It is deliberate. They need visible marks as a permanent reminder, in case they should forget what they are."

"Even the facial scars?" I asked.

"Especially those. The human nose is a weak point, as you must know." His gaze flicked momentarily to my own nose, broken long ago and showing it. "I have a procedure to strengthen it. This is mandatory for my fighters."

He stood up suddenly and stood by the wall, removing

some bottles on a shelf to reveal a spyhole looking out into the gym.

"Look here, Mr Stubbs: that man on the other side."

I had not noticed him before, an inconspicuous figure in overalls wielding a mop and bucket. I looked closely to see what was so interesting about him.

"He's limping," I observed. "He can't bend his right leg."

"Exactly so," said Vengler, with satisfaction. "A week ago he was training with the others, now he is almost a cripple again."

"What happened?"

"He broke the rules, so I withheld treatment," said Vengler. "He has been demoted to scrubbing and cleaning toilets. He is a reminder to the others."

He went back to his desk, rubbing his hands.

"I have rebuilt these men into efficient living engines. I have given them muscles they did not have before, perfected their physique, built everything from the skeleton upwards. And they will stay until I have taken this technique to its furthest limits."

"They need continuous treatment?" I said.

"At present, the surgery is sustained by regular injections," he said, a little irritably. "It could be made permanent, by increasing the dose to complete the nerve regeneration, but then I might lose my test subjects."

I found it difficult to return his smile.

"And Mrs Smith is satisfied with your work," I said.

"She sees its potential. But more than that…" His expression softened. "She is a beautiful woman, of course. All such women want to preserve their beauty. I have explained how my work can also achieve this."

I felt he badly misjudged Mrs Smith's motives. Vengler was not, perhaps, a great judge of people, His preferred relationship was one of rulership rather than anything more complicated.

"So, in addition to restoring broken men, you can offer eternal youth?"

He scoffed.

"Not at all! But the restoration of the external appearance of the epidermis to a youthful state is well within my power. My men are ugly because I choose ugliness for them, but I can make women beautiful. This is something you might mention to your employers."

They may already have it, I thought, considering Miss de Vere's flawless, ageless complexion. Not to mention that they also appeared to have the ability to restore mobility to the lame, recalling my conversation with Ryan, the tiger hunter at the start of my last case for TDS.

"I will certainly let them know of your progress," I said.

"You do not like me, Mr Stubbs," he said. "I am the evil doctor, experimenting with boxers, men who you identify with." His eyes fell on my scarred knuckles, and again it was like the touch of a moth. "In reality, you are nothing like them—you who can quote Paracelsus and with your experience of greater things. Your employers, they will appreciate that I am a man who can obey instructions and that, if they trust me, I can shape human flesh however they wish. The world wants strong men and beautiful women, but so much more is possible if we free our imaginations."

The doctor's eyes were wide now. I could only guess where his imagination was roaming, and I suspected he was contemplating modifications and extensions to the human body beyond anything found in nature. Mr Wells' Dr Moreau had nothing on Dr Vengler.

My employers, I knew from experience, would happily burn this whole place down and Vengler and his experimental subjects with it. But maybe they wanted something from him first.

"Very true, Dr Vengler," I said. "I thank you for a most interesting discussion."

"I look forward to hearing more," he said.

It was something of a relief to get back out onto the street, where young Arthur, in his guise of mock-urchin, was eager to hear all I had discovered.

"The thread continues," I told him. "We have our mad scientist and his crew. But I don't think he's at the end of it."

"We'd better keep investigating then," he said.

I suppressed a smile at his thirteen-year-old's air of

importance. He was simply mimicking what he had read in stories, seen on the stage and heard on the radio. In truth though it was what many grown-ups would have said too, and nobody would bat an eyelid. The intellectual difference between adults and children may be less than we like to believe.

Chapter 10: The Fall

Unless you are a police detective, with all the authority which accompanies that post, investigating a death years after the event is a fools' errand. There is no chance of finding physical evidence, and witnesses, if they can be found, will remember little and make up facts to cover the gaps. Nevertheless, honour demanded I make the attempt. A letter would be ignored, so one evening, when I could see a light on in the top-floor apartment that was my goal, I rang the doorbell.

A window opened and a face looked briefly down at me. Before I could call out they were gone, but a minute later a shadow darkened the glass panel in the door, the bolt slid back and I was face to face with a pale young man.

"You'd better come in," was all he said, before turning and tramping back up the stairs.

The youth seemed middle-class, his long hair and old-fashioned, earth-tone clothing giving me the impression he was posing as a Victorian landowner. He said nothing as I followed him up the three flights and through the apartment door, down a short passage and into a spacious living room with windows on two sides.

The young man flung himself on an overstuffed armchair as though he had just scaled a mountain and could not walk another step.

"Got him," he said, and fell into a trance contemplating a reproduction of a painting by Lord Leighton.

"Hello there," said a woman from the other armchair, waving with the tips of her fingers. "You must be Harry Stubbs."

She was all in black, with long dark hair, a pale complexion and kohl around her eyes. Her fingernails were also painted black. I guessed she was in her early twenties, like her companion. I had seen this distinctive individual before, more than once, most recently in South Norwood cemetery.

"I am indeed," I said. She had not invited me to sit on the sofa, but I did so anyway as it seemed politer than towering over them. They seemed to be highly informal people. "I believe I know you by sight, but—"

"Claudia," she said. "Claudia Oldham." She did not introduce her companion. "I know you through Annie. Annie Frey, you know? My fellow bone-hound in the graveyard."

"Ahh," I said. "Miss Frey has mentioned you, yes. You're a poetess, I believe."

"A shopgirl with pretensions," corrected her companion. She ignored him.

Miss Frey had mentioned a friend called Claudia who also haunted the cemetery, and who affected a gothic style. Sometimes it really is a small world. Mathematically speaking there must be hundreds of people with whom I have mutual acquaintances.

"And you!" she said, almost squealing, "You're the investigator of Mysterious Things. Now, Adrian will get you a drink—if you're allowed to drink on duty?"

"I'm not a police officer, Miss Oldham, but—"

"It's Claudia, please," she said. "When you call me Miss Oldham I feel a hundred and three. Go on Adrian, hop to it."

Her voice was enough to reanimate her companion, who shuffled over to the cocktail cabinet and held up a bottle in either hand.

"Whisky or gin? We've a passable burgundy, or absinthe if you prefer, or...we have most things."

"I'll have a small whisky, if you please," I said. I did not especially want a drink, but I needed to foster the growing rapport.

"So," said Claudia, leaning forward confidently. "How can I help? Is it about the mysterious death of Mr Parrish?"

"As a matter of fact, it is."

"Told you!" she said, triumphantly, to her friend.

"You'd be more like Hercule Poirot if you had guessed

anything else," said Adrian, passing me a glass with a generous quantity of Scotch.

"Parrish's the whole reason I'm here," she said. "You see, after he met his end they had difficulty finding a tenant at any price. Everybody knew this was the suicide apartment, and if they didn't know, the neighbours would tell them pretty quick. I had people telling me months after I moved in that a man killed himself here."

"You wouldn't believe how cheap she gets it," said Adrian. "Full-size place, one-and-a half bedrooms, hot and cold running water."

"It's not the price," she said. "It's the fact that I don't mind a ghost. In fact, I revel in the etheric vibrations of a melancholy spirit around the place. I don't know why people are so upset by the idea."

"Would you consider it rude of me if I took notes?" I asked, holding up my notebook. Both gestured their indifference with practised shrugs. "So it's common knowledge around here the death was suicide then?"

"Common tittle-tattle," said Adrian.

"Well, come and see for yourself," said Claudia, moving to the bay window and striking a pose. "This is the fatal fenetre."

It struck me then that both of them were quite some way down the bottle, if coherent and perfectly amiable. I stood close to the glass and looked down, noting the wide window ledge which was occupied by several flower-pots, each with a sprig of dead vegetation.

It was slightly dizzying. I never much care for views looking vertically downward. There is a power of suction there which seems to draw you over the edge, and I am all too aware of my weight and the smashing impact that waits at the end of any fall. Miss Oldham, by contrast, looked like she would just float down in her long dress.

"You would have to throw yourself out some way to hit the ground," I observed.

"Well, exactly," she said.

She fitted a cigarette into a holder and lit it, then belatedly offered me one which I declined.

"He could have fallen," I said, "if, for example, the window had been stuck, he was trying to force it, and it gave way suddenly. Does it stick?"

"Not that I've noticed," she said vaguely.

It was not a very likely explanation.

"Or perhaps if he was very intoxicated and very careless— was there any indication of that?"

"He must have had the odd drink, everyone does. But none of the neighbours said anything about his being a dipsomaniac."

"Which leaves suicide," I said, looking down.

I was judging the fall and how he might have projected himself out. It might have been quite simple, especially if he was drunk. One stage to half-fall out of the window, say if he had been forcing it open, and second stage to slip and overbalance over the edge. Not a very likely accident, but, then, the newspapers are full of unlikely accidents.

"'Nine days he fell, until hell at last yawning wide received him whole.' Do you read poetry?"

"Nothing you'd approve of, I suspect," I said. "I was raised on Rudyard Kipling, and some of it stuck. I'm partial to Robert Browning and W.B. Yeats but I don't get on with T.S. Eliot and the modern crowd."

"You've read The Waste Land?"

"But I didn't understand it."

"Good for you," said Adrian. "The last honest man in England."

"Yeats though," said Claudia. "Yeats is terribly important."

The Horniman case had involved the Golden Dawn group of occultists of which Yeats was a member, but this was no time for side tracks.

"He didn't leave a note," I said. "I believe that's unusual."

"Extraordinary," she said. "Because he was a writer. Very much a writer of letters and a bit of an obsessive about those women…" She snapped her fingers, trying to recall.

"The Widows Society," I supplied.

"Yes, them. Do you think they're frightfully sinister?"

"Look who's talking, Miss Dracula," said Adrian with a snort of laughter. Claudia was herself dressed entirely in black, down to the rings on her fingers. She ignored him.

"Mr Parrish found them highly suspicious," I said.

"He thought they were witches," said Adrian. "Maybe they used their powers to compel him to leap out into space, by telepathic hypnosis."

"A difficult theory to substantiate," I said, before realising he was being sarcastic.

"Unfortunately, Adrian is not just an ignoramus when it comes to the supernatural, but a proud one," said Claudia.

"Claudia had a psychic medium around to talk to our ghost," said Adrian, looking into his glass, "so of course she knows everything about the fatal fall."

"An interesting approach," I said. "Was it successful?"

While plenty of self-professed psychics contact the police and the newspapers in regard to high-profile murders, their track record is generally a poor one, and it is not a recognised means of investigation. But that is not to say that, in certain types of cases, they cannot turn up any evidence.

"Well," said Claudia. "It was and it wasn't."

She darted a look at Adrian as if daring him to say anything witty. He merely looked smug and sipped his drink.

"I invited a lady called Elizabeth Belhaven to the flat," she said.

"I know her," I said, looking up. She had conducted the fateful séance at the Theosophical Society during the Roslyn D'Onston affair. She was certainly no fraud, though she might be prone to allowing her imagination to get the better of her at times.

"She did not sense any restless spirits here," said Claudia.

"The creaking of the boards and the howling of the wind at night did not impress her," said Adrian. "At that point she was talking sense, and I thought she was going to say it was all your neurotic imaginings."

"But then," said Claudia, "when she stood here by the window, she had a vision."

Adrian made an expression of mock surprise as if to say, "well what did you expect?"

"She saw something land on the ledge beneath the window,"

said Claudia, in a low voice. "A spectral presence. Something evil."

"And it opened the window?"

"The window was opened," she admitted.

It was a sash window with no lock, so opening it from outside would be no great challenge if you could gain some purchase. But this would presuppose not just a material being but a winged beast with hands.

"And it caught Parrish by surprise," I said.

"I'll bet it did!" Adrian interjected.

"It menaces him, and he ends up leaping out the window to his death. The thing squats on the windowsill, like a gargoyle contemplating its work, then it flits away into the dark, leaving an empty room with a locked door."

She acted all this out as she spoke. She was a lady with a powerful imagination.

"Which is all just telepathic hypnosis with shiny knobs on," said Adrian. "It comes to the same thing, just a dark spirit rather than psychic power."

"Unless it was an actual being," I said. "Though there is the question of aerodynamics."

"I'm sorry?"

"I believe it's a matter of lifting power and the limitations of avian physiology. My understanding is that science tells us that a human-size, or at least human-weight bird is not possible. So, while the great albatross may have a wingspan of twelve feet or more, it weighs less than the average turkey and is strictly a gliding bird."

Claudia blinked twice before taking another puff from her cigarette holder.

"I suppose we can allow that there might be flying creatures with wings more powerful than any on Earth," I said. "But it might have to have the wingspan of an aeroplane, or else beat its wings as fast as a dragonfly to gain enough lift."

Adrian looked at me closely, as though not sure whether I was making fun of Claudia and, if so, whether he should join in the joke.

"You've considered the matter," he said.

"I believe there were some signs of struggle, indicating there may have been an assailant."

"There were," said Claudia. "Two pictures were knocked off the walls, and Parrish's pipe was crushed underfoot."

Of course those were just the sort of things that happened when someone was staggering drunk. But pictures being knocked off the wall might have inspired someone with an active imagination to think of a large, winged creature brushing against them.

"It wasn't much of a struggle," said Claudia. "Elizabeth said Parrish was paralysed with fear, like a rabbit confronted in its warren by a stoat."

Investigators at the time might have checked the window for signs of interference from outside. Any blood spatters on the floor or walls might have been an indication too, though those can have many causes. Anyone who has worked in a butcher's with sharp knives knows how much even the tiniest accidental cut can bleed.

"The perfect murder, you might say," I said. "A supernatural entrance which nobody would believe, and no forensic evidence left behind."

"Unless you believe in crumbs of ectoplasm," said Adrian, with another eye roll.

"I had forgotten that," said Claudia, excitedly.

"This will simply astound you," said Adrian, his voice dripping with irony.

Claudia darted to a bureau and opened a small drawer. After rummaging she came up with a matchbox, which she passed to me.

"Look," she said.

At first I thought it was empty, before I perceived a couple of dozen black flakes. They might have been crumbs of burned toast.

"I swept up in between the floorboards," she said. "Nobody had done that since he died. I think it's some sort of residue, like the scorch-marks left by infernal fire."

The flakes were more regular and curled than toast crumbs. But without any experience of what you find in normal floor-sweepings I could not begin to judge their significance.

"If you can look under a microscope and see 'Made In Hell' stamped on them it might convince a jury," said Adrian. "But if we put the demon aside for one minute, we have the blindingly obvious conclusion that the man was pathologically depressed, or drunk, or both and threw himself out of the window."

I weighed the matchbox in my hand.

"People throw themselves off skyscrapers all the time in New York, you know, it's quite the thing."

"This is not a skyscraper," she objected. "I've thought of throwing myself out there at times, but you can't just do it on impulse. You have to crawl out and graze your knees, bark your shins and tear your stockings getting out there. And—there was no note!"

"Claudia loves suicide notes, she writes a new one every week," said Adrian. "She doesn't realise that not everyone shares her obsession for documenting innermost thoughts."

"I have been driven to extremities," she said, addressing me. "There have been times when I have contemplated self-destruction, and the act of focusing on one's emotions, of expressing feeling in words on paper, is marvellously cathartic. It gives one such a perspective, to see life from the Other Side, to look back on existence as a thing in the past, and it's excellent raw material afterwards. It makes no sense that an expressive man, one with strong feelings, would not leave a note."

In her emotion she fitted another cigarette into the holder and lit it.

"That apart," I said. "Given his obsessive pursuit of the Society, I would have thought he might have secreted a notebook or other writing somewhere about the place."

"Been through it a hundred times, darling," she said. "Not a thing. Not even an enigmatic warning chalked on the inside of a cupboard. That's why I was checking between the floorboards."

"She doesn't ordinarily stoop to housework," Adrian added.

"We used to get the odd letter addressed to him, mainly from North America."

"You did not take down the return address, I suppose?"

"Sorry. But," she said, brightening, "one of them was from

a private detective with one of those American names, in Chicago."

"And there was one from New England," Adrian added. "From a Dr-something-or-other."

"Not Dr de Vere?" I asked.

Miss de Vere apparently held a doctorate in psychology, and went by doctor when it suited her.

"Don't know. Organisation had a funny name ... Total Something Something..."

"'Total Development Syndicate'," her partner said with an American drawl.

TDS. That would be Miss de Vere, and Parrish would have been her creature, knowingly or otherwise. A canary sent into the coalmine with the usual results. Just like Gillespy in the asylum case. I was privileged to be slightly further up in the rankings of the organisation's cannon-fodder.

As I retrieved my hat, Adrian indicated I could show myself out—he did not want to go down and have to climb the staircase again.

"We're not really together you know, him and me," said Claudia. "I'm sure you'll tell Annie, and I wouldn't want her to think he was my lover."

"Her lovers are so much more bohemian than I," he said. "Drug fiends and sexual perverts to a man, you know. I'm just a very good friend."

"Thank you so much for your help," I said. "And for the whisky."

I heard her voice as I descended the stairs, "Drop round any time, darling!"

The investigation in Parrish's death had yielded more than I could have hoped. I left with a few notes, the results of Elizabeth Belhaven's psychic investigation, and a matchbox containing some—possibly—mysterious material.

Chapter 11: Making Some Enquiries

Sometimes there are not enough hours in the day. I had to get up early to walk Sally to work from her lodgings. This was because she was seeing a wedding dressmaker that evening, and the next evening she was with the florist. I would not have a chance to see her for two days without this early-morning excursion.

"I could come to the florist with you," I said.

"And sit around getting bored and fidgety, and trying to hurry me, and then being resentful about it afterwards?"

Her words stung, mainly because they were true. The burden of organising fell mainly on Sally, and she was determined to make a good go of it.

"Maybe not," I agreed.

I did not know how anyone could take hours simply selecting flowers for a wedding reception. But then, I reflected, this is based on ignorance of the process. For men, flower arrangements, like laundry, are simply something that happens.

"You leave the flowers to me," she said, gently. "Stick to what you're good at. You never finished telling me how you got on with that boxing gang thing."

I had been telling her about my visit to the warehouse, and my meeting with Dr Vengler. She looked thoughtful when I described him.

"A German doctor with grey hair, wearing black spectacles?" Sally asked. "Sounds like someone I knew. Only his name wasn't Vengler, then; Schmidt was what he called himself. Used to help girls who were in trouble. Probably still does."

Pregnancy was an occupational hazard for those who worked the streets. Abortion has always been illegal except under certain special circumstances, but there were always a few doctors, or pseudo-doctors, willing to carry them out, for a price. Vengler had made no bones about his need for money, and his ethics were certainly flexible enough, but that did not mean it was him.

"Maybe all German doctors wear those glasses," I said, trying to remember Vengler's other distinguishing features. "Did your doctor have a cane?"

"Not that I know. He had a cruel way of talking, even when he was pretending to be sympathetic." She frowned with concentration. "I heard he had a silver cigarette case with a dog's head on it."

"Ah," I said. "That's the man. What do you know about him?"

"He turned up, must have been about three years ago. He even handed out business cards to some of the girls."

"Cards?" I asked, astonished.

"With a telephone number. You left a message with a name, and a taxi would come around outside the White Swan pub late that night. Dr Schmidt would blindfold them in the taxi so they did not know where they were going.

Doctors in that field relied on the discretion of their clients. But Dr Vengler, or whatever his name was, even went to the length of hiding his location.

"Sounds like Teutonic efficiency," I said.

"He was safe, and he only charged what you could afford. And he didn't come around asking favours like some of them. He used a place in Balham which was very clean—a room in a clinic or something—and sent the girl back in the same taxi after. But nobody liked him, and that's not just because he was German."

"Funny about the charging," I said. I would have expected him to have extorted whatever the market would bear. Paracelsus only asked for what his patients could afford, but I suspected something other than altruism here. "What's his game?"

I wanted to know what Vengler was up to, and why. I wanted to know who was behind him, feeding him ideas about palingenesis, and what their plans were. I had been doing some research into nerve injuries, and, as I thought, they do not heal, and no surgeon had any real success in reconnecting nerves once they were severed. Vengler was way ahead of the world, and clearly he had help.

"I can see if any of the girls know exactly where that clinic is," she said.

Finding out where he worked could be a big step towards finding out what he was really up to, and it might give me a bit of leverage. But I did not want Sally to have to see her old acquaintances on the streets: the Fifi, Mimi and Lulus as they called themselves, whose real names were Rose, Lillian and Elizabeth. It had been a bad time for her.

"I don't mind," she assured me, as though reading my thoughts. "It'll be a chance to tell them the good news."

She twisted her engagement ring, with the five-pointed green stone from the Antarctic on it.

"It would be a great favour," I said. "I'll pursue other lines of enquiry."

"Leave it to me," she said.

We went our separate ways, she to her work at the pickle factory, and I to pursue my own occupation.

My first stop was the Electric Café, where Arthur Renville was holding court as usual. He was at his preferred table with a number of associates arranged around him, a few in an inner conversational circle, others at the outer tables, ready to be called on.

My eye was drawn to the four tin cans in front of him. They were the sort of tins in which you might buy baked beans, except there were no labels on them.

"Here's Stubbs," said someone. "Maybe he knows a psychic who can help us."

It was not mockery of me, but the sort of facetious comment thrown out when other ideas have failed. At Arthur's gesture I swung a chair around to take up a place at the table.

"I'm picking the brains of everyone who comes in today," he said, in the tone of one issuing a challenge, "over this here little conundrum."

He indicated the four tins.

"These are four samples from a consignment that came into my possession from the docks, bound from the good city of Boston. It seems some of our American cousins sent over a shipment of tinned foods from their brand-new canning plant. Due to stormy conditions, water got into the hold and a good fraction of the cargo had the labels washed off." He shook his head. This sort of thing could not happen with decent labelling. "Because the crates were not labelled and nobody thought to record what order they were packed in, we end up with a few thousand mystery tins. Unsaleable of course, and so picked up at a very reasonable discount."

He said this with a straight face. Everything would have been technically legal; the purchasers would have refused delivery of the goods, the sellers would not want them shipped back, so they would have been waiting on the dock for someone like Arthur to make an offer.

"From the ship's manifest, and from opening some, we know that some are tinned peaches, some pears, some peas, some green beans...and some of them are vegetable soup and some Boston Baked Beans, with pork, I am told."

He switched a couple of the tins around, like a confidence man doing the shell game in the West End, then switched two more.

"If it was all vegetables," I said, "or all fruit, you could sell it as such without too much fuss."

"That would be a breeze," said Arthur. "I've found a man with a labelling machine, so we can get them all labelled up. As you so rightly say, veg is veg and fruit is fruit, and nobody minds too much if they get beans or peas, or, on the other hand, peaches or pears. But while vegetable soup and baked beans might have a higher retail value, they queer the pitch entirely."

Nobody would buy a tin not knowing whether it was peaches or soup. The assembled commercial brains had been puzzling over this matter for some hours, so it was unlikely I would be able to add much.

I picked a tin up, shook it experimentally, and checked the base for markings. There was a small, diamond-shaped indent, but the same appeared on the other.

"Not so easy to tell, is it?" said Arthur, wryly. "Could be baked beans, could be peas. Only way to find out is to open it, but there's no going back once you've done that."

I shook it harder. There is such a thing as viscosity, which is the technical term for resistance to flow, and is how you can tell water from syrup. I was rotating the tin about an axis perpendicular to its length, which would agitate the contents. I tried another tin for comparison.

"They're not the same," I said. "I'd wager the contents were different."

"As we have observed. So what we need is a skilled tin-shaker who knows which is which," said Arthur. "I knew a chicken sexer once. All he did, all day, was pick up newborn chicks and sort them into bins for male and female."

"Is that so?" It sounded like the set-up to a punchline, but he was serious.

"And, so he told me, it was a skilled art that few ever mastered. He earned good money for it, too, his whole working life. Because hens lay and roosters don't, so you need to get them sorted out as soon as possible."

"What's he like at tins?" I asked.

"That's not the worst idea I've heard today," Arthur said, as Mario placed a cup of tea in front of me, a curl of steam rising from its surface.

Arthur took a sip from his own cup, and his expression relaxed as he laid the problem with the tins aside.

"You're keeping my boy out of trouble then?"

"Young Arthur is a credit to his father," I said. "He's saving me a lot of work."

"He seems to be enjoying himself, from what little I can get out of him. All very hush-hush, from what he says. He can't even tell his old dad."

Arthur's eyes twinkled. There was not much that went on in Norwood he could not find about if he wanted to.

"He's my Latin expert," I said. "Doing some historical research."

"I dare say it'll come in useful somewhere. But I don't expect you came here to give me a school report."

"As a matter of fact, I was wondering about a character reference," I said, "for a person you might be acquainted with. You know the boxing matches at the old fire station?"

"Mickey Power's racket?" Arthur knew about every enterprise in the borough, and nothing took place without his approval. He had a stake in some of them, and some of them paid him a cut—not protection money, just on the understanding they might need his assistance one day.

"That's the one."

"I don't need to tell you about Mickey, do I?" His smile was confiding. "You've seen his sort by the truckload. They're all the same. He's flash and he talks a mile a minute, and he can splash the marigold about when he needs to impress. But you know, and I know, that one fine day he's going to shoot the moon, and the next morning there will be debts owing from here to Hackney, and nobody to answer for them."

"Not him," I said. "His partner. The doctor."

"Oh, him," said Arthur. "Now that's a rarer sort of bird."

"He does wonders with getting maimed soldiers back on their feet. Unless that's all trickery—but he certainly has a way of adding some pounds to man's punch. I can attest to that firsthand. But is he a quack, or a dangerous lunatic, or something else?"

"That 'Dr' 'Vengler'," said Arthur with some disdain. "I wouldn't want him operating on me... I expect you to take this with a pinch of salt, but there's an interesting rumour concerning that doctor."

Arthur spread his hands wide to indicate he was going to recount a tale.

"Now, I don't know whether you encountered this at the time, or whether it has fallen under your purview since, but there was a tale about The Hound of Mons. Ah, I can see that it's new to you.

"Well, the story goes that, fairly early on in the war, Germany set its scientists to developing horrible new weapons. We all know about chlorine gas, and germ warfare, and all that, but this was something different. It seems that one scientist was set on using animals as weapons. He had bred a huge and enormously vicious beast from Siberian wolfhound stock. On its own, this would not have been of much use, so he somehow transplanted the brain of a man into this hound—a lunatic who had a fanatical hatred of the English.

"With its combination of speed, power and human cunning, this Hound was set loose in No Man's Land. Then patrols started disappearing, and sentries were found dead with their throats ripped out, and even messengers between our own trenches were taken. Soldiers heard unearthly howling at night, and some of them said they had seen the silhouette of a monstrous hound.

"Now, we've all heard this sort of story—horrors lurking in the night, just out of sight in the trenches; strange shapes seen by flare-light, moving faster than a man in the shell holes; mysterious tracks, and of course, men who go missing with no explanation. It was a deadly time, and, as if we did not have enough to worry about, men's imaginations were fertile and grew plenty of new things to scare themselves with."

"It's pretty far-fetched," I said.

"And it's not the sort of thing most people set any store by. But I have it on very good authority that in his discussions with Mickey Powers, the doctor has been known to boast that he was on the surgical team that did the brain transplant."

I recalled Vengler's cigarette case with the engraved wolf's head. Or should that be wolfhound's head?

"Funny thing to boast about," I said.

"The thing is, the whole exercise was a flop. According to Vengler, they did succeed in putting a man's brain in a dog, but that wasn't the point. I mean, what good is a dog against machine guns and barbed wire? What they were being paid for was to put the brain of a dog into the body of a man."

"Why that way round?" I asked, but I could already see his point.

"Think about it, Stubbsy. It's trained to total obedience, and with the aggression of an attack dog. He can learn to use a gun, he's got no compunction about killing. He can take orders, but he can't answer back. A pack of them are the perfect fighting unit. Werewolf stormtroopers! Well, it didn't work. But they had the dog body and the human brain left over, and they did what they could with those, just so they had something to show the Kaiser."

"And what did he think?"

"Well, Vengler got away to Switzerland and he was the lucky one. Then he comes here, for some reason."

"From what I heard," I said, my voice lowered, "He performs a service when women get into difficulties. Under the name of Schmidt"

Arthur looked more serious, dropping his voice to match mine. He made a vague gesture as though a cloud of fog stood between him and his subject.

"Girls die at the hands of unqualified, drunken, or just careless practitioners. In the interest of the public good, I made myself aware of this man's activities." He was as uncomfortable on this topic as I had seen him. "But his record is impeccable. Not one girl has died, or even suffered serious consequences as a result of going to him. Harley Street could not do better, but he provides his services for a fraction of the going rate."

"Seems unusual," I said.

I wondered if he was doing it as practice. As an experimental surgeon, maybe working in Harley Street or somewhere under a different name, and needing to hone his techniques on patients not from wealthy, influential families.

"No," Arthur went on. "According to my information——
the doctor carries out this trade purely for the purposes of gathering raw material for his other work."

"Ah," was all I could say.

One of the things my reading on the nervous system had taught me was that newborn babies can regenerate nerves in a way impossible for older children and adults. The connection was obvious. There were plenty of quacks selling fake rejuvenation treatments that involved injecting the blood of young people into old veins, but Vengler seemed to have found a procedure that actually worked.

"In his boxing racket, he treats his men hard and he doesn't pay them, but that's about par for the boxing game, as well you know. They are not there under compulsion and they get medical treatment they wouldn't get otherwise, along with bed and board and maybe fame and riches when they become champions. So he is, I suppose, a public benefactor, of a sort, and I haven't the slightest grounds for running him out of the area," Arthur concluded at normal volume. "Nevertheless, Stubbsy, nevertheless ... I have a bad feeling about that man."

He gave me a look, and raised his eyebrows meaningfully.

"I share your concerns," I said.

There was no need to tell Arthur all I knew about Vengler and his sadistic treatment of his men. He did not need, or want, to know such details.

"Might I be correct in believing that Vengler may be departing from us in the near future?"

"That seems likely," I said.

"Good. If you have a brainwave about those tins—don't keep it to yourself!"

Back at the office, I found the younger Arthur Renville studiously bent over his Latin translation. I doubted he had been at it the entire time I had been out, but he did seem to be making progress.

I dashed off some letters, one to Claudia Oldham thanking her for her assistance with the investigation into Mr Parrish, one to Mrs Bridges to let her know the investigation was proceeding satisfactorily, and a longer one to Miss de Vere to keep her up to date.

"I'll just get these to the post box," I said, reaching for my bowler.

"Can I come with you?" asked young Arthur, jumping up from his books like an excitable dog at the sight of the lead. "Please?"

"I don't generally require an escort," I said. "But maybe you can give me a precis of the latest chapter on the way, and we can both make use of the time."

I checked before setting out that it was not raining, and we walked companionably down the High Street.

"Have you ever seen a ghost, Mr Stubbs?"

"I don't rightly know what ghosts are," I said, "but I've seen men walking around when they're supposed to be in their graves."

"Aw, pretending to be dead doesn't count," he said.

That was not what I meant at all, but I held my tongue.

"When we left Paracelsus and his Friar Tuck, they were in the woods being held up by outlaws," I said. "A whole band of them."

Young Arthur, taking three strides to my two, had no trouble keeping up while continuing the story.

"That's because, you see, the people who are outlawed don't hide in the woods on their own. They band together to help each other and rob other people," Arthur explained. "His guide is scared and tries to run away, but Paracelsus isn't scared at all. He makes friends with the outlaws, and he treats one of them who has a bad eye, and one who broke his arm. And he treats a sick baby."

He seemed to think the latter was a bit of an imposition on the great man.

"They had their families with them, then," I said. I supposed they had to, though from Arthur's expression I could see that, to him, it would take all the fun out of outlawing if you had to have girls and babies along.

"Paracelsus says he doesn't mind outlaws, because he's an outlaw himself. The outlaws tell him how to find the people he wants to see, who are the 'Aegypti qui feruntur' who live in the woods."

"The who?"

"Well it literally means the 'ones from Egypt', and he keeps calling them 'Aegypti' which is Egyptians, but Mr Hoade thinks he really means the Gypsies or Romanies."

"So Mr Hoade was consulted?"

"He was very interested. He looked at the bit in the book and said he thought it sounded as though Paracelsus must have come to Gypsy Hill, because he comes to a big encampment of the Romanies with a lot of tents and fires. And they all draw weapons, but when he can get his guide to talk, he tells them he has come all the way from Helvetia—which is Switzerland—to see their queen."

Now we were getting to it.

"What happened next?"

Arthur took a piece of paper out of his pocket and scanned it before going on.

"There is a lot of talking. He tells them he is a great physician, and he talks to their physicians and they argue about herbs, and healing and things. At the end of it they say he can only see the queen if he goes through an ordeal. It's a sort of trial. He has to drink a deadly poison."

"Wouldn't that kill him?"

"The ordeal is, he has to prove he's really the greatest physician in the world by finding an antidote."

Given the account was written by Paracelsus himself, there did not seem to be much doubt about the outcome, but it would take a man confident indeed of his own powers to take up such a challenge.

"So, he did take poison?"

"Oh yes," said Arthur, as though he had been there himself, "He drank the whole goblet in one swig, down to the last dregs. He actually says 'ad ultimam faecem' which means the last dregs, but also means poo."

Schoolboys find what entertainment they can in their Latin translations.

"He says it didn't taste very nice."

The Romany physicians and herbalists must have all been watching the trial. Paracelsus was a big, blustering type, always blowing his own trumpet, who did not know the meaning of modesty.

"He puts the goblet down, and he then explains to the audience what his symptoms are—his hands and feet getting numb, and a pain in his chest and he gets dizzy. After a bit, he goes looking for herbs, finds one called Pennyroyal, and crushes it up and takes it. That makes him really sick, and he sicks up most of the poison. Then he goes to the campfire, and he gets some charcoal and grinds that up with water, and drinks it to counteract the rest of the poison. Then, he calls for a goblet of wine and sits down and starts telling them about all the different types of poison he knows. He's perfectly alright afterwards, but he says some of the others had too much wine because they tried to keep up with him."

"So he gets to see the Gypsy Queen?"

"I haven't got to that bit yet. There is a lot of talking and some recipes that he gets from them, but I can't translate half of the ingredients, even with the big Latin dictionary in the library and Mr Hoade helping me."

He was clearly taking some trouble over this. And Hoade was involved again.

"Well done, lad," I said. "I think we're beginning to make some progress."

I posted my letters through the slot one by one, wondering which way the case would go next.

Chapter 12: Guardian Angel

"I won't say it's a pleasure to meet you, Mr Stubbs, because it isn't, but we can at least be amicable, can't we?"

Mrs Hardcastle's accent betrayed Northern origins. I could not say if her roots lay in Yorkshire or Lancashire, but her no-nonsense manner would have been a credit to either. Her expression was milder than her words. She extended a hand glittering with rings, which I shook. It would have taken a braver and more foolish man than me to kiss that hand.

"I certainly hope so, Mrs Hardcastle," I said.

She was stout rather than otherwise, her complexion ruddier than fashion called for, but she looked to be in good health. Her dark outfit was neat and proper.

"I wasn't going to respond to your invitation, but when the others did I thought I'd better," she said, as though apologising to herself.

"And I thank you for the opportunity to talk," I said, offering her a business card.

We were in the offices of the London Mineral Exploitation Company Ltd, which occupied three floors of an undistinguished building on Westow Street. I assume it was the board room or similar, because of the grand walnut table surrounded by high-backed chairs.

Between Parrish's fatal fall, Dr Vengler's experimental work and the mysteries hidden in the Society's ledgers, I already had plenty of leads, any one of which might constitute the misdeeds hinted at by the anonymous letter. But, given the chance to talk to the third member of the Committee, I had accepted at once.

"It's a big place for just the two of us," I said, looking about.

"It's not the fanciest place, but it does."

Against the walls were glass-fronted display cases such as you might find in a museum, each holding samples of minerals. I glanced too briefly over one marked 'Meteorites,' which seemed to have quite a number of curious specimens. The walls themselves were adorned with paintings of foreign landscapes, but I did not have much chance to examine any of them.

"It seems very congenial," I said, as she guided me to the end of the table where tea things had been set out for two. "I gather this is a firm in which the Society has a financial interest."

"We own a third of the shares," she said. "The tea has already brewed some, I'll pour yours unless you like it very strong."

"Thank you. I understand the Society owns one third of the company directly, and another third indirectly," I said. "A majority shareholding, in effect. I can't trace exactly who owns the final third, but I have an idea the thread might end somewhere nearby."

She held my eye for a moment.

"You've been doing your homework, then," she said. "Good. That should save time over foolish questions. Yes, this arrangement makes it easier dealing with the board, which I have a non-executive seat on."

Mrs Hardcastle was listed as a director of eight companies, all of them in the mineral extraction line.

"And your role in the Society—"

"Is looking after our investments and keeping an eye on the companies. I protect our interests."

"That's rather a tall order given how far flung their operations are," I said.

"I'm not so frail that I can't stand a bit of travel," she said. "It's not like it was a few years ago. Steamships these days take you anywhere in no time. I've been to mines in Africa, Europe, Asia and South America. I'm no mining engineer, but I can see who's pulling their weight and who's swinging the lead."

"I gather the mining game is not entirely straightforward," I said.

My house mates, Barnes and Thompson, had both been able to tell me about the financial aspects of mining. After an hour in the library I felt at least superficially informed.

"Half the battle in precious metals is weeding out the cheats and swindlers. I've seen more fake gold mines than you've had hot dinners." She looked me up and down. "Well, almost as many."

"It's a field notorious for fraud," I said. Shares in gold mines are peculiarly fertile ground for swindles, and the newspapers were full of stories of fellows losing life savings over fictitious mines in the Andes or on the Zambezi.

"I just look harmless and beetle about saying how interesting it all is. I get to see a lot more than they would show an actual mining engineer. You can soon tell how much of it is for show, and how much real work is going on. The frauds are never bothered about running a tight ship." She picked up the teapot, swirled it about a bit to improve the mixing, and poured herself a cup of liquid the colour of mahogany. "When you see the workers coming and going without being checked if they've got any dust in their turn-ups, you know there's not a farthing's-worth of gold in the place."

It seemed Mrs Hardcastle had learned some of the tricks of the trade.

"The other side is knowing where to look for these pretties," she said. She held out her hand and waggled her display of jewelled rings. "These always impress the ladies."

She spoke as though she viewed them as mere baubles, but she could not disguise the pride she felt at having amassed such a magnificent collection.

"That's a real diamond," I said. "And rubies, sapphires and, I believe, emeralds."

While in the debt collection business I'd had a number of informal lessons on the valuation of jewellery. Many times I've been offered items for settlement of a debt, sometimes by a woman trying to help her husband, sometimes by a husband who treats his wife's jewellery-box like a piggy bank. Sometimes the items offered are genuinely valuable, but I had never seen anything as impressive as those Mrs Hardcastle wore.

"You know your gems. You know what some girls will do for a diamond! Well, I go out and get them myself. And that's twenty-four-carat gold," she said. "Not the best sort for practical purposes, but the purest. There's nothing quite like gold."

Again, almost a purr of pleasure as she gazed on the precious metal.

"Do you know where gold comes from?"

This sounded like a trick question. I was not inclined to make more of a fool of myself than I could help, so I opted for a simple answer.

"I don't. My schooling in that line never extended beyond coal and iron extraction. I believe they reserve teaching of precious metals for the boarding schools."

She laughed out loud.

"And finishing schools, Mr Stubbs! A well-born young lady can tell how many carats a diamond is from ten paces. They train you lot in coal and iron, and your sisters get domestic science. Very proper and fitting, I am sure."

I was beginning to warm to Mrs Hardcastle.

"It was the opinion of Paracelsus," I said, "that gold is formed from base elements which mature in the womb of the Earth. I expect they laugh at that now."

"He wasn't that far wrong, but he should have looked up rather than down. Gold comes from the stars."

She was clearly used to amazing audiences with this fact, and I do not think my reaction disappointed her.

"It's true. Like other metals, gold is formed by nuclear furnaces in the heart of giant stars. When these expire they scatter their fruits across the heavens, joining the gas clouds that condense into planets. And gold, as you probably know, is heavy—heavier than lead."

I nodded. You learn how to tell real gold in the debt business. Alloys give themselves away by being lighter than the real thing.

"All of the gold on Earth sank to its molten core—you might say our world has a heart of gold, though you wouldn't think it. The only way it gets to the surface is through volcanic processes which bring material up from the depths. So, the places you find gold are all lava flows of prehistoric volcanoes."

"And panning for gold..." I started, not sure where I was going but keen to stay up.

"Is where water has eroded these lavas flows and washed

grains of it downstream," she said. "Those poor men panning glean a few ounces a week if they are lucky. Wiser men go upstream and look for the vein of gold in the rock."

"So, it's all about geology."

"And whoever has the best grasp of geology finds the crock of gold. You might say," she added with a knowing smirk, "that I'm a rather successful gold-digger."

The comment seemed a bit off-colour, but she had already changed tack.

"That's gold. Now, do you know where diamonds come from?"

Diamonds are a form of carbon. I had heard it said that if you compressed coal you could make diamonds, but I had never heard of diamonds found in coal seams and I decided not to hide my ignorance.

"I've no idea," I said.

"Volcanoes again," she said. "When the lava comes bubbling up from miles underground, it has gases dissolved in it, and they come fizzing up like ginger ale when you shake the bottle. Some of those gases crystallise into diamonds."

"Again, a matter of geology."

"Exactly. The scientific application of geology, and especially what we call volcanology: the study of volcanoes. A bit of science, and having an eye for these things, will find you plenty of gold and diamonds."

Her complacent satisfaction was amply justified. In a nutshell, she seemed to hold the whole secret of the Society's vast wealth.

"Which is why you provide funds for academic research," I said. "Though in a rather roundabout way, and not in such a fashion that anyone else would connect it with gold mining."

I had found half a dozen papers which I could trace back to organisations which were, ultimately, funded by the Society. They all had titles with a lot of long words in them. Vulcanology may well have been mentioned.

"Oh, you have been busy at your homework again," she said. "An educated guess is better, the more educated it is. We like to give ourselves all the advantage we can, without tipping off the competition to how we do it."

"Very wise," I said. "The results speak for themselves. I gather your prospecting has enjoyed a decent success rate."

"It has," she said. "But you should see how quickly we're improving!"

Her pride had gotten the better of her. She had spoken out of turn, and we both knew it.

She nodded towards the case of meteorites, having obviously noted my fascination with them earlier.

"Did you want to have a look at those?"

"Merely a personal interest," I said, "but I wouldn't mind a look."

My interest was more than casual. The Stafford case, which turned on the deadly cargo that arrived on a meteorite, was only the most obvious example of celestial intrusion. Any meteorite might contain a hazardous cargo.

She was already leaning over the case and gesturing for me to join her.

"You'll know that they are split into the rocky ones, the metal ones, and those that are both rock and metal," she said, indicating the exhibits.

"'Martian'," I read, next to one small pebble with a reddish hue. "What does that mean?"

"Just exactly what it says. That there is a piece of Mars."

"Surely not," I said. It had to be a joke or word play.

"Oh yes."

To my surprise, she opened the glass lid of the display case, which was not locked, picked up the reddish pebble and passed it to me with an impish smile.

"There you go," she said, "You're holding a piece of Mars."

"That's not possible," I said.

"Oh, but it is," she said gleefully. "The surface of Mars, you may know, is pockmarked with craters, like the moon. Now, they may be volcanic craters, or they may be the result of meteorite impacts. They're fighting out that question in the universities. Maybe they're both right, and there are some of both. And what do craters mean?"

The only craters I had seen were on the Western Front.

Thousands of them, an entire landscape blasted full of holes.

"That there have been explosions," I said.

"Either volcanic explosions, or meteorites. Either way, they blow thousands of tons of material into the air, and some of it gets blown so high that it never comes down."

Mrs Hardcastle loved her subject. She would have made a good teacher, although perhaps she had found a higher calling, and one that few women could aspire to, in the field of practical geology.

"So, pieces of rock from Mars end up on Earth," I said.

"A few. Junk from the whole cosmos rains down on us here. There are a few gold meteorites, and a few with diamonds, though not many." She indicated rocks in the display case with bright specks in them. Not enough to pique the interest of a smelter or jeweller. "That's why the company is interested. Find where a gold meteorite came down a million years ago and you'll find the biggest pot of gold ever seen. So they say."

She rolled her eyes, indicating she was not one to believe everything she heard.

"I had never heard of golden meteorites," I mused.

"Better give that back," she said, taking the red pebble. "Before you forget yourself and walk off with it."

She replaced it in the case and we returned to the table.

"And that's all about me," she said. "Going out to far-flung places, looking at mines, and seeing how much the manager sweats when I ask him about supplies of pit props. The fake ones don't bother with doing any digging, so they can't answer questions like that. If there's anyone who doesn't like the way I do my job, I'd like to hear about it."

"I don't think it's that," I said.

"Maybe not. The problem is that nobody trusts you when you have secrets," she said. "The Widows Society is not a secret society but we do have commercial secrets, and we don't let everyone in on them."

"I wouldn't say you have more secrets than any other organisation, but what you do have is mystique, thanks to the exclusion of males. Without that, the mystery and envy would dissipate."

"Pshaw," she said, or something like it. "When there are all those men-only Masonic lodges and men-only clubs? And men-only professions? Why can't we have a women-only benevolent society, for those who need it most?"

"Nobody is suggesting you can't," I said, "but somebody in the organisation is unhappy with the way things have been run."

She sighed.

"Women are not permitted to express their displeasure in masculine ways. Some of them adopt more underhand means. There's always spitefulness, like that business with Mrs Smith's predecessor in the Good Works department."

"What was her name again?" I asked, a little too innocently.

"Mrs Find-It-Out-Yourself, you lazy dog!" she said, leaning back with a hearty laugh. "I've told you more than enough. They pay you to do a job of work, don't they? You can blooming well do it!"

"I suppose I can," I said, "if I wouldn't be wasting my time."

"Not up to me to say." She folded her arms in front of her, a black castle of a woman, with the drawbridge up. "I don't know what she's been spreading since we dispensed with her services, but I'm not going to say a word more about her. If you want to know more, you know what you need to do."

"I certainly do, Mrs Hardcastle," I said. "I'd like to thank you again for this interview, not to mention augmenting my education in geology. And the journey to Mars."

"You're very welcome, I'm sure."

We parted on much better terms than we had met. Perhaps Mrs Hardcastle was deflecting interest from her own activities, but for the first time someone in the Society had been willing to point the finger at a Committee member. Given my suspicions around Mrs Kennedy's accounting and Mrs Smith's 'good works,' the mixture was becoming a rich one.

Chapter 13: Mr Briggs the Burglar

It should never be suggested that Briggs was not a serious man. He was cheerful and sociable, known to all at the Conquering Hero as a talented piano player who could bash out a tune at the drop of a hat. Now pushing forty, he ran a scrap metal yard and dressed accordingly. It was a quiet trade. His two sons were widely known to be layabouts who were rarely at their supposed place of work. Briggs was not bothered. He was content to wait for business to come to him, and by all accounts spent much of his working day napping in his shed.

Metal can come from anywhere—copper wiring, pipes, old iron bathtubs—so a scrap metal dealer must establish the bona fides of his suppliers, else he runs a risk of being charged with handling stolen property. A lot of men are desperate for money and are making off with iron railings or the lead from old church roofs, so Briggs had plenty of opportunities to get metal cheap. But he is a stickler for the rules and did not purchase from casual callers, however much trade it cost him. Nobody ever caught Briggs out in an illegal act.

Not because he was honest, exactly; more that he was a genius when it came to concealing his main source of income. Briggs was a burglar, and a very competent one at that. A real master of his trade, in another field he might have been celebrated and won prizes.

Nobody who knew him resented this because we were never likely to be the target of his activities. Briggs only thieved from the well-off, the sort of houses with several floors and a side entrance for tradesmen, and he was only interested in gold and silver. Nobody at the Conquering Hero had more gold than you would find in their mouth or round their finger.

"'Ere Stubbs," said Briggs in his raspy voice, encountering me in the pub. "I have something to communicate to you. Arthur Renville has always been good to me, and I said I'd communicate with you as a return of the favour."

He wanted a private conversation. I finished my pint, wished a good evening to my companions and went to join him. He stood up, and I followed him outside. He had with him a small bull terrier. This was Nelson, the scrapyard's guard dog, but altogether an amiable beast.

"That's very good of you, Briggs," I said. "I know you don't talk much about professional matters."

He winced a little, as though even in this low-voiced conversation with nobody else present I was being indiscreet.

"I must adjure you to silence on this matter, Stubbs," he said. "Don't never breathe a word."

"I don't need adjuring," I said. "Discretion is the stock-in-trade of my business."

"Even so, I'd oblige you to swear an oath of confidentiality for my own peace of mind."

This was an unusual procedure.

"You mean, swear on the Good Book?"

Briggs' showed distaste.

"No offence, but I've seen men perjure themselves blind on the Bible," he said, "I need you to swear on something that means something to you. On your life, or your mother's life, if you don't mind."

I went through the routine of swearing, something I have never had to do before excepting in court.

Briggs watched me very closely throughout, and when I was finished, he nodded to himself as though I was appropriately bound and could be trusted.

"Very good," he said. "Now you, me and Nelson can go for an evening stroll, and I can show you something of significance. Lucky it doesn't look like rain tonight."

A man walking a dog looks much less suspicious than one walking the streets alone. I suspected that Briggs regularly criss-crossed the neighbourhood, familiarising himself with every new development.

He insisted on talking about the weather and what sort of summer it had been and how it compared to last summer. The dog's claws clicked along the pavement beside us, and it was a pleasant enough evening, but after some initial puzzlement I could soon tell exactly where this was leading.

"There was some talk about the Widows Society," he said, suddenly businesslike. "In specific, their centre of operations on a street which we are now approaching. A premises previously being a private house, now converted to commercial use, with the exception of the top floor which is occupied by a person who acts as caretaker. And with an unusually large safe."

I had mentioned to Arthur Renville that it would be convenient to my purposes if I could get inside the offices, and I wanted to make sure that would not cause any trouble, even though I would not burgle the place.

Further discussions, and a little more dissection of their accountancy suggested some high-level jiggery-pokery. Barnes, my book-keeping expert, was of the opinion that the more detailed ledgers would give an exact breakdown of the trading in bullion, and this would confirm the nature of the trick being pulled.

It might be that the Society was simply accumulating assets, which was no crime. It might be they were taking measures to avoid taxes, which might be questionable and cause trouble. Or it might be, as Thompson believed, that someone was skimming something off the top in the form of gold bars.

I was positive that Mrs Kennedy would keep everything in writing, and some perusal of the detailed account books, and the particulars of some of the companies they did business with, would settle the matter.

If Mrs Kennedy was in the clear, that meant Mrs Smith, young and beautiful as she might be, was the prime suspect, for her involvement with Dr Vengler.

However, that type of activity was best undertaken after checking with Arthur that it would not rub anyone the wrong way. He had noted that there was no particular objection, so long as I was careful and did not actually take anything. It seemed he had extended an enquiry to Briggs, hence this meeting.

"You have familiarised yourself with this property," I said.
Briggs flashed a crooked smile.

I am only slightly oversimplifying the matter when I say
there are two sorts of burglar. The first and commonest types
are young men who want money quickly. They creep around
the backs of houses at night looking for unlatched windows
or unlocked doors. If they think they can get away with it,
they will force an entry. They will grab whatever they can,
preferably hard cash, and make a quick exit. Their careers are
short and eventful, and end in long prison sentences if they are
not diverted into more organised forms of activity.

The other burglars are men like Briggs, experienced
professionals who know their trade.

"Floor plans, details of construction, security measures and
the sturdiness of the drainpipes," he said. "Good cast iron jobs
from 1897 with nary a trace of rust. As good as a ladder, if you
know what you're about."

"But you never acted upon this information."

"I did and I didn't," he said. "Which is to say, my activities
did progress beyond the assemblage of plans, and into the
actual actuation thereof, and I stumbled on a mystery, one
which bothers me and which you might resolve."

Even though the street was empty his voice had dropped
even lower, and he bent close enough for me to see the stubble
on his chin. Briggs was a man with the habit of secrecy.

"You have to use all your faculties and capacities when you're
at work," he said. "Observation of fine detail and attention to the
seemingly inconsequential are the difference between triumph
and disaster. You have to attune yourself."

"I'm with you," I said, recalling occasions where I, too, had
to effect entrance covertly.

"Faculties and capacities," he said, tapping his head. "Things
which other people might not understand, never having had to
use them. You understand me, Stubbs."

"I believe I do."

"It was half past one in the morning, there was only light
cloud and the quarter moon was high in the sky," he said. "All
favourable conditions. I made a complete circuit of the streets

around the premises, getting a view of it from several angles and satisfying myself of the complete lack of activity in the area.

"I made my approach over the back fence and down the garden path, then paused by an outbuilding for a final assessment. You can only judge so much from a distance. When you get up close you have a far more accurate picture of the challenge ahead. I had a hand-cranked pocket-torch, and I played the beam over the house."

I must have looked surprised at this, because he smiled again.

"If anyone is awake and sees a light shining in, what do they do? They come to the window. That's my signal to scarper, no harm done and nobody's any the wiser. You don't want to be tiptoeing down the back hall before you meet a householder in his dressing gown, with a loaded shotgun."

"Very true," I said.

"This premises, as you probably know yourself, is protected better than most," said Briggs. "Locks and bars on all the windows, electric alarm bell, and of course a large safe of very good quality, but a little out of date. In addition to which the caretaker has a couple of Jack Russell terriers which roam freely through the property in the night. And the caretaker has her own private telephone line, in addition to the one downstairs in the offices."

"Formidable defences," I said.

"Not so much in the physical line," he said. "No high walls in the way, more a matter of not raising the alarm. On making a closer inspection, I decided the game was not worth the candle."

Briggs was too canny to try and take more than he could easily carry. My guess is if he could get into the safe, he would have taken a single gold ingot from the back, rearranging the others to cover the loss. It might be days of weeks before the loss was discovered, and Mrs Kennedy would likely suspect pilfering rather than burglary.

And maybe, if he had succeeded, Briggs might have come back some months later for more. But one gold ingot will last a cautious man a good while.

"An unusual decision considering the stakes," I said.

"I know exactly how much I could have realised but my faculties and capacities told me not to proceed," said Briggs, "and I heeded them. So, you can take it from me, Stubbs, one who ought to know, that you'd have a better chance of breaking into Buckingham Palace than the Widows Society. That is the essential kernel of what I have to communicate to you. Don't do it."

He was stern and serious. But, as we both knew, he was not telling me everything. There was a gaping lacuna in his account where an explanation was called for.

"I take you at your word, Briggs, and I am grateful for your advice, which I will certainly heed, if I can just understand one thing." I looked at him straight. "What was it that caused you to turn away?"

"Well, as we are approaching the property, I will allow you to see for yourself," he said. "Absolute discretion now?"

"Absolute."

We were approaching the property when Briggs quite casually opened the rear garden gate to the adjacent property and strolled into their garden, with no more than a glance at the house.

"Been empty since spring," he said. "Can't find a buyer in the current market conditions."

Even in the failing light none of the curtains had been drawn and there was no light inside. It was a good place to view the rest of the neighbourhood without being seen, and Briggs slipped a pair of field glasses from an outside pocket. Nelson sat down quietly at his feet.

"That, you will observe is the property of the Widows Society," he said. "Lights only in the caretaker's quarters on the top floor. Notice anything odd about it?"

"I can't say I do," I said after a minute.

"Have you ever seen an owl?"

"Can't say I have."

"I've seen plenty. You learn to recognise the silhouette of an owl against the sky, and not to be spooked when they suddenly fly off or start hooting." He was looking up through the field glasses. "Have a butchers' on the roof ridge, just by the main chimney stack. Got it?"

There was something where he indicated and the hairs on the back of my neck prickled. A hunched shape, but surely much bigger than any owl, seemingly perched in the lee of the chimney. You might have thought it was part of the room, except that it was rounded rather than having straight lines like the pipework and chimneys.

"I see it," I said.

"Now have a close look," he said, passing me the glasses.

The binoculars not only magnified the image but they also drew in more light. I could make out the rough surface of the thing, its peculiar lumpiness, and on its head, what first looked to be antlers but later seemed to be more like antennae as though it were a colossal insect. I stared at it, trying to make sense of the thing, for a whole minute.

"Let's go now," Briggs said, taking the glasses back, and he led Nelson and me back out on the street where we started the stroll back to the pub. "It doesn't do to look too long."

Nelson seemed glad to be heading away from the house, keeping the lead taut.

"I can see why you wanted me to see it."

"First time I came here I was careless, and it turned around and looked at me. Not like an owl—you can see their eyes in the dark, I don't know if it's got eyes, but it saw me, and Nelson here whimpered like a puppy and we beat it pretty sharpish." He sucked air through his teeth at the memory. "I don't mind telling you, Stubbs, I was afraid. I ran. Well, I've made a living these twenty years by trusting my faculties and capacities and I stand by them."

"I can see why."

"I've been back here at full moon, at three in the morning, just to have a good look. That didn't make it any clearer. Exactly the opposite. But, I was thinking, this is your speciality, isn't it? Strange things. Spooky things. Because I would like to know what it is. It's been bothering me all this time."

I had never heard Briggs speak like this before, And no wonder. He had trusted me, and I did what I could to reassure him.

"I have an idea," I said. "Only a vague one at this time. It's

something unnatural and it's to do with the Widows Society."
I struggled for an explanation and settled for the simplest. "Let
us say, Briggs, that most likely it is exactly what it looks like."

"Ah hah," he said, releasing a long breath and nodding at
the long-awaited confirmation. "And of course, of course, that is
why Mr Stubbs is involved in the first place."

It seemed that everyone knew, or thought they knew, about
my business, but given everyone knew about Briggs' business,
which was equally clandestine, I could not very well complain.

"Yes," I said simply, "It's one of those cases. I think that
thing is guarding the place."

"It is. I know what a watchman looks like," said Briggs.
"This one is alert."

He put a hand on my arm.

"You're a big man, Stubbs, and you're a fighter," he said.
"But you take my advice and do not go anywhere nearer that
place than we already have. Because I do not like the look of that
thing one bit. There are men in my business who just disappear
one night and are never heard of again, and I would not want
that to be you."

Chapter 14: The Fallen Angel

Iwould not want you to believe that this case was entirely straightforward. I have omitted dead ends and false leads, and the many occasions when doors were shut in my face. In truth, those took up most of my time. But persistence is rewarded and every so often fortune smiles on the unexpected caller and the door opens. This was one of those times when I was gifted with a friendly reception and a few vital clues.

"Stubbs, Lantern Insurance company," said the manservant who answered the door, glancing at my card without taking it and looking at me again. "The lawyers did not apprise us that you was to be visiting, but seeing as things are slack, please do come in."

He looked very proper in his servant attire, but his manner was remarkably offhand. That is generally a sign that the mistress is away, though it was curious that he would let me in if that were the case.

"Thank you," I said, as he took my coat, shook it out and hung it up as though I were a duke rather than a tradesman. Under my breath I added "Meredith, we're in."

It is a line from a music-hall sketch, which I picked up as a kind of charm whenever I gain access unexpectedly.

The servant had long, dark hair, tied back in a style decades out of date. His outfit had the addition of a black armband. I had observed how some of the widows in the Society took their mourning further than others, but this struck me as extreme. Mrs Travis' husband had died at least ten years ago.

"Mr Stubbs," he said, regarding me again. "Now, haven't I seen you in a boxing ring somewhere?"

"That's more than possible."

"Believe I lost five bob betting on Kid Berg against you," he said with a rueful smile. There was more than a hint of Cockney in his accent, and he was letting it show.

Now I was confident his mistress was away.

"It was a close match," I said. "I'm sorry you didn't have better advice."

An untidy line of tea chests occupied half the entrance hall. Others were stacked in a corner. The place was in some disarray, and the household looked to be mid-move.

"I am sorry to disturb you," I started, but he waved my apology away.

"It's been all disturbance since she died, believe you me," he said. "Whole place is higgledy-piggledy. One more caller doesn't signify." He turned and shouted over his shoulder. "Man from the insurance is all!"

That explained the armband, the chests and his attitude. A neat solution, but one which invalidated the entire point of my being there. I was at a loss on how to proceed, since I could not simply walk out.

"Do you want to see the roof terrace then?" he asked. "I've shown so many people I've practically got the whole thing down as a guided tour."

"The roof terrace," I said, halfway between statement and question.

"Where the distressing event occurred," he said, sounding very matter-of-fact about it.

That gave me the final pieces, more or less. I anticipated a brief visit, mainly for show, but it would at least give me a chance to quiz the staff about the Widows Society, Maybe they would have less compunction about sharing confidences now their mistress was gone.

"Would you mind if I took notes?" I asked, taking out my pencil and notebook. "I don't need to mention your name, but—"

"Jerry Williams," he said promptly. "Put my name to it, go on. It's all on the record with me. I've nothing to hide. It's up this way."

He led the way up a wide staircase with gleaming brass stair rods.

"And you've worked here for how long?"

"Six and a half years all told," he said. "It's been a good gaff. Be sorry to leave, but Madam provided for all of us so we shan't starve. Even if I won't be able to get a proper character from her."

His tone was ironic. With the market for well-trained, well-groomed staff these days, I suspected Mr Williams would have his pick of positions. He might even move up to a grander house and serve a titled family.

"Who's left in the house?" I asked.

"Just me and the missus," he said. "She's the cook. We're just staying on until everything is cleared away and shipped off."

Husband-and-wife servants and cooks, once common, are rare and valuable commodities these days.

"You're not staying with the house?"

"Seems there's an American millionaire buying this place, so we're all being turned out as fast as Pickford's can get it moved. I expect he'll have everything done for him with machines."

Williams' tone expressed his feelings on American millionaires in London.

We crossed a landing, went through a large room which had been stripped of furniture—pale rectangles on the wallpaper signifying missing mirrors and pictures, the windows bare and curtainless—and emerged through French windows on to a roof terrace, perhaps twenty feet square and paved with marble tiles, surrounded by a low stone balustrade. It afforded a fine view of the garden, and half a dozen giant urns filled with swaying greenery gave the sense of being in the garden itself.

"Very pleasant," I said.

Being only one floor up, it was not so high that I felt uncomfortable approaching the edge and looking over.

"There were a few items of outdoor furniture, but those went." Williams rested a hand on the balustrade. "To set the scene: this was at seven forty-five in the evening, and Mrs Travis was out here, enjoying the prospect as she often did of an evening. It was getting dark, but not too dark, and mild."

Wherever Sally and I ended up would not have a view half as nice as this, looking out over gardens and the park beyond.

The place was on a slope and it gave quite a vista.

"On her own?"

"Yes. She had entertained visitors at dinner, the Moores, earlier. After they left she asked for a cocktail on the terrace. I left a tray with a gin rickey in the shaker, with a glass, a napkin, a saucer of lime wedges and some nuts on the side table just here."

I had an inkling of why Mr Williams had been kept on. His style was more relaxed than the stuffiness of servants of the older school, less formal. He was a world away from Mrs Bridges' frosty butler, but he gave the impression of prompt and exact efficiency.

There was a knowingness about his performance, like an actor playing a butler, so that everyone understood it was not meant to be taken too seriously. Perhaps that was the only way he could do the job these days. Mrs Bridges was right: things had changed since her youth.

"Was it her habit to drink of an evening?"

"Just the one cocktail, usually, and not every evening even. But—in my personal opinion—the Moores are not necessarily the easiest company, and I think Mrs Travis needed something afterwards by way of a restorative."

"Understood," I said, taking this all down.

"Having served Mrs Travis, I retreated to a discreet distance," he said. It was the job of servants to be always on call without needing to be shouted for, but never so close that they were intruding. "The last words she spoke to me were, 'That will be all, Williams'. Very appropriate, really."

"So you were waiting—in there," I nodded to the room we had come from. He would have stayed out of her line of sight.

For the first time it struck me just how tedious it was to be at someone's beck and call, when you did not have anything particular to do. Servants cannot chat among themselves if they are within earshot of their employers, nor be found playing patience, let alone smoking.

"She generally stays—stayed—out for twenty minutes to half an hour."

"What happened next?"

"Nothing, really," he said. "I heard the usual sounds of her pouring and drinking. I think she walked up and down a bit, probably enjoying the view of the rose arbour. After ten or fifteen minutes I heard a sound. Like she was clearing her throat, was all."

"Clearing her throat?"

"Yes. She didn't speak or call for me or anything, just a sort of slight cough. But, maybe five minutes after that, I realised she wasn't drinking anymore, so I just took a peek around the curtain just in case she wanted something, and, of course, there she was, lying dead. Right about on that spot there."

He indicated a spot a few feet away. I made some quick notes then waited, pencil poised. Silence is often more effective than a direct question at eliciting what is on a subject's mind.

"The coroner said it was heart failure," he said. "Though there wasn't anything much wrong with her heart. She wasn't one of your hypochondriac ladies but she saw a doctor when she needed one. And she hardly ever did need one, tough old bird that she was. I shall miss her." He sighed. "But for your insurance boys, I suppose the main thing is whether it's natural causes, or accidental death, or something else."

Several trains of thought started running through my head and I attempted to marshal them.

"Did she talk much about the Widows Society?"

He looked nonplussed at that.

"Not after she left a few years back," he said. "She was vexed, as you might say—by which I mean hopping mad—when she left. Pride is easily wounded in that class, and word gets around. She recovered, and she always found plenty to do with herself. But she was never the confiding sort, if that's what you're asking. Never told me the ins and outs."

"It was a few years ago."

"About four years," he said after a moment's thought. "One funny thing..." He trailed off, caught my eye and continued. "Before she left them, a few months before, she got rid of her old clothes, her widows' clothes. I thought something must be up then."

"Like she was through wearing them?"

"Could be. Had her maid pack them up and took them off somewhere."

He spread his hands, as if to ask whether he could be expected to have inquired further. I had to admit he could not.

"She was in charge of the Society's good works, I believe," I said.

"That's right: orphanages, hospitals, slum schools, soup kitchens, usual sort of thing. She liked helping people who were less fortunate, but there was some disagreement over exactly who they should be helping, or how, or how much...she never said much about it."

Then, years after she had left the Society, but just after I started investigating it, Mrs Travis had died suddenly, and under what might be construed as suspicious circumstances.

"What might have brought on this heart attack?"

I was wondering about that gin rickey. Would the police have been suspicious enough to have carried out toxicology tests?

"They've been looking at every possible cause, Mr Stubbs," said Williams, raising his eyebrows, "believe you, me. Because of the money."

"Her estate," I said.

"Exactly. The inheritance is straightforward, straight splits between the three children, but..." He shrugged, because this was just the way the world was. "Some suggestion was made that someone might have been in a hurry to get their portion, and of course if that happened to be true, they would not be permitted to benefit. Lawyers have been hired, you can imagine the rest."

I certainly could. I walked up and down a few steps, looking out at the garden, the rose arbour, and the marble beneath my feet.

"Heart attack in a healthy lady of her age is rare."

"They checked for everything," said Williams, taking a turn up and down himself. "I've been interviewed half a dozen times and I just wished I had more to tell."

"Were there no signs of a disturbance?" I asked.

"The tray was overturned, and the glass was on its side," he said. "Just about there."

He pointed to another spot on the terrace, some feet away from where the body had been.

"And what did the investigators make of that?"

"Nothing much. It seems she knocked it over as she was stumbling. Took a few steps and then ended up there."

I paced between the two locations. If Williams were in any way involved, he could easily have set things up to be less suspicious. He might be a good actor, but I sincerely doubted complicity on his part.

"She did not die easy," he said. "It was quick, it can't have been more than a minute or two but...she did not have a peaceful expression on her face."

"She didn't leave any notes, or write a last-minute letter to her family?"

"Suicide? It's not a family prone to scandals," he said, shaking his head in a way that told me I was barking up the wrong tree. "It's not like she had a past that was going to catch up with her. A thoroughly respectable woman all round." He gave me a confidential look. "We always know, you know: the staff. You can't take laudanum, or have an affair, or lose everything on the stock market without staff knowing—what's that?"

He was puzzled at the way I crouched down.

"Just checking," I said, running my fingertips over the marble, feeling for particles of dirt or sand. It had not rained in some days, so if there was any residue it might still be there. As Williams turned away, I carefully wiped my handkerchief over the tiles.

"For what?"

"Relevant forensic material."

He was not satisfied, but knew that was all he could get from me.

"Well, there's no scandals," he said, looking out over the park. "No illegitimate children or past lovers waiting to appear. Himself, the late husband, was as straight as they come, you know. Some people would call that boring—they love it where it's all gossip and scandal, family rows and high drama all the time—I call it a nice, quiet life."

"It was evening you say," I said. "After dusk I believe."

"Yes, it was just about dark."

"Was she scared of mice?" I asked. "Could there have been a mouse or a rat to give her a fright?"

"She wasn't one of those terrified women, if that's what you're thinking," he said. "That would be a good one for a murder mystery though, wouldn't it, if she had been? The murderer releasing a trained rat into the victim's room which runs back out afterwards..."

"You read murder mysteries?" I asked.

"We get a certain amount of standing-about time in this line." He said, pulling a paperback from a back pocket. The cover had a picture of a detective woman in a red dress pointing a gun at a detective.

"I hope you didn't tell the police that," I said.

He raised his hands, again suggesting he had nothing to hide. If Williams had been reading while awaiting his mistress's next instructions, he might not have been alert to every sound. Like a dog with its owner, or a mother with a baby, his brain would be finely tuned to the sounds of his charge, while ignoring anything else.

We walked back to the front door and he gave me a summary of medical views on the matter.

"The coroner says natural causes," he said. "We've got no suspect, no method and precious little motive. Not much of a case for murder. Not much for you insurance boys to do."

"Maybe we will surprise you, Mr Williams," I said.

"Maybe you will. Pleasure meeting you, Mr Stubbs."

"And you, Mr Williams."

The timing was altogether too suggestive, and the situation in which the deceased has been found altogether too reminiscent of Parrish's death. I would transfer the few black crumbs I had found from my handkerchief to a matchbox and see if someone could tell me whether my wild theory could possibly be correct.

Chapter 15:
The Opinions of Dr Evans

Y ou would not look twice at Dr Evans if you saw her in the greengrocer's. A bespectacled, untidy woman, with wisps of greying hair escaping from a bun, she might be mistaken for a slightly scatterbrained housewife. You would not suspect her of being a renowned scientist and explorer into worlds little suspected by the ordinary people she passed on the street.

Dr Evans was an invertebrate zoologist, which is not to say that she lacked backbone herself—far from it—but that she studied tiny creatures, generally only visible through a microscope. Consulting her on the Shackleton case had given me an awareness of the invisible worlds that co-exist with our own. Not just the tiny creatures that swarm and multiply on every surface, that everyone who has seen an advertisement for antiseptic knows about, but the menagerie of small and bizarre animals that look like miniature versions of more familiar creatures.

She had kindly agreed to an interview. She opened the front door herself. I could see her husband busying himself in the kitchen behind her.

"I'm sorry to take up your time, Doctor," I said, "but I felt you might be uniquely qualified to help—and this might turn out to be an interesting curiosity."

Dr Evans looked at me over her glasses.

"As a general rule, I'm wary of people bringing things in matchboxes," she said in her lilting Welsh accent, "but in your case I'm willing to make an exception, Mr Stubbs. Come with me into the laboratory."

Dr Evans worked at a prestigious university in central

London, but her work was also her hobby, and she had a small facility in her own house. This home laboratory was not one of your Hollywood scientist lairs, with bubbling test tubes and electrical apparatus throwing off hissing arcs of light. It looked more like a kitchen, with a sink and hardwood work surfaces, and little chests with dozens of tiny drawers. An ordinary crockery cupboard was crammed with odd scientific glassware.

Down one side was a row of fishtanks without any water in them, just heaps of mossy stones. Her microscope, a big brass thing like an inverted telescope, held pride of place on a desk at the centre of the room.

The place smelled, ever so faintly, of damp earth and cleaning fluid.

"That's very good of you," I said. "Do you get a lot of requests from members of the public, then?"

"A few," she said. "It tends to be people with delusions. They think they've got mites or something crawling on them, and they bring me matchboxes with bits of lint and flakes of skin, and expect me to tell them what sort of insects they are."

"I have never heard of such a thing."

She seated herself on a wooden stool in front of the microscope. It was a one-person laboratory with no provision for guests.

"If people knew you had a microscope you soon would," she said cheerfully. "People do cut up rough if you won't support them in their delusions, but science is there to find the truth, and it does not take sides. So if I tell you this is just ordinary house dust, please don't be offended."

Slightly self-consciously, I placed the two matchboxes in front of her, one from the scene of Mr Parrish's death, the other from the terrace where Mrs Travis had died.

She used tweezers to lay out the grains from the first matchbox on a glass slide not much bigger than a postage stamp.

"I will not be in the slightest," I said. "Mainly, what I would like to know is whether these samples came from the same source."

"You mean the same place?" she said, doubtfully. "Forensic geology that is. Not my sphere at all, I'm afraid."

"The samples came from different locations but I'd like to know if they were the same composition. As though, for example, they were all scraped off the same creature."

"Creature, now?" she said, rolling the 'r' and raising her eyebrows.

"That does sound melodramatic... Or, the same person— maybe they had exotic leather footwear."

"Like alligator skin," she said, turning on a light underneath the microscope and putting her eye to the eyepiece. "I don't rightly know. As I say, I'm not a forensic scientist."

She turned a knob and then adjusted the eyepiece.

"No, it looks like vegetable matter," she said after a minute. "Is that what you were expecting?"

"Not exactly," I said. "Is it at all distinctive?"

She continued to stare through the microscope. I would have liked to have seen what she was seeing, but I knew that whatever it was, it would not mean anything to me.

"I would say it is," she said, raising her head. "Let's take a look at the other."

She repeated the procedure before going back to the first one to compare it.

"Interesting, that. This is not a formal investigation, look you," she said, "and I won't be repeating this in a court of law. But if it's any use to you, my professional opinion, for what it's worth, is that both of these are samples of the same type of lichen. Further than that, I can't say much."

"That's still saying a great deal," I said. "But you're sure it is lichen?"

She looked at me over her glasses again.

"As you know, it's tardigrades I mostly study," she said, "but I think that even as an undergraduate, twenty years ago, I could tell lichen with a reasonable degree of certainty."

Her sarcasm was light, but hard to ignore.

"Forgive a layman's ignorance," I said.

"Not in a hurry, are you?" she asked. "If you've a few minutes I might be able to tell you something more, because it's a little bit unusual."

Her voice danced over those last words, and I surmised that 'a little bit' meant 'extremely'.

"Take all the time you need," I said.

After all, it was her unpaid time. From being offhand, Dr Evans had become absorbed. I recognised the same sort of reaction from Mr Hoade when presented with an interesting question, or Dr Blake when he comes upon a new enigma, or Miss Frey when she is presented with a new intellectual puzzle. Like bloodhounds sniffing a new trail, they are all curiosity and enthusiasm.

I felt myself vanish from her world as she adjusted the focus, moved the slides around and took notes. She took a book from the shelf and consulted it, and another, and then went out of the room and came back with two more books. She drew a couple of little sketches. Her expression betrayed a changing pattern of interest, puzzlement, frustration, and intrigue. The hunt was on.

I remained still, not helping—as if there were anything I could do in a laboratory—not fidgeting, just watching the stages of the investigation as it unfolded.

"The sensible thing to do would be to pass these on," she said at last. "Have a specialist who knows about these things make an exact identification. It doesn't correspond to anything that I can tell, but maybe I'm missing something that would be obvious to an expert."

"We could try that," I said, "if it isn't too costly."

"Then again," she went on, giving me a penetrating look. "Then again, maybe there aren't any specialists who could help. Perhaps if I told you what I can say, you could tell me more."

"What can you tell me?"

"These samples are, without doubt, specimens of a type of lichen," she said, opening to a page in a textbook.

She tapped a colour plate, an artists' impression in which strange, piglike creatures which I knew were tardigrades moved through a miniature jungle of giant yellow and green leaves, and sprouting yellow stalks.

"The stuff that grows on tree bark and bare stones?"

"Yes. Except that technically speaking it's not a plant at all. It is not a single organism either, but a co-operation between a fungus and an alga."

I knew a fungus was like a mushroom or toadstool. Beyond that I was guessing.

"But alga...is that pond slime?"

"Very good," she said. "Yes. These are samples of an unknown lichen—unknown to me at least. The funny thing is, look you, that I've been looking at samples from all around here for the better part of ten years, off roof tiles, slates and brickwork. It's the tardigrades I'm interested in, but obviously I'm familiar with their habitat and the vegetation they inhabit. And this..." her voice dropped an octave. "This is an odd one. There are fracture lines on every bit I look at; they've all been scraped off the surface off something bigger. So, can you relieve me of my misery and tell me where this came from?"

That put me in a tight spot. I could hardly blurt out that the samples both came from the scenes of horrible murders which had not been identified as murders at all, and that they might be from the skin of an unknown flying creature, quite possibly of alien origin.

"They were found in two different places. I was expecting it to be animal tissue."

I had not meant to speak the second part out loud. Her eyebrows went up.

"Animal tissue? Well, that's a curious thing you should say, that," she said, "because it isn't green at all."

She broke suddenly off to open a textbook and read a few paragraphs.

"The way lichens work, you see, is that the fungus provides the structure, the skeleton if you like, or the trunk and branches, and the alga is the leaves. The alga has chlorophyll to makes sugar from sunlight, and that sustains the fungus. One provides support and the other provides sustenance. A mutually beneficial arrangement."

I had the feeling that if I were a bit more educated this might have been illuminating, but all I could do was nod dumbly.

"So, it's very strange having a lichen that's not green, or at least yellow, you see, because that means it's got no chlorophyll. You saying that it might be an animal—well."

It was as though I were under interrogation and she expected me to confess to something.

"It's as strange to me as it is to you," I said. "I didn't even know what a lichen was before today."

"After seeing this, I'm not so sure I know what a lichen is myself any more. Would you mind if I kept the slides? I have some friends at the South London Botanical Institute who would be very interested."

Miss de Vere might not approve. She believed in keeping a very tight lid on information, but I saw an opportunity for a bit of horse-trading.

"Maybe you could tell me," I said, "if there's any lichen that combines a fungus with an animal?"

"No, nothing like that ever existed."

"But could it exist?"

For the first time she took off her glasses and started polishing them.

"Lichens are funny things," she said. "Many of them are exactly the same sort of fungus as you get in common toadstools, and the algae are the same as you'd find in any pond, they just combine in different ways. The fungal spores are the way it spreads. The algae are just sitting there, and a spore comes along and they combine. So they are, you might say opportunists, the fungi, they just join up with whatever happens to be thriving in a particular area."

She shrugged and put her glasses on.

"So they could join up with some sort of animal organism, I suppose, if it was in a larval form and could adapt to the symbiosis. But it's never happened. Not that anyone knows of."

"That sounds like the fungus is the one that gets all the benefit," I said. "It spreads to a new area, using the alga so it can survive, then sends its spores leapfrogging off to the next spot, leaving the alga where it was."

"Well, it's like a sliding scale you see. At one end you have pure symbiosis, then there are arrangements where one side benefits more than the other, along to outright parasitism."

"But it could spread to an animal," I said. "In theory. Evolution makes greats leaps."

"Not usually it doesn't, no. Usually it just makes tiny little steps. A little mutation that gives just a one per cent advantage in survival spreads throughout the whole population in no time, in evolutionary terms. Little advantages win out in the long run."

That shot my theory down, but a new one took its place. Not natural evolution, maybe. Perhaps something deliberate, something as unnatural as Dr Vengler's experiments.

"By all means share the samples with your colleagues," I said.

"They'll want bigger samples for a proper identification, especially if it really is a new species. Don't get your hopes up about fungus-animal hybrids, but it might be something just as interesting that gets energy from heat or another source. You know, I remember reading recently about strange lichen around chemical factories in the waste outflows."

We chatted a bit more. Most of what Dr Evans said was over my head but I believe I had the important points down before I left. I had a host of ideas revolving in my mind which continued to develop as I walked back.

In previous cases, I had found that beings from other worlds were poorly adapted to our planet and so tended to infiltrate Earthly organisms. The mysterious thing in the Stafford case, others that occupied human bodies, and the bizarre entity in the wax museum, all relied on a host to maintain a presence on our planet. Captain Cross had hinted that some things even interbred with humans to create hybrid spawn which could breathe our air and ingest Earthly food as their makers could not.

I was imagining, then, an intelligent fungus whose spores could drift through space, and which might latch on to organisms on a new planet by some special process, creating hybrids to colonise a new world.

It was evening, and I was deep in contemplation as I passed through the underground walkway which connects Crystal Palace Park with Crystal Palace Parade and the shopping streets.

Not so deep that I was not aware of my surroundings, though. The walkway is a vaulted space in the Moorish style, with red-and-white striped brickwork, enormous pillars and soaring arches. A dozen or so stalls sell snacks, drinks and souvenirs, but they were all shuttered now and the place was empty and echoing.

I turned as soon as I heard the rapid footsteps behind me. Maybe it was just someone hurrying to catch a bus, but the fact this was the first completely uninhabited spot I had passed was probably significant.

Wary, I moved sideways to take a look on the other side of the nearest pillar.

He was a big man, dressed in dark clothing, face covered by a balaclava helmet, hands encased in black leather gloves.

A pulse of terror washed over me like a bucket of icy water. The black outfit and concealed face, even the gloves, mean that no inch of skin was visible. If I had not been thinking of things that looked human but were not, hybrid things, it would not have occurred to me, but I wondered just what I was facing.

Maybe he, or it, just wanted to talk to me. This was not an orthodox way to go about it, but secrecy was second nature to some.

"May I help you?" I asked. "Did you want a word?"

He said nothing, but stepped towards me in the crouched pose of a fighter ready to move in any direction.

I glanced left and right, and of course saw nobody, just boarded-up stalls.

As I have often said, it is the height of folly to get into the ring with a man without knowing his form. Only fools willingly fight an unknown opponent. The wise fighter studies his adversary, learns his strengths and weaknesses, talks to others who have seen him fight or sparred with him. That way you can build your plan of campaign. Or, if you discover that your potential match is with a homicidal maniac, you can decide whether the game is truly worth the candle.

Of course, there have been many times in my career, working as a doorman, debt collector and general dogsbody, that I have been in fights with complete strangers. In those cases though, I usually had a chance to at least scrutinise the other and the advantage was generally in my corner, which was why my employers selected a heavyweight boxer for those jobs.

There is no dishonour in refusing a fight which is not of your choosing. I would have turned and run, but that seemed risky. So, I did the next best thing.

"Help!" I shouted at the top of my lungs. "Help! Police!"

The words echoed hollowly through the halls.

"Help!"

He came forward at speed and threw a strong right at my jaw. I had been watching closely and, anticipating the movement as it was made, was able to dodge left and backwards.

"That's enough of that" I said. "If you have a grievance, speak your piece and I'll listen. Come at me one more time and I'll show you some real boxing."

He made a sound, a grunt or snort. My bowler hat had fallen to the ground. I could see it out of the corner of my eye, but all my attention was riveted on my assailant. Both of us were in boxing stances. He was a trained fighter alright. I would have preferred to take my jacket off, but I knew from experience that it would tear along the seams without impeding me too much. Another job for Sally.

He came forwards again, feinted twice, then threw a one-two combination. My defence was slack, and the blow to my ribs hit very hard indeed.

Another snort, and this time the contempt was unmistakable. It was also slightly reassuring in that it was a very human sound. Perhaps this was a man after all and not a monster.

He surprised me then with a kick, not a straight-legged swing at the groin, but a pivoting kick like a French savate fighter. It struck me hard in the chest, almost knocking me off balance. He failed to follow up fast enough though, and I blocked or dodged the rain of punches that followed it, and now I started jabbing back at him.

We traded a few blows, and again I got to feel the force of his punch, which was more than it should have been. I suspected his gloves were weighted. Certainly I did not want to get in the way of too many of those.

The balaclava concealed his features but did give me one benefit. Bare-knuckle is hard because of the damage to the knuckles, but even a little bit of padding makes all the difference, Just as the ladies in the China-packing concern know that a single sheet of newspaper between items of crockery is enough to absorb shock and prevent them from cracking, even one layer of cloth makes quite a difference to impacts.

He tried another kick. This time I was able to dodge and press the attack while he was off balance, putting him back a few steps.

As I got the measure of him, things started to fall into place. He was strong and fit, but in no wise superhuman. He was not a boxer as such, rather he was a graduate of some version of military hand-to-hand combat training, something a bit more advanced than the simple moves they taught during my basic training. Modern hand-to-hand combat is a rough-and-tumble game based on street fighting moves, along with a smattering of exotic disciplines like jiu-jitsu and savate. Blows were delivered as much with the feet, knees and elbows as the fists.

It was a style of fighting more effective in brief, sudden and brutal assaults at very close quarters. My maintaining my distance like an old-time fencing duellist was giving him few opportunities to deliver the sort of punishing blow he probably relied on to finish a fight.

He dropped back suddenly, disappearing behind the pillar. I paused, reluctant to be too much the aggressor if I might get an opportunity to just leg it and leave the field. There is no dishonour in leaving a fight you did not join willingly.

But he returned a moment later and we rejoined battle. He blocked my straight right to his face, but the left that followed it was well under his guard and caught him solidly below the ribs. He was back immediately though, and the force of his punches confirmed something I had suspected before: those gloves were weighted, and that gave him a substantial advantage. And, unlike most weapons, they would rarely be recognised as such.

For my part I was bare-knuckle. This might be nature's way of doing it, but is not my preferred style, Give me gloves any day, or a knuckle duster when I'm pushed.

He mixed in a few kicks for variety, but these were slow to arrive and an alert fighter with plenty of room could stay well clear. They were his way of telling me that if I stayed back I could not count on beating him with long-range strikes, although my arms gave me a slight advantage in reach. And with those gloves he very much had the advantage in hitting power.

It was a more evenly-matched fight than I would have chosen. At the same time, my mind seethed with questions. If this was an attempt at murder, why choose such an inefficient means when he could as easily have used a knife? If it was not murder, just what did he have in mind?

As the fight wore on, I began to get an inkling. He was not going for the knockout punch, so much as wanting to hurt me and keep hurting me. Perhaps, as I was a boxer, he wanted to humiliate me by beating me at my own game.

It occurred to me that this might be someone from my past, someone not related to the current case. Certainly, I had dished it out to a few men approximately the size and build of this one, and they might want a chance to square the account and give me a beating in turn.

We sparred a bit, neither committing too far, both landing a few good blows, including one that momentarily made me see stars. He was not confident enough to finish it off though, wary that I might be faking in order to lead him into what the Americans call a 'sucker punch.'

We circled around each other. He was aggressive and he wanted to hurt me, but he was cunning too.

I did have a secret weapon up my sleeve: the Chinese punch Mr Yang had taught me. That was literally a killer blow which would likely leave the recipient dead on the ground, but it was slow and required a build-up.

I had never shown anyone the secret punch. I had practised it on my own and had verified that I could break planks and even roofing tiles, but I had never used it in a fight, and I had not yet worked out how to make the breathing and focusing quick enough that a trained opponent would not knock me down while I was getting ready.

I would need to count on the fact that my adversary would not know what I was doing, and if he could be distracted for long enough it could be brought off. However, that particular desperate gambit was reserved for the direst emergency.

He caught my shoulder with his blow and my counterpunch grazed his cheek, pushing the balaclava slightly out of alignment, so that he was forced to turn his head to see me properly. That gave me a better idea than the Chinese punch. Of course it entailed some risk but it was the best I could do in the circumstances.

The use of fingers in professional boxing is not only illegal but impossible. The gloves see to that. Bare-knuckle though gives some other offensive options not possible to the gloved hand, which is why eye-gouging and strangling were outlawed in the earliest rules.

In our next exchange, I feinted with my right. At he blocked, taking advantage of his restricted vision, I aimed a solid kick at his right knee.

He had not expected that. Sauce for the goose is sauce for the gander, and he got his good and hot. He emitted a grunt and hopped backwards.

I ducked low, and for the first time, stepped in close while he could not get away. He caught me on the side of the head with an elbow that made my ear ring, but I succeeded in hooking a finger through the balaclava and jerked it smartly sideways.

Now his vision was properly obstructed and he could only see me through the corner of one eyehole. As I swerved, jinked and feinted he was having trouble following me. The matter was proved conclusively when I put together a sequence and he failed to block the punch from his blindside. The tide was shifting in my favour.

We danced around for a bit and slackened off, one of those changes in tempo that all fights have, as the contestants digest the outcome of the last pass and decide on tactics for the next engagement. He foolishly assumed that he had a fraction of a second to raise a hand and improve his vision. But of course this was exactly what I was waiting for. He just blocked my left, and the right, but the next left caught him in undefended midriff.

I kicked his knee again in the same place as before. His hands went up to protect his head, but this time I just stepped forward and shoved as hard as I could.

I had maneuvered him to within a couple of feet of the wall, and as he was thrown back his head whiplashed against the brickwork. Again, not tactics for the ring but sometimes you just have to take advantage of whatever presents itself. Lucky for him he was wearing that balaclava, but he would have a grand lump there tomorrow.

That stunned him, as it would any normal human, and he was in no shape to defend himself against the well-drilled combinations that followed.

The few seconds after that owed more to all-in wrestling than the Marquess of Queensbury, but suffice to say it was not long before he was prone on the ground with all the fight knocked out of him and my knee on his chest.

I had a sudden flash of self-consciousness. I could not believe this was really happening, but, yes, I was about to remove the mask and discover the identity of the disguised villain. This was definitely the sort of thing that only happened in adventure stories. Except that, in those, the hero does not get beaten black and blue first.

"And who are you when you're at home?" I asked, ripping the balaclava off in one quick movement.

At first I did not recognise him, but, making allowance for facial injuries, the different lighting, and the absence of a uniform cap, it came to me, and I was confident of my identification. My assailant was Mrs Smith's burly chauffeur-cum-bodyguard. Marks, she had called him.

The man had been hostile, and had been discomfited by the idea of my taking her in to the old fire station to see the boxing without his protection, but there was nothing in our brief history which would have prefigured this level of violence.

The obvious explanation was that she had sent Marks to beat me up. That made a certain kind of sense. If she had wanted me rendered incapable of pursuing the case but did not want me to be seriously injured, then this would have been the way to go about it. I would have recommended he use a stout stick rather than being overly reliant on the padded gloves, but his general approach was on the right lines.

Marks stirred, swore at me, and tried to lash out, then tried to kick me.

Knowing when you are beaten is important to a boxer. Tenacity and hanging in to the finish are well and good, but you will take a good deal of unnecessary punishment if you do not learn to bow to the inevitable and keep trying to get up after you have been knocked down for the umpteenth time.

This man was in the grip of strong emotion. He gave a great heave and tried to punch me again.

I blocked him easily, and hit back, just to let him know that I was not putting up with any of that nonsense.

"She's mine!" he said, in between swearing. "You keep your filthy hands off her!"

Well, that answered that question. Not the first employee to be hopelessly smitten by his mistress, and Mrs Smith was more alluring than most, and perhaps gave more encouragement than she should. I wondered it had taken him so long to take action. But perhaps he had been following me for days waiting for an opportunity and I, caught up in my investigation, had not noticed. That was a worrying thought.

I gave him a couple of gut punches to keep him quiet. By rights I would have hurt him a lot worse as a lesson, but I did not have the heart for it. He was, after all, just a man doing his job, like me. At this stage in the game, I would not have sworn that I was the one on the side of right.

Instead, I just gave him a look in the eye.

"She's yours and you can keep her," I said. "But I know you, Marks. If I see you again, you're a dead man. Understand?"

It was tough-guy talk lifted straight from some gangster story. It might have sounded ridiculous, but maybe coming from someone who had just knocked seven bells out of him gave the old line some authority. He croaked something that might have been 'yes' and did not try to hit me again.

That was good enough for me. I sprang to my feet, not quite as agilely as I would have liked, and walked briskly away, pausing only to stoop for my hat.

Chapter 16: Mrs Bridges' Secret

Mrs Bridges was probably wearing the same black dress as before. We were in a different room this time, another parlour or drawing room, but decorated in a different style. Stag heads adorned one wall, and hunting prints, a family coat of arms, some trophies on a sideboard and other decorations suggested a masculine taste.

I guessed this would have been her late husband's room, where he could gather with his friends and be out of the way of the gentler sex. The smell of cigars had long departed. There was no speck of dust, and if there was any odour it was of floor wax and metal polish, like a well-run museum.

I took up a place opposite her, noticing how thin her legs were under her black dress, and her almost translucent skin. Time had worn her, but Mrs Bridges abided, like the last autumn leaf clinging to a branch. Again, I wondered whether she had walked to the chair or been carried and set down in it, she looked so frail.

Mrs Bridges had been contemplating a glass case full of stuffed animals. Second-hand shops have entire walls given over to the things; modern taste has left such Victorian décor behind, but they are common enough items, especially among older folk.

These, though, were prize specimens, masterpieces of the taxidermists' art. A glass dome the size of a dustbin held a tree stump and an imitation forest floor. A fox posed beside the stump, oblivious to a red squirrel on a bare branch and a rabbit almost at its feet. Looking more closely, I also made out a hedgehog among the leaves, and a field mouse. More were doubtless hidden for the patient viewer to find.

After the incident of Grim the Collier of Croydon, I believed Mrs Bridges wanted to communicate with me, but was constrained from doing so. I thought she might become lucid in the absence of Mr Bailey, but her stiff manner suggested she was still very much on her guard.

"I often think about them," she said, looking in the glass case. She was more sober and serious than before, and, I thought, more anxious. "When I was a girl, I endured many tedious visits—middle-aged men do go on—and they were my only distraction. I used to make up stories about the animals."

I nodded politely to show I was listening.

"They have their revenge," she went on. "We killed them, but they have now watched everyone die, one by one, from their glass case. I do not want to die, Mr Stubbs, but I would not want immortality, not like that."

The fox looked on with a glassy eye. If Mrs Bridges would not talk directly, I was expecting some subtle clue, like Grim the Collier of Croydon. Maybe this was it. Looking more closely I could see a mole emerging through the leaves.

"Immortality is not what people imagine," she said. "It's only young people who want to be immortal. The world changes...You see children grow up, marry, have their own children, grow old. You start to recognise the bright sparks and the troublemakers, the clever ones and the fools, from an early age. You learn to recognise liars early on. You see patterns of behaviour, the girls who will make good marriages that last, and the ones who will throw themselves away. The boys who will die in wars, and the ones who will write textbooks about military strategy."

In her century of life Mrs Bridges had been forced into the role of passive observer. She was a clever woman, and I did not doubt she had noticed things that would have escaped the attention of others.

"My Mr Bailey," she said, "I know what his fate will be. He thinks he's clever. He makes his living off me, and a very good living too, with no work. He's loyal enough, but he's lazy. His friends have proper legal careers. He likes the easy life, the good dinners in his club. In a few years he'll be wondering where it has gone. His friends will do better, have impressive careers and move up in the world. Mr Bailey will get bitter and jealous. In time he will blame me for having taken the best years of his life, robbing him of the opportunity to make a name for himself."

"I wouldn't presume to comment," I said, uncomfortable at hearing my betters talk about each other like that.

"Oh, I'm a reliable Sibyl," she said. "If you look up Mr Bailey in twenty years—if he hasn't drunk himself to death by then—you'll see I'm right."

"I wasn't—"

"If I have learned nothing else, and I am not at all sure that I have, I have learned that time passes. Even the huge iceberg of a hundred years slowly melts. Time runs away like water until nothing is left, and everything changes."

Whatever her point, she was approaching it obliquely.

"When I was a very little girl, my father took me and my brother—it must have been George, because he was older—around our estate in Hampshire. We watched a ploughman with a team, running furrows straight down the long field, turning the plough and running back. I thought it was wonderful how he drew lines on the blank earth, like filling up a page with words.

"'This will never change.' my father told us. 'The ploughman sows in spring and reaps in autumn. This is your heritage, and your fortune.'

"Well of course, he was a landowner, as everyone of consequence was in those days. He knew the old aristocracy was in danger. Yes, even then, certainly by the time I was a debutante, rich Americans were coming over here to marry into noble families. And there were plenty of Northern industrialists with soot on their shoes who wanted to buy their way into society. Of course they were never admitted. If he could only see what London is like now! That Mrs Hardcastle with her flat vowels, pretending to be as good as anyone else. And Mrs Smith, an actress for goodness' sake...

"You're young, you don't know what change is. You see the name of a shop change, a new house built at the end of the street, fashions changing, but you think the fundamentals remain. The big things do change."

I could have mentioned the War to End All Wars, which I had fought through, had seemed like a big enough change in the world. Her thoughts were elsewhere.

"Like servants. The sense of respect has dissipated. These days they are more like employees than family. When I was a girl they always had reverence, they made one feel special. They looked up to father and he led Sunday prayers. Now they do everything on suffrage, they're like restaurant waiters. They'll give the same grudging service to whoever happens to be paying them."

She looked up at that, knowing there would be servants within earshot, just outside the door, ready to take orders, or make judgements. Or report what they heard to someone else.

"My father saw threshing machines come along, and then there were combine harvesters. Now there are motor-tractors pulling ploughs, instead of horses. Five thousand years of horse-ploughs gone. All changed."

"And motor-cars, and aeroplanes, and trans-Atlantic steamers," I said, seeing if I could hurry her on to a point. "Telegrams and telephones and radio."

"Yes," she said. "All those things. Express trains, and electric lights. But the ploughman—you see, the ploughman and his team, and the horse and carriage, the hearth fire, and rush lights in the village church… that was always the same, for thousands and thousands of years. And now it isn't."

"In some ways…" I started.

"It's an alien world," she said. "It's not my world. Bigger changes are coming. So much power, and power to be misused."

I decided to risk being more direct.

"Does this have any direct bearing on the Widows Society?"

Mrs Bridges froze as though turned to stone, a look of polite horror on her face.

"Forgive the question," I said hastily. "All I meant to say was that the Society has also had to experience changes over the decades—what with the changes in labour laws, and education, and the women's property act, and suffrage, and all the women working in factories in the war, and women MPs and doctors and all that."

I was gabbling, but her expression had unfrozen as though a spell had been broken.

"The situation for women has changed beyond all recognition since my day," she said. "A girl born today might become an aviator, or a professor. Or maybe an archbishop or a prime minister."

While she was speaking I had pulled my notebook out and scribbled—IS THERE SOMETHING YOU WISH TO SAY BUT CANNOT SPEAK OUT LOUD?

I showed the note to her while she talked about how orthodoxy had changed, how women had been increasingly restricted in the last century but were now being freed again, how the freedoms of the 90s were being reasserted.

She read, and nodded once.

CAN YOU WRITE IT? I wrote and held up the notebook and pencil for her to take.

She shook her head and held up her hands, her knobbly, arthritic fingers trembling. While she might be able to write carefully at a desk given enough time, Mrs Bridges could not dash off a note as I could. I wished she had just written a note beforehand and passed it to me, but maybe she felt she could not even do that.

"Having said that," I said, "Women of earlier generations have always been able to achieve remarkable things. The late Queen, of course—Empress of India. Or Florence Nightingale. Or Josephine Butler."

My mind was not up to carrying on the two conversations, one verbal and the other written and signalled, at the same time. Mrs Bridges was sharper.

"Or indeed the members of the Committee," she said. "All remarkable ladies in their ways. And I am lucky to have been elevated to be the head of the Society."

"You are the chair of the Committee."

"Or perhaps just the figurehead of the society, you might say," she said with a small laugh. "If you see what I mean."

She put particular emphasis on that phrase: figurehead of the society.

As she spoke, she leaned over and, with infinite care,

extracted something from a black handbag and passed it to me. When I withdrew my hand, I was holding a key ring, with a brass door key and a smaller but still substantial key, embossed with the name of a firm known for the manufacture of safes.

"It is a notable achievement to be in charge of such an august institution," I said pocketing the keys.

"The figurehead," she repeated. "If you know what that means. I am not really in charge of things, not anymore. Others are."

The references to the figurehead in combination with the keys suggested one thing to me.

SHOULD I GET THE BUST? I wrote.

She nodded an affirmative.

"Mrs Kennedy, Mrs Smith and Mrs Hardcastle do all seem to be highly capable," I said, "however humble their origins. The Society has prospered in the past few years."

The butler appeared at the door. I concealed my notepad under my hand, like a boy caught passing notes at school.

"Will Madam and the guest be requiring refreshments now?" he asked. His expression did not invite a positive response.

"Tea? No, not now," said Mrs Bridges. She seemed rattled. A few seconds earlier and he would have caught us. He may not have been snooping, but it looked like it. "In fact, if you don't mind, Mr Stubbs, I'm rather fatigued by all this talking. You had better send me your report in writing, if you don't mind. "

"Of course," I said, getting to my feet. "Thank you, Mrs Bridges. Please pass on my respects to Mr Bailey."

The butler escorted me to the door, keeping an eye on me as though I might steal the silver knickknacks.

"Mrs Bridges is in remarkably good fettle for a lady of her years," I said.

He ignored me. Speaking about his employer to strangers was beneath him, unless, perhaps, they had something substantial to offer him by way of financial incentive. Then, maybe that mask would slip.

The door was shut very smartly behind me.

Arthur had been waiting at the gate and was in the process

of stripping bark off a stick. He dropped it and jumped up as he saw me, like a faithful dog.

"Did she spill the beans without the money man?" he asked, adding belatedly, "Mr Stubbs."

"In a manner of speaking, yes,"

There was no doubt, now, of Mrs Bridges' intentions, and that she was behind the original letter which had triggered the investigation. No doubt she had included it as an enclosure in a letter to a friend, so the servants who posted it would not be aware who she was writing to. She knew subterfuge.

"What did she say?"

"It seems I need to get hold of the bronze bust that is the symbol or figurehead of the Society."

"The oracle!" he said with great excitement.

"I beg your pardon?"

"I've been translating Paracelsus," he said.

"Tell me more."

Chapter 17:
Miss Frey Breaks the Code

A rthur and I continued from Mrs Bridges' house towards our appointment with Miss Frey, whom I had set on the trail of the mysterious radio transmission. I urged him to take up his story again.

"So, Paracelsus is in the woods, with his guide, and he's been through the ordeal where they poisoned him, and finally he gets to meet the Gypsy Queen," Arthur recapitulated, all in one breath. "He says she's famous because she can tell the future."

"The end of the quest," I said.

"They take his sword away, which he isn't happy about because it's magic and it's called Azoth, and they take him and his guide to a secret place in the woods, to a shelter set up between four big oak trees. It's really dark inside and there's a smoking fire in the middle, and bits of dead animals hung up on the walls, and this really old woman with matted hair is sitting on a bearskin.

"Paracelsus has his guide translate for him, and the Queen needs a translator, too, because she doesn't speak English, so it's a really slow conversation and he isn't sure that she's getting what he says properly, or that he's getting what she says. Paracelsus says both of the translators are ignorant and don't know what they're talking about."

"What were they talking about?" I asked.

Arthur scratched his head.

"He's a bit vague. He wanted to ask her questions, but she wanted to ask him questions too. About mining, and minerals and 'the deep places of the earth,' which he happened to know a lot about. He wanted to know about medicine and healing herbs, and things. He says he learned many things, but he didn't say what they were."

That was typical of Paracelsus. He was careful about sharing his secrets too freely; he always liked to make his readers work for them.

"The strangest bit was the oracle," said Arthur. "He didn't see it at first because it's so dark in the tent, but then he sees this metal thing, like a helmet on a wooden chest. He says that sometimes the Queen seemed to talk to it like it was a person, but of course it never said anything back, even though she acted like it did. She said it was an oracle, and very old and sacred, and that it spoke to her.

"He goes and looks at it—and the guards jump out and nearly stab him, but the Queen says it's all right. The oracle is like this brass head, all battered and rusty, and really old. The Queen says it speaks to her, but the word she uses in Latin isn't like 'speak', it's more like 'signals.' It's the same word they use when the Romans sent smoke signals from watch towers."

"What did she mean by that?"

"Paracelsus doesn't say. They talk for the whole day and then they tell him he has to leave, and he sets out with his guide for Londinium—which is London, obviously—on their way to Dumnonia, which is Cornwall, because he wants to see the mines. That's all he says about the North Wood."

"A brass head, you say?"

"Well he calls it aes, which can be bronze or brass, but Mr Hoade says it was more likely to be brass because of Roger Bacon. Bacon had a brass head that answered questions too."

I paused for three steps, trying to think if I should know who Roger Bacon was. Arthur must have picked up my perplexity, because he chimed in at once.

"They called Roger Bacon, Doctor Mirabilis, the miracle doctor. He was a friar and an alchemist, and they say he was a wizard but Mr Hoade doesn't think so. He was alive two hundred years earlier, but the story about him having a brass head doesn't appear until after Paracelsus. So, Mr Hoade thinks it was added later. With Bacon's head, some people said it was a mechanical thing he made, and others said he trapped a cacodemon in it. Do you know what a cacodemon is?"

I shook my head.

"A bad demon. I asked if that was because caco is Latin for poo." He laughed suddenly. "Mr Hoade didn't think it was funny."

"Mr Hoade is an educated gentleman," I said, "but he is not supposed to be involved."

I would have to have a talk with Mr Hoade. He was taking far too much of an interest.

"I'm sorry," said Arthur after a few more steps. "He kept asking questions and I couldn't ignore him after he had helped me."

"Don't worry about it. You've done good work there, Arthur, good work indeed."

"The oracle in the wood and the bronze bust, they sound like two of the same thing," he said.

Or one and the same, I thought. The bust was nineteenth century, but there was no reason why the old, battered oracle of Paracelsus' time could not receive a new covering.

The timings were all coming together. The Romanies had been driven out of Norwood in the late eighteenth century. I had heard rumours that the masked gangs who attacked them had been sent or employed by TDS. The camp had been dispersed, but certainly some Romanies remained—such as the Whately family who caused so much trouble in Dulwich. And the Widows Society was set up during the Napoleonic Wars, just about then.

"What do you think the oracle was?" Arthur asked, breaking into my train of thought. "Was it mechanical, or a demon, or just a trick?"

"It's not exactly unknown for Romanies to use a bit of trickery when they're telling fortunes," I said. "But I think our man Paracelsus isn't so green as to be caught out so easily. He spent a lot of time exposing fakes."

"But what is it really?"

"Something weird," I said. "Something wondrous and terrible."

The hint from Grim the Collier of Croydon was that the bust, whatever of was, was of infernal origin and, whatever it pretended, it meant harm. It might be acting as an oracle like the one Paracelsus saw. Mrs Bridges had realised, rather belatedly, that it had ulterior motives. The challenge was getting hold of it, but, with the keys, that might not be too difficult.

"Oh," he said, not greatly impressed. "I forgot to say, I saw her again."

"Who?"

"That strange woman in the veil."

"Indeed. Well, make sure you note the time and location."

I was more concerned at this point with talking to Mr Hoade. I had asked him not to pursue the case, and it seemed to me he was getting far more information than he should from young Arthur. I should be able to conduct an interview fairly soon, as I was meeting Miss Frey at the library. As soon as we were through the front door, Arthur made for the adventure novels. He did not greatly enjoy Miss Frey's company.

Miss Frey lived with her aunt, who did not, on the whole, approve of me, and who would take a very dim view indeed if she thought her charge was getting involved in questionable practices. As the legal guardian, she has the final say in such things, but Miss Frey is a resourceful fifteen-year-old. Her aunt is lucky her charge is not getting into any worse trouble.

Miss Frey is an inveterate reader, of the three-books-a-week variety, and the library is her lifeline. Her aunt does not have the patience to stand over her while she browses the shelves for the latest works on science and mathematics, instead dropping the girl off at the library while she goes to the hairdressers. This arrangement suits both parties and also gave me the ideal opportunity to pursue a discussion.

I could not see her immediately, so I found the science section and was leafing through a book on the theory and practice of wireless operation when she appeared at my elbow in a navy-blue outfit.

"That's not the best one on radio," she said, with her usual lack of preliminaries. "I've just returned a couple of others and they'll be back on the shelves soon."

"I gather you took delivery of the radio set without difficulty."

Obviously it would have been very much easier if Miss Frey could have come to my boarding house and listened in on the wireless set there. That was impossible, both because of the prohibition on female visitors on the one side and the strict controls on Miss Frey's visits on the other.

The mountain would not come to Mohammed, as they say, but Mohammed could certainly be moved to the mountain. It was Sally who pointed out that Miss Frey was an habitual winner of magazine competitions, who solved complicated puzzles just for fun. The prizes are rarely anything useful or valuable, most are donated straight to the church raffle, but she liked winning.

While a radio might be an extravagant sort of prize, it would not be the most valuable thing Miss Frey had ever won—that apparently had been a self-assembly garden shed, which she had been forced to donate to a church fete, although she would have liked to have put it up herself.

"Aunt wasn't very interested in the radio," said Miss Frey, taking my lead and speaking more quietly while pretending to look at a book. "I did try to show her, but some people, you know..."

"She didn't suspect anything?"

"My aunt, well, she's not a very imaginative woman, you know," she said with an intonation, expression and gesture borrowed directly from her friend Claudia Oldham. "Mainly, she was worried about where to put it, but it fits perfectly well on the chest of drawers in my bedroom."

Miss Frey, not being prone to the sort of pointless knick-knacks other girls accumulate, probably has more room and less cluttered spaces than most. I cannot imagine she ever played with a doll in her life.

"Setting it up was very interesting," she said. "There's quite a lot of assembly required."

"Nothing too difficult for you, I trust?"

"Obviously. The mystery broadcaster started up at eight o'clock, just as you said."

I was surprised she had managed to get the thing installed,

set up and tuned in so quickly—but not very surprised.

"Definitely code," she added.

"Aha," I said.

"It's frustrating not being able to draw anything and show you," she said, glancing about. "But I suppose I'd better not."

Not least because her explanation would probably make me feel more ignorant than ever, without shedding any light on the matter. If she said it was a code, it was good enough for me.

"What sort of code?" I asked.

"It's a phrase code. The only examples I've seen before have been Elizabethan. Messages were hidden in religious literature. Each particular phrase—'our blessed redeemer' or 'the blessings of the almighty' or 'the sacred word'—stood for a letter of the alphabet, and they were sprinkled in a much longer text. It's not too obvious when you have a sort of writing that uses lots of repetitive phrases anyway."

"That sounds pretty cryptic," I said.

"Not really. It's sending a twelve-digit number."

"But what does that mean?"

"Actually," she said, "It's two six-digit numbers with a space between them. That was what made it sort of obvious."

Miss Frey was enjoying her superiority, teasing me with clues to see how many she would need to give me before I got it. Playing the game, I dredged some dimly-recalled Army training from the recesses of my memory.

"Grid references. Northing and easting," I said.

"Ex-actly. But it didn't make any sense—codes within codes!" Her eyes were wide with excitement. "So I did the obvious thing and treated it as decimals, rather than base sixty degrees and minutes, and the latitude I got was 51.4279 degrees, which is exactly right."

"For what?"

"For here, silly. The longitude didn't make any sense, but then it wouldn't, because they wouldn't be using the Greenwich Meridian. They'd be using their own system. So I assumed that it was the latitude for Norwood in their system, and I worked back from that to find their Zero Meridian, which is in the middle of the Pacific."

"That's certainly quite remarkable," I said.

"But it probably isn't that," she went on. "I don't think it's anything on Earth. I think they take their Zero Meridian from an alignment with something celestial. Their home star."

Miss Frey was making a lot of assumptions here, but so far they all sounded rather shrewd. I had not even hinted at alien beings, but she had been involved in previous cases and made inferences. They were not necessarily accurate, but, unlike her aunt, she did not lack imagination.

"I haven't quite figured out what it is yet," she said. "I'm working on it."

"So, let me get this right," I said. "Someone is sending out a coded broadcast which gives a location here. But then we know it's coming from near here anyway, because the signal is so strong."

"Someone a hundred miles away would not know," she said. "Unless they can decode it. Then, it is a beacon guiding them to where it is. Oh, don't tell anyone, but I vandalised a book for you."

From her pocket, she took out a folded page torn from a London street directory, showing Norwood. A neat line had been ruled across it.

"That's your fifty-one point something something degrees of latitude line," I said, scanning the path of it.

It ran through roads and parks, and across railway lines. Sure enough, there was a familiar street name: the line ran squarely though the offices of the Widows Society, where, of course, the bust was located. Written neatly in the corner of the map was the latitude of the home meridian.

"I'll listen to see if it transmits anything else, but it only seems to put out the one set of numbers. So, that's that," she concluded. The puzzle had been solved, the message decoded, she had an answer to the mystery as far as she was concerned, and it was of no further interest. She moved on to the next topic without a pause, giving me no time for further questions. "Do I really have to wear that dress to the wedding?"

Sally had appointed Miss Frey as bridesmaid, which she saw as an essential part of the young woman's education. Sally had decided Miss Frey needed to at least be able to act the part of being ladylike, even if she had no particular interest in it.

"Absolutely," I said. "Wearing the uniform is an essential part of the job. I'm sure Miss Oldham will have told you about the requirements for weddings."

"She said she always wore black to weddings. It gets her noticed."

"Not when she is a bridesmaid, I suspect."

Though with some people these days, you never knew.

"She told me about you visiting her flat and asking all those questions about Mr Parrish and the dark spirit, or whatever it was."

"Did you draw any conclusions?"

"Of course not. I don't have enough evidence."

"Me neither," I said. "Did she say anything about the bridesmaid's outfit?"

"She thought I'd be very pretty dressed up. Huh." She made something like a pout, another mannerism she must have learned from her friend. "Do I get to choose my present for doing it afterwards?"

Gifts to bridesmaids are not normally made in such a spirit of quid pro quo. But then, Miss Frey was not the usual sort of bridesmaid, and she had just done me a great favour.

"Within reason," I said.

Her head bobbed.

"Then tell Sally I'll do it," she said.

"I will." I glanced up and down. None of the other visitors to the library seemed to be paying any attention to us. "I hope you enjoy your radio. Don't go broadcasting anything I wouldn't. Now, I need to talk with a librarian."

Chapter 18: Mr Hoade Goes Too Far

I must have had a serious air because Hoade's face went from a warm greeting to a more sombre expression. He looked rather tired and careworn, with dark circles around his eyes, as though he had had a long and difficult week, but he was eager to help.

"Good afternoon, Mr Hoade," I said. "Might I trouble you for five minutes of your valuable?"

He pushed aside a stack of books.

"Stubbs, I am at your service," he said. "In fact, this is rather opportune as I have some discoveries for you. I gather young Renville is your assistant these days. I hope I was able to help him find his way."

"I would say you did somewhat more than that," I said. "Exceeded your brief."

Library customers passed by on both sides, seeking out the latest historical romance or books on cultivating rhododendrons, oblivious to serious matters in their midst.

"I am sorry," he said. "I was honestly just trying to help, and I couldn't properly do that without knowing more about it. You know I wouldn't pry into your affairs, and you know I know how sensitive your work is. I have maintained absolute discretion—I haven't even told my wife."

This came out in more of a rush than he may have intended.

I sighed, feeling myself weaken.

"I know," I said. "I don't blame you a bit, but this is a dangerous business. I've been attacked. A man was killed."

Parrish had been murdered because his investigations were too successful. Mr Hoade was going down exactly the same path.

"Really—who?"

"For obvious reasons I cannot share that information. I'd please ask you, for your own safety and for my peace of mind, not to involve yourself or to quiz young Arthur."

In answer, he reached into a drawer and removed a sheaf of handwritten notes.

"Before I drop out of the case, I should share some things with you. They may be important."

"What sort of things?"

"Well," he said, glancing down and spreading his notes, which were compendious. "You were asking me about Grim the Collier. As you know, it's a play, a comedy, in fact, first published in 1662, author unknown. But it appears to be a version of another play, Like Will to Like, which dates 1568."

"Is that also about Grim the Collier?"

"Sort of—he's a minor character in it. It's mainly about a devil called Belphegor, who is sent to Earth to investigate reports that women are making the place worse than Hell itself. Belphegor has a servant, a minor demon called Akercock, who helps Grim win his fair lady, but that's a subplot." He looked at me meaningfully. "The supernatural element and the local setting seem significant."

"Perhaps so," I said, thinking that this was meagre pickings.

"It's also similar in theme to Ben Jonson's The Devil as an Ass. That was 1616, and in that one the servant character is a minor demon sent to fashionable London. Now, with him we get slightly more substance—Pug, the demon, possesses the body of a hanged thief to gain human form."

He sounded as though this was a revelation but I could not see how possession would be relevant.

"Then," he said, glancing at a note, "We have another version. Henry Milner rewrote the story in 1825 as Grim Will, The Collier of Croydon or the Death of the Red King. He makes Grim a coal miner, who tunnels so deep he can overhear talk in Hell and discovers a diabolic plot to take over the kingdom. So, Grim is behind the death of William Rufus—the Red King—in 1100, in a hunting accident many believe was actually an assassination."

"I see," I said.

"But, do you?" asked Hoade. "What's interesting with Milner's version is how the story mutates but certain essential elements continue to run through it."

"Who's to say if those are the true parts?"

"There's also another Grim the Collier," he said, too caught up in his explication to heed me. "Not a play or a book, but a flower. A type of hawkweed, technically Pilosella aurantiaca. In an herbal of 1633, Gerard describes it and called it 'Grim-the-Collier.' Also known as Fox-and-cubs, Devil's Paintbrush, Golden Mouse-ear, King-devil, or Orange Hawkweed."

Hoade was speaking with great animation, and as he leaned close I noticed he was unshaven.

"Gerard says it could be used to treat respiratory infections, digestive issues, and skin conditions. Its leaves were also used to make a tea which promoted sleep. And it originally came from the Carpathians!"

"I see," I said.

"The other clue we have is the name of the demon," he said, speaking even faster. "Belphegor is a real being, or at least one from established mythology. Machiavelli wrote a play about him, La favola di Belfagor Arcidiavolo around the same time as Grim the Collier. You've heard of Macchiavelli?"

"By reputation."

"It has exactly the same plot as the others," he said. "But the interesting part is that Belphegor is one of the seven princes of hell, in charge of promoting the deadly sin of laziness. He tempts people into become idle by offering them knowledge, so they can become rich without work, with new inventions."

The connection between Belphegor, the oracular bronze head and the Society started to become clearer.

"That's why, in Like Will to Like, the devil character is called Nicholas Newfangle. Not very subtle. Newfangle's origins are hinted at, and once you know about the Machiavelli it all becomes obvious. I've done a sort of explanatory diagram."

It was an elaborate sketch with the different plays and the characters in them, with arrows joining them all up. The name

Belphegor had an arrow going into the middle distance with the word 'Moab'.

"Belphegor goes back further though! He was a god of the Moabites. His name derives from 'Baal of Mount Phogor,' or Peor, who became a demon in the Hebrew mythology. Phogor is identified with modern-day Mount Nebo, which is exactly where Moses was given a vision of the Promised Land in Deuteronomy 32:52."

He gesticulated wildly, knocking two books off the desk and causing people to look round.

"I'm afraid you're losing me a bit," I said, leaning to retrieve the books. "Perhaps we could just stop at Grim the Collier."

Hoade ran his fingers through his hair in a gesture of what might have been agitation or frustration. He took a deep breath before starting up again.

"It's difficult to explain," he said. "I don't quite grasp it fully myself yet, but it all joins together—Ben Jonson, Machiavelli, Grim the Collier, the flower, Moses, the Ark of the Covenant, the Knights Templar—they had a prophetic head!—I haven't had a chance to read all of it yet, there's so much more, but it's all connected..."

"We don't need to go any deeper than we already have."

"But it makes sense!" he insisted.

He was too loud for a library and people were noticing. He dropped his voice, but the urgency was still there.

"The more you read, the more you see these threads running through all the stories—the devils, the communication, everything..."

From my upside-down viewpoint I could make out the word BAAL written out several times in block capitals, sometimes circled and underlined.

"You remember Elagabalus who we talked about before? The Roman emperor who worshipped a stone that fell from the heavens, which was also called Elagabalus, which means Ba'al of the Mountain?"

Hoades's mind, normally as neat and orderly as the Dewey Decimal System, was jumping about like a grasshopper on hot bricks.

"That was a different case entirely," I said. "Not related to this one. We do not need to—"

"That Latin book that Arthur is working on!" He had leapt topics again in his excitement, pulling out another sheet from his notes. "Most English people did not mix with the Romanies, but the charcoal burners, the colliers, were another caste. They mingled with the outlaws and the Romanies and intermarried. Like to Like as the play says, meaning that birds of a feather flock together. There's another source—the Historie of Friar Rush from 1620—which also mentions Belphegor coming to earth in human form and playing tricks on the monks in a monastery in Germany. He ends up being driven out and fleeing to England—"

"Stop!" I said abruptly, giving up hope that he would wind down of his own accord. "Please. Mr Hoade, just how much time have you been spending on this?"

"More than I should have done," he said, with a weak smile, and gulped. "Days and nights. Whole nights. I've been making myself unpopular at home, and here. I'm getting terribly behind with my work, but—I can't sleep for thinking about it sometimes."

"I never meant anyone to spend hours and hours looking all this up. You need to stop."

"I know."

"Mr Hoade," I said as gently as I could. "Please. You are getting much, much too carried away in all this. It's not good for you."

I had seen stark raving madness in the asylum. This was a more genteel manifestation, but for a librarian to behave as Mr Hoade had done was a sure sign of the same level of mental disintegration.

He opened his mouth to say something, but stopped. After a long moment, Hoade let out a long, juddering sigh. He put his face in his hands.

"You're right," he said faintly. "Oh god, you're right."

I thought he might be about to start crying but after a minute he mastered himself and lowered his hands, rearranging his features into a facsimile of normality as I patted his shoulder.

"I'm very grateful for all you've done," I said. "You've given me plenty of food for thought but can I please ask you to now desist and get back to doing whatever it is you ought to be doing? For your own good. And please do not try to get more out of Arthur."

"Stubbs, this thing, it's like an addiction…" He swallowed. "I have tried to stop. I have tried, believe me, but I can't. I can't sleep! I just fantasise and daydream about it. Am I going mad? Am I?"

His eyes were big and shining. I marshalled my diplomatic skills.

"If it's causing you distress, you should talk to someone about it," I said. Not his wife, obviously; she must be richly fed up with the whole thing. Probably not a priest. "Do you have a sympathetic doctor?"

"Well…I suppose my general practitioner…"

I recalled how useful sedatives had been at the asylum for cases of mild disturbance.

"See if he can't give you something to help you sleep," I said. "Get some sleep and that'll give you a whole new perspective on it. You have a job and family matters to attend to. You can leave this with me, at least for a few days."

"Yes, just a few days," he said.

"You can come back to it refreshed."

"You're right, Stubbs. I need sleep. I need perspective. I'll see my doctor."

The whole thing was embarrassing to both of us. Eventually, he calmed down somewhat. I decided to leave, on the grounds that I was the cause of his distress and, if I left, he would be able to concentrate on other things—which was cowardly of me.

I retrieved young Arthur, who had picked up a couple of novels and began telling me about them as we walked back, when he suddenly punched me on the arm. He would not normally forget himself like that, but his excitement was extreme.

"That's her," he hissed, nodding at a black-veiled figure on the other side of the road. "The widow-woman I told you about, the suspicious one."

I barely remembered that he had pointed out a woman he thought was 'suspicious' near the office of the Widows Society, and had claimed to have sighted her on subsequent occasions.

She might have been a little unusual, being hidden from the world in her black outfit and dark veil, but not that extraordinary, and there are plenty of eccentrics about. I had asked Arthur what he thought a widow was supposed to do other than go to the shops, the doctors and church as other people do, and told him seeing her out and about was no great mystery.

"She's going into the cemetery!" he said.

Again, this was hardly peculiar for a widow. Many visited their husband's graves on a regular basis. However, given it was now getting on for evening and West Norwood Cemetery would be closing in minutes, it was slightly odd.

"Can we follow her?" he asked.

I was ninety-nine per cent convinced it would be a waste of time, but just to check, I took out the little storm glass I had retrieved from Gillespy's belongings. The thing was a kind of detector for occult forces. The liquid inside it was sometimes clear, or bubbly, or cloudy, which did not signify anything that I had discovered. But now something had congealed inside it. The shape was hard to decipher; it might have been a squashed beetle. But the fact that there was anything at all was alarming.

"We should," I said. "Or rather, I should. You can wait at the gates here. If a bloke comes to lock them before I'm out, give a whistle so I know time's up."

He looked at the cemetery gates, and the gathering gloom in the graveyard, with a mix of fascination and anxiety.

"I suppose I'd better stay outside," he agreed.

I followed the dark figure up a paved path, then down one of the narrow lanes between rows of gravestones. In some places, the cemetery is a lawn, in others it is overgrown, and in the upper sections it is all shaded by trees, with thick vegetation threatening to swallow up the tombs and monuments.

She stopped at a crossroad, and I made a sharp left just as she was turning around, so she would not see I was following her. Her turning was as slow and deliberate as the sweep of a searchlight, and there was something about the rotation of her waist that did not seem normal, something that could not be accounted for by even the stiffest of girdles.

The storm glass and Arthur had both warned me that this 'widow' was not at all what she appeared to be, but getting it confirmed when we were alone in the shadows of a cemetery at twilight was a chilling experience.

She moved on and I continued along a parallel path somewhat behind her. My view was intermittent, as she disappeared and reappeared between the screening vegetation and gravestones, like a figure on a slow-rolling reel of film.

Then, I lost her. I concluded she had stopped at one of the graves behind a tree. I paused, breath bated, listening, then crept behind one of the vaulted tombs, attempting to get a better view.

I craned my neck and listened intently. There were no footfalls, but another sound, a busy rustling sound of cloth on cloth. I kept moving, keeping my head low, trying to establish the exact spot it was coming from.

A moment later, I ducked back as I saw movement, the top half of a figure emerging above vegetation. Either my vision deceived me or what I glimpsed was not a bit human, but more like Briggs' monster owl, with waving feelers above its head.

A sound like a slap followed and I looked up to catch an even more bizarre sight: the thing had unfolded vast wings. My jaw dropped. The thing twitched, wings blurring, and, with a flurry of displaced leaves, ascended vertically. I ran a few steps to see it through the foliage, flitting like a gigantic bat towards the North before I lost it.

It was not quite like a bat though, or a swallow, or even those strange fish you see in an aquarium. It might have had more than two wings, and it seemed to move with a kind of gyratory, corkscrewing action, but at great speed: faster than any bird I ever saw, for certain.

As the last dried leaves settled to the ground, I made my way to the spot it had taken off from, occasionally looking up to the sky in case it returned as quickly as it had disappeared.

I found a broad, flat stone at ground level, the size of a double bed, sacred to the memory of somebody or other and their family. Casting about, I found a loose stone nearby and underneath it a neat black bundle. I unwrapped the bundle and laid it out on the flat grave marker. A long black dress with black gloves sewn on to the ends of the arms, tall boots, a handbag—empty—and a veiled hat. The hat was itself a complex garment, with a wig sewn into it and a wax mask at the front behind the veil. There were no eye holes for the wearer to see out.

The dress still had a laundry tag attached. In the dim light I could just make out it was a six-letter name starting with 'T.' That would be Mrs Travis then, who had donated her old clothes.

Shaking out the dress on the slab produced a sprinkling of gritty black particles. I gathered these, sweeping them up with my fingers and saving them in a twist of paper from my notebook. I would have another matchbox of material for Dr Evans to examine, though I knew full well what the results would be.

A fungus or animal-lichen creature. A flying thing, the size of a human, which could perch on a rooftop and stand sentry, or land on a windowsill or roof terrace and carry out murders no police investigation would ever suspect. It was all far madder than even Mr Hoade had begun to suspect.

"Did you lose her?" Arthur asked when I returned to the gate.

Clearly, he had not seen anything and I was not about to tell him what I had seen.

"After a fashion," I said. "But I think we'll be seeing her again."

Chapter 19:
An Extraordinary Meeting

LANTERN INSURANCE Co Ltd—Norwood London SE Branch
FIELD INVESTIGATION REPORT FORM—OFFICIAL USE ONLY
To be completed as soon as possible following investigation.
Contemporaneous notes to be attached.
NAME OF OPERATIVE: The soon-to-be Mrs Sally Stubbs
DATE AND TIME OF INVESTIGATION: Yesterday
ADDRESS OF INVESTIGATION: St. Margaret's Church Hall, Upper
Norwood
SUBJECT OF INVESTIGATION: WIDOWS SOCIETY
EXTRAORDINARY MEETING
OBSERVATIONS (CONTINUE ON ADDITIONAL SHEETS AS
NEEDED):

I was not in disguise, more what you might call incognito. I had my old widows' weeds dry-cleaned and I wore those. That brought back some memories, I can tell you. I felt the pangs of losing a husband again, and I cried some more tears for Freddie, which is no more than his due and I'm sure you won't begrudge me this once. Then, I blew my nose and topped the outfit off with a new hat with full veil (see expenses claim with receipt in Appendix 1. Without the black band and veil, and with a ribbon, it will do for the reception.)

I arrived at the church hall in good time, but there was a crowd already there, every one of them in black. This was my first meeting as a member of the Widows Society, and the invitation had not mentioned any such thing but everyone seemed to understand. Like me, they put on the black to show they belonged. Our own uniform.

Not a few were carrying their little blue Society passbooks, the one you send when you pay money in or take it out, in their hands or sticking out of handbags. The members were ready to cash in and leave the Society.

I showed my invitation at the door. The lady gave me a look, but did not ask me to lift my veil. It was plain enough I was a woman, and not some man trying to sneak in on a dare or for a bet. By whatever grounds she was judging, I passed muster.

There was a low murmur from the crowd, as from a beehive, and not a peaceful one neither: a beehive that has been disturbed, maybe, the bees all roused up and worried about the honey, wanting answers from their queen. All we needed were some yellow bands around those black outfits and the effect would have been perfect.

I was not eavesdropping on purpose but everyone was saying out loud what they were thinking.

"What about our money, that's what I want to know," said one woman near me. She had curls of tight grey hair and looked like the less sympathetic kind of teacher. She seemed to be speaking to the world in general as much as her neighbour. "Is it safe?"

In another setting, people might have ignored her, but we were all sisters together.

"I do hope so," said a plump, nervous woman, wringing her hands. "Let's see what they say."

"They'll explain everything," said a woman on my left. "They always do. They're very good."

Her confidence sounded a little desperate. What with the banking crisis and everything, everyone was worried about their money these days. We all knew how easily banks could go smash.

Maybe that was the reason for all those veils. Coming

here might be taken as an admission that they had made a horrible mistake, and that's a good reason to keep your face hidden. It made them look as though they really were a secret society, and everyone had come in hoods.

As a new member, I had the same rights as any of the others to attend, even if my stake was more of a widow's mite than the golden treasures some of the others must have had. There were a good many new shoes, fine handbags and hats on display.

We were all herded into the seating area and took our places on rows of wooden chairs. I saw your landlady there, two rows ahead of me, but I made sure she did not see me. And Mrs Stafford was there at the front row, but she would not know me from Adam even without a veil.

Up on the platform was a long table on which sat a vase of flowers and another object, which I shall describe shortly. After a minute, the four members of the committee ascended the steps to the stage. Old Mrs Bridges was a little unsteady, and she was helped by two of the others as they took their places.

I knew Mrs Bridges' name from the invitation, but I was not able to take down the others as writing notes was not practicable. There was a bossy one, whom I have since identified as Mrs Kennedy, a Northern one who seemed more friendly, called Mrs Hardcastle, and the pretty, blonde Mrs Smith, who used to be an actress and certainly had the look about her. I would not want to be on stage being compared to that figure and that complexion. (Don't think I've forgotten that you went out with her, drinking champagne, the other evening!)

Mrs Bridges spoke first. Her voice was not loud, but the room went so quiet you could have heard a pin drop.

"Some of the newcomers among you, and I know there are plenty of new faces here who have not attended meetings before, may be wondering about our figurehead, here." She indicated the item on the table, a life-size bronze bust of a woman wearing a helmet; the sort of thing you see in a museum.

(I thought that would get your attention! You see, I do listen when you talk about Paracelsus and the oracle in the woods, and all that.)

"She represents the spirit of wisdom who guides us—we call her 'Prudence'—and she presides over all the committee's meetings, and has done for a hundred years. She reminds of the wisdom of women, freed from male impulsiveness and greed. We invest our mutual funds not out of avarice, but out of a wise concern for the future. Pride and arrogance, qualities which rightly belong to the male sex, are alien to us."

I am not so sure I would agree with this, but the rest of the audience seemed to like it.

"Ours is the strength of the eternal mother, the homemaker, the one who knows what money is needed to feed and clothe her family, and how to make it go as far as possible. As widows, we have outgrown the need for show and finery, but we will never outgrow the need to shelter and protect our sisters in hardship. The Society is our bulwark against a hard world which would strip us of everything.

"Prudence is at the heart of the Society. We do not promise to double your money or make you all millionairesses, as some do. The Society has never invested in speculative, insubstantial funds that inflate like bubbles before popping. No, we invest in gold, and diamonds, and things of solid value and lasting worth. We survived Canal Mania, and a few of you will remember Railway Mania. We survived the Great War, and while banks and bankers may come and go, the Widows Society will always be here."

There was no applause, but a slight murmur of appreciation. The bees had calmed down a little.

Passing over to the bossy one was a mistake. Mrs Kennedy had a pile of notes, and fired off facts, figures and percentages which all went over my head, and, I think, everyone else's too. I don't think she was trying to hoodwink us, as I might have expected. I think she was actually trying to explain the financial situation, and expected us all to be as knowledgeable about it as she was. All we could really glean was that it was all very complicated and we had better just trust her to do complicated things.

This time, there was a buzz more of irritation and concern. Questions were not being answered. The hive was restless.

This was when the Northern woman spoke up.

"You're worried about your brass, your money, aren't you?" she asked, and a few members of the audience answered 'yes' as though it was a musical hall turn. "Well, you needn't worry. If you look to the back of the hall, Mrs Beaumont is ready to pay you out right now, if that's what you want."

Heads turned to look at the woman sat at a folding table by the entrance with some ledgers and a large black bag.

"You can take your savings at the end of the meeting," she went on. "With no penalty, no administration fee and no delay. She's got enough to pay out the lot of you."

More attention was now focused on Mrs Beaumont, who looked uncomfortable.

"Go on, show them the money!" urged Mrs Hardcastle. "Hold it up girl, show them what you've got in that bag! Wave that cash!"

Flushing, Mrs Beaumont duly held up two thick bundles of banknotes and waved them over her head. An appreciative murmur went up from the crowd. Nobody had stood up yet, but several had shifted in their seats as though they intended to be first in the queue.

"You can have it all back, if you want it. We haven't lost

it, and aren't likely to, as my colleague explained in such illuminating detail." She pulled a comic face, and some audience member laughed. "But if you do that, you'll be missing out. Nobody else is going to give you the returns we do—because nobody else cares about widows like we do."

Her tone was harsh, but it struck a chord with the audience.

"Hear, hear," said one.

"Now we know where we are," said old Mrs Bridges in her quiet, clear voice. "I think we are ready to take questions from the floor. Does anyone wish to ask the Committee anything?"

A dozen hands shot up at once, most in black gloves. Mrs Bridges pointed to the nearest, and the question-and-answer session was on.

For the most part, these were prepared questions, read out in best Sunday School voices. Some of them made references to the annual report and the state of the stock market or the price of gold. Mrs Kennedy came right back at them like a well-bred terrier. She had her notes but she hardly consulted them.

If Mrs Kennedy's assurances were not enough, the banknotes in front of Mrs Beaumont had more of an effect.

"Is it wise to have so much money here, unprotected as it were?" asked an elderly lady. "There are so many robberies these days."

"Don't worry, Mrs Griggs," said the Northern lady. "No robber would dare try taking money from us!"

That earned her a laugh.

There were two other questions from unexpected directions. One was a woman who wanted to know what the Society was doing with what she called "An 'eathen idol" in reference to the bronze bust.

"I think you'll find Prudence is one of the Christian

virtues," Mrs Kennedy shot back. "Prudence stands with Justice, Temperance, and Fortitude, which we also value, but do not call upon for guidance."

"We are as Christian as anyone," added Mrs Smith, speaking up for the first time, and her voice was as lovely as her face. "The Society is known for its good works and charity. We help the sick, the needy and the helpless. I think it's hurtful to say we're heathen."

"There's nowt wrong with Prudence being the figurehead on our ship," chipped in Mrs Hardcastle. "Look at any other financial institution—the only god they know is Mammon!"

The questioner was not quite mollified, and might have followed up had her neighbours not been tugging at her sleeves. The next questioner was a tall woman with the powerful diction of a governess.

"I understand that the Society is under investigation," she said slowly. "Can the Committee enlighten us why this is, and what is to be done?"

There was an audible sigh, as though many had been waiting for this to be asked. It was followed by a ripple from the others. An investigation? An investigation! That whole hive was abuzz. I thought, it's just as well they don't know who I am, because Harry Stubbs' name is mud around here. They would tar and feather me if they knew I was here on his account!

The Committee members exchanged looks.

"There is indeed an investigation under way," said Mrs Kennedy, "but this is a purely administrative matter. It does not concern the police, nor the Inland Revenue, nor any other authorities. There is no suggestion of any irregularity in the conduct of the Society."

The mutterings in the crowd told her this answer was not going to wash.

"We have had some enquiries from an insurance firm,

not the police," said Mrs Smith. "These are about a matter tangential to our activities, and they're not about the money."

She spoke much louder than you might expect—actress training, I expect—and delivered the word 'tangential' with great gusto, knowing that half the audience would not know it, but she also used the magic word 'money' which everyone did understand.

"If you want your money, you can get it now, in pound notes or gold sovereigns for those who prefer," said Mrs Hardcastle, at the finish. "There's nothing like hard cash. But I'm telling you flat, this society is a gold mine and you won't find the like anywhere. All you'll find out there are false promises and confidence tricksters with smooth tongues."

"Stay with us," said Mrs Smith. "Or face the world on your own."

"The Society is as strong and true as it has ever been," added Mrs Kennedy.

Nobody stood up and said, 'three cheers for the Widows Society' at the end, but the speakers seemed to have won over most of the waverers. A few women did queue up at Mrs Beaumont's table, blue books in hand, to clear out their savings, but most of the blue blooks were now tucked back in handbags, their possessors believing they'd had a narrow escape from a poor decision.

As the meeting broke up, we slowly shuffled out, moving at the speed of the oldest and slowest with their sticks. Nobody was going to push past anybody, however busy and important they wanted to think themselves. That gave me a chance to eavesdrop a bit more, and make a few other observations.

"Well, thank goodness that's all over. What a load of fuss over nothing."

"You just don't know who you can trust these days."

"My son is in the City, and he says I should take my money out and put it into Treasury bonds. Now I just don't know who to believe."

"Look at all these people, Mavis, we shall never be able to get a taxi."

"We used to have meetings in nice places which had character, not draughty old halls with rickety chairs."

"It's because it was an emergency meeting, dear. I'm sure we'll be somewhere better next time, when they have more notice."

"Couldn't they make an exception and let someone who knows about banking look over the books? A man, I mean? I know she's good with numbers but it's not the same".

"Pshaw, if you ask me, it should be women running all the banks and building societies. Mrs Kennedy knows her onions."

"Did you see those diamond rings she was wearing?"

I noted a young woman wrapping up the bronze head in cloth and putting it in a wooden box lined with green baize. It did not look as heavy as I thought.

"It is an 'eathen idol too," said the woman who had objected to it, seeing me watching. "They might have given it a new name, but they won't talk about where it came from, oh no. They won't tell you that."

"Where did it come from?" I asked.

She just scowled as though I was being stupid, and turned away.

My other observation was a heavily veiled widow standing motionless at the other side of the hall, who seemed to be watching everything. At first I thought she was aged and someone ought to see if she was all right, she was standing so still. Then, she moved, with a peculiar jerking energy which was not like an old woman at all. Quite unladylike, I would say. From the way the members of the committee walked past without looking, I gathered they knew her.

We came out into the open air, and I made a beeline for a nearby doorway so I could have a cigarette. I don't smoke as many as I used to, but sometimes I still need one, and this was definitely one of those times.

Someone else was there before me. A young widow with her veil thrown back was already lighting up. She smiled and offered me one, which I gratefully took. She had the weary look of a mother looking after children on her own, working part-time and stretching the small income from her savings just as far as it would go. What happened to the Widows Society might be not far from a matter of life and death for her little family.

"Some days," she said. "Some days you've just got to count your blessings and hold on for dear life."

She could have been my younger self, widowed and with a small child. Maybe things would have been different if I had joined the Society, rather than letting that parasite Collins ruin my life.

"Don't worry," I said. "This will all blow over."

"You think old Prue will see us right?" she asked.

"I expect so."

She looked wistfully into the cloud of smoke she had exhaled, as though she, too, was looking for auguries of the future. The crowd of women was dispersing from the church hall now, black bees flying from the hive to find their flowers.

She must have seen my engagement ring, with the unusual five-pointed green stone, because she suddenly spoke up.

"Better than getting married again," she said. "I've had quite enough of men, thank you very much."

"They're not all bad," I said.

Though, to tell the truth, a lot of so-called respectable

gentlemen are nothing of the kind when they think they can get away with it.

"I tell you what, rather than marry again, I'd rather have a heathen idol, if that's what she is. I don't care if the devil himself was looking after my savings if he gets a decent rate."

I nodded and took another drag. Maybe that's the whole story of the Society in a nutshell.

You must not judge the Widows Society too harshly. Things are not easy for widows, and the committee were not to know there was something evil using the Society for its own ends like you have told me.

A woman came out of the church hall carrying the wooden box, and bore it to Mrs Kennedy's car. The driver helped her get it into the back seat, then drove Mrs Kennedy, Mrs Hardcastle and the box back towards the office. Mrs Smith and Mrs Bridges were escorted to their own cars and went their own ways, but I think I know where you will be going next.

Chapter 20: Eavesdropping

The next episode might have belonged in a West End farce, were it not for the potentially fatal consequences.

I had accepted Briggs' assessment that burgling the offices of the Widows Society was not a viable proposition, but Mrs Bridges had given me the very keys to the front door and safe. I could swan in, take what I wanted and swan out again, without any suggestion of breaking and entering.

It was all a matter of timing. I had to act in that interval between the departure of the office staff and the arrival of the guardian Briggs had witnessed. I was aided by my confederate, Arthur Junior. The boy fancied himself as invisible as a Mohican scout. While he was assuredly not one, even out in the open he could be inconspicuous. While pretending to be an avid car-spotter on the main road, a common craze among boys his age, he had been able to note, count and document the office workers as they arrived and left. The only person remaining in the building when I arrived was the caretaker in her top floor flat.

At his signal that the last worker had left, I strolled insouciantly down the road, and without looking to my right or left, entered the grounds via the front gate. I maintained an equally casual pace past the croquet lawn, the gazebo, and the large ornamental pond in which orange fish flicked their fins. I checked the roof of the house, but though the sun was getting low it was still daytime and nothing lurked there.

The key slid easily into the lock and the door opened.

"Meredith," I said, not too loud as I stepped through. "We're in."

Unlike Briggs, I am neither an experienced nor a confident burglar, and I did not want to rush, so I proceeded at a measured pace. I first made a careful, cat-quiet circuit of the ground floor, to assure myself the caretaker was not about. I listened at every door for some time, opened it cautiously and peeked through the crack before going through. Taking a leaf out of Marks' book, I had supplied myself with a balaclava helmet, which I proposed to don if the caretaker appeared.

The bronze bust was, as expected, not in its pride of place in the main office. I assumed it was locked away in the strong room safe.

I went to the strong room, and found it locked.

Mrs Bridges had given me two keys: the front door, and the safe. For some reason, she had not given me, or did not have, the key to the interior door to the strong room.

I began a careful inspection. It was, in fact, an ordinary house door, with an ordinary lock, and not the type of reinforced door you would find in a bank. Breaking it down would be easy, but would cause a certain amount of noise. I could just kick the door down, open the safe with the key, grab the bust and run before the housekeeper was halfway through calling for the police.

Briggs would not approve. Quiet and stealthy was his way, not taking any more risks than necessary. A man running away from a building with alarm bells clanging, clutching something under his arm, is likely to get spotted, and there are not too many who fit my description.

I went into the office in search of tools I could use. A file would be too much to ask, but paper knives, steel rulers and other implements might give me the means to pry open the lock without major disturbance. I located the stationary cupboard and was going through it when I heard women's voices and the front door being unlocked.

There are times when real life rivals a farce. Like the lover caught out by the early return of a husband, I quickly and quietly shut myself in the cupboard I had been inspecting seconds before.

Hardly had I done so when the door to the office opened.

"The German is our only weak link," said one voice, "Cut ties with him and we are untouchable."

That was Mrs Kennedy.

"He's a criminal," said Mrs Hardcastle.

"Nothing has ever been proven against him," said Mrs Smith.

"Don't be so naïve," snapped Mrs Hardcastle. Chair legs scraping the floor, more than one set. "We all know what he is."

"You both seem to have taken a lot of effort to spy on my business."

"Lucky we did," said Mrs Hardcastle. "Otherwise you'd've gotten yourself into even more of a mess."

"You bribe my servants to spy on me," said Mrs Bridges. "I don't know what you need me here for, you know everything I know anyway."

"It's in the constitution," said Mrs Hardcastle. "You swore the same oath as us. You know she won't answer without all of us here. Now, let's get this over with."

By this time I had maneuvered myself around in the cupboard and by placing my eye next to the crack in the door I could see a narrow sliver of the room beyond. Sweeping to and fro, I discerned that the women had drawn up chairs and were seated around Mrs Kennedy's desk in attitudes of mutual hostility.

A moment later Mrs Kennedy, who had left the room, re-entered carrying a wooden box which she placed on the table. She opened it and, with a certain reverence, placed the bronze bust in the centre of the desk.

I had a good three-quarter view of the bust's face, when Mrs Smith was not blocking it. It had a kind of stylized, abstract quality that made it timeless. It was the face of a woman, and definitely one of the more severe Greek goddesses: Athena, goddess of war, as well as wisdom. Said to be as pitiless as the rest of the Olympians when dealing with mortals.

"Please, let us always be guided by your wisdom," said Mrs Bridges, and the other three repeated the same plea together.

They were silent for a moment.

"That bloody German has to go," said Mrs Hardcastle, resuming as before. "I don't care what he's working on. He's a threat to the Society."

"Elegantly put, as ever, Mrs Hardcastle," said Mrs Kennedy

tartly. "But your sentiment is correct."

"I understand the sentiment," replied Mrs Smith. "I don't disagree with the sentiment one bit. The practicality, however, is another matter."

"Give him his marching orders. What's he going to do?" Mrs Hardcastle's voice had an edge to it. "You haven't given him anything he could use against you, have you?"

"I wouldn't be so foolish," said Mrs Smith, bristling. "I do have some experience of the world."

"So I've heard," said Mrs Hardcastle.

"And what's that supposed to mean, exactly?"

"Don't bicker," admonished Mrs Kennedy.

"He has a band of violent men who are utterly loyal to him," said Mrs Smith.

"Pfft," said Mrs Hardcastle in a most unladylike way. "We have a whole police force on our side. Herman the German can like it, or he can lump it."

"Ask Prudence," said Mrs Smith. "She'll settle it."

There was an odd sort of silence, then. I moved my eye back and forth. All four women, including Mrs Bridges, who had remained almost silent during the entire dialog, were looking at the bronze bust.

"Will you speak to us?" asked Mrs Smith.

"Yes, do," said Mrs Kennedy. "If you'd be so kind."

"Share your wisdom," said Mrs Hardcastle, sounding half ironic.

"We beseech you," added Mrs Bridges. "Answer this question, Prudence, please: should we dismiss Dr Vengler?"

I was concentrating so much on looking at the bronze lips that I almost missed a faint ripple or shiver that ran over the surface of the bronze face. I blinked, and it happened again, like a momentary blur that came and went almost at once.

I managed not to make a sound.

"Two, that means 'no,' doesn't it?" said Mrs Smith.

"I'm afraid so," said Mrs Bridges.

There was a collective exhalation. This reply was obviously what Mrs Smith had hoped for, but the others were surprised.

"Well, that's us up the Swannee River," said Mrs Hardcastle.

I felt an acute vulnerability. The widows were unaware of my presence. All I needed to do was to sit tight and stay quiet, and they would be none the wiser.

That brass head, whatever it was, did not have eyes or ears as we understood them, but apparently it did have senses: senses which might not have human limitations. How can you hide from something that might be able to sniff you out or perceive your aura through a wall?

My advantage lay in the fact the thing was dumb, but I was thinking hard about what I would do if I was discovered, and whether I might make a bold move.

"What about this investigation?" asked Mrs Smith, as though sensing an observer.

"A little bird tells me," said Mrs Hardcastle, "that Mr Stubbs is working for some old friends of ours, though he may not know it."

"Who?" asked Mrs Smith confusedly.

"TDS," said Mrs Kennedy. "Their people have been poking around. I, too, have my sources."

"Are they a sort of secret society?"

"You haven't been with us long enough to remember the difficulties we've had with them," said Mrs Bridges, speaking up at last. "They harbour a relentless and unending grudge. They will go to any lengths to undermine us."

I wondered whether Mrs Bridges had known of my connection with TDS. If so, that would explain why she had chosen to invite me in, as a way of disrupting things.

"But why?" Mrs Smith protested. "It doesn't make any sense. We just help people."

"We have a great gift which benefits those in need," said Mrs Kennedy. "TDS have other ideas."

"Mrs Kennedy is right," Mrs Hardcastle interrupted. "These are unscrupulous people, and, for whatever dark reasons, they are set against Prudence. All of us can be replaced, but Prudence is the Society. Without her…"

"…Without her, we're just ordinary women, with no protection from the world," finished Mrs Kennedy.

"Talking about replacement, I saw Mrs Travis died just

recently," said Mrs Smith slowly. I could see her spreading her hands and attempting to calm herself. "It was just that the timing seemed rather coincidental."

"What's that got to do with the price of fish?" demanded Mrs Hardcastle.

"That man, Parrish, who was bothering Mrs Kennedy, died tragically, but conveniently for us. And Mrs Travis, a woman who held a certain animus for the Society, dies just while we're under investigation. Also tragic, but convenient—for us."

"What are you suggesting?" asked Mrs Hardcastle.

"And there is this mysterious veiled woman we're not allowed to talk about." Mrs Smith darted a look at the bronze bust as though expecting a reaction. "There are times I feel I'm not privy to everything anymore."

"My dear," said Mrs Bridges, "when ignorance is bliss, 'tis folly to be wise."

Mrs Hardcastle and Mrs Kennedy murmured agreement. Did they know, or at least suspect, that they might be complicit in murder? And did they just accept this as necessary for the greater good of the Widows Society?

All of them believed in the cause, but there was more to it. The Society, or Prudence, had given Mrs Kennedy dominion over a business empire she could have only dreamed of. It had given Mrs Hardcastle all the jewelled baubles she could have wanted. They had succeeded on their own merits, but only because they had been given opportunities rare for women.

"What we should be asking is whether we need to do anything about this investigation," said Mrs Hardcastle.

"That is a better question," said Mrs Kennedy. "A more useful question. Speak to us, Prudence."

"Speak to us," Mrs Smith and Mrs Hardcastle said in unison.

"We beseech you," said Mrs Bridges. "Answer this question, Prudence, please: do we need to do anything about Mr Stubbs' investigation?"

That shiver across the bronze face, and then another. This time there was a sigh of relief.

"No, again," concluded Mrs Kennedy. "Well, that makes things simple then."

I was increasingly aware of my cramped confinement and the risk of discovery. The bold thing would be simply to step out, take the head by force and run away. The four women could not stop me. Mrs Hardcastle, who travelled to dangerous places with expensive jewellery, was just the sort of woman who would keep a pocket pistol in her handbag, but I could not see her getting it out and shooting me down on the spot.

The real difficulty would come immediately afterwards. They all knew who I was—two of them had my business cards—and the police would be after me in minutes. I could keep running and lie low, but there would be all sorts of difficulties, even if I had Arthur Renville's assistance. As they had reminded me, they had Vengler on their side, with his band of devoted thugs, and they would be hard on my heels. Worse, there was the threat of that deadly winged creature in the guise of a widow.

No, it would be infinitely preferable to accomplish the theft by stealth and remain anonymous.

The door opened, out of sight, and a new voice spoke up.

"Mrs Kennedy!—I didn't know you were in here. Begging your pardon, ladies, I thought it might be intruders."

"If we were intruding, we wouldn't be sitting here having a chat," said Mrs Hardcastle.

"I'm very sorry not to have forewarned you, Mrs Sanders," said Mrs Kennedy. "We urgently needed to have a confidential meeting."

"You should let me know before you go doing something like that," said the caretaker. "I might have phoned for the police and I'd have had to explain to them."

"Very sorry," said Mrs Kennedy again. "My apologies for troubling you."

"I'm just doing my job," said the other woman, "but I can't very well do it unless I'm given proper notice."

"As Mrs Kennedy explained, this is a very important and urgent meeting," said Mrs Hardcastle. "The situation has been explained. You may leave us to it now."

"I know when I'm not wanted," grumbled the other, followed by the sound of the door closing.

"Mrs Sanders is very efficient," said Mrs Kennedy. "But she has been upset by the irregular visits lately."

"What was that?" asked Mrs Smith. "Prudence just signalled."

A chill ran through me. I was sure that my movements, slight as they were, had been detected. I held my breath.

"She did," said Mrs Hardcastle. "That's funny. She never does that without being asked a question."

From her tone, funny meant anything but amusing.

"She wants to tell us something," said Mrs Smith, half excited and half worried.

"Is it about Dr Vengler?" asked Mrs Smith.

"It's no use asking questions at random," said Mrs Kennedy. "Prudence, spell it out to us. A, B, C…"

She started reciting the letters of the alphabet in a steady monotone.

"That was it!" said Mrs Smith when she reached S.

"Definitely S," confirmed Mrs Hardcastle.

The procedure was repeated and the letter P was selected. It was a painfully slow process, perhaps deliberately so. The idol doled out answers at its own slow pace, controlling the flow of information.

"Is the third letter Y?" asked Mrs Smith.

"You can't—" objected Mrs Kennedy, but was shouted down by the others.

"Yes!—it's 'SPY'," said Mrs Hardcastle.

"I knew it," said Mrs Smith. "We're being spied on."

They say the human gaze exerts a subtle pressure, and that is what makes the back of your neck prickle when someone is looking at you. That is all nonsense, according to science, but maybe Mrs Smith did have some kind of sixth sense, the worse luck for me.

"Or there is a spy in the group," suggested Mrs Bridges.

"I think Mrs Smith may be right," said Mrs Kennedy. "Prudence, are you trying to warn us that we are being spied on?"

"Yes!" said Mrs Smith, with a rustling that suggested the widows were looking about the room. I was breathing again, but staying very still.

A chair scraped as someone stood up and footsteps moved across the room. The door opened, then closed.

"I thought Mrs Sanders might be listening at the keyhole," said Mrs Kennedy. "I don't see where else we could be spied on from."

A sash window grated.

"There's nobody in the garden under the windows," said Mrs Smith. "I can't see where...unless..."

Footsteps came closer and the cupboard door was briskly opened wide.

"I don't think so," said Mrs Hardcastle.

"Evidently not," said Mrs Kennedy.

Mrs Smith closed the cupboard door, and I let out a silent sigh of relief.

I had not gained the power of invisibility. Though I have been involved in the practice of magic in the role of an assistant, and have attended more than one séance, and though my reputation might credit me with unusual powers, I cannot claim any such for myself. The magic involved was much more of the stage variety, of the type perfected by Mr Harry Houdini.

Mr Houdini was celebrated as an escape artist until his recent untimely death. Originally known as The Handcuff King, he moved on to grander things and escaped from padlocked crates thrown into rivers, sealed barrels, milk churns and any number of prison cells.

Houdini's publicity material suggested that he performed these feats through a process of dematerialisation, and some are convinced to this day that supernatural forces must have been used. In fact, the great showman used a whole box of tricks, often very simple ones to achieve his effects.

I was thinking of Houdini from the moment I found myself shut in that cupboard. Discovery seemed all too possible, and I needed a way out.

Disappearing was hardly feasible. In some situations, a man in a dark space can cover himself with a black cloth and escape being seen. Many stage illusions use this as a trick. In this case there was no question of it; even if I had a suitable cloth, at this range the illusion would be seen through at once.

I was surrounded on all sides by solid walls and an impervious floor. But, as I have noted, the office was made from what had previously been a living room, and the cupboard had been created by walling off an alcove. The building, being of Victorian vintage, had a twelve-foot ceiling. The builders installing the cupboard had decided, sensibly enough, that it did not need to be so high, and had given it a false ceiling or internal roof at a little over six and a half feet,

I had been exploring this false ceiling by placing my hands on it and exerting steadily-increasing upward pressure, listening out for sounds of damage. Fortunately for me, as it was not a load-bearing structure, the builders had simply nailed it down rather than bolting it or affixing it more firmly. After a few experiments with leverage, I found that on one side it gave way quite easily. When the caretaker came in and created a distraction I made my move.

I removed my shoes, placing them at the back of a shelf behind a box of stationery, and hauled myself up, clambering on the shelving and trying to distribute my weight as widely as I could so that nothing collapsed.

There was less room up there than I might have hoped. The space above the cupboard being considerably less than six feet high. I was left crouching, bracing myself against the walls to hold my weight, a decidedly unsustainable posture. The illusion would have been complete if I could have closed the lid, but there was not enough toom for that. I hoped that poor lighting and the human tendency not to look at things above eye level would protect me.

And that is why, as Mrs Smith opened the cupboard, she saw nothing. From above, I saw the top of her head as she looked left and right, but she never thought to look upwards.

"There is an intruder somewhere," said Mrs Kennedy. "We should depart and find a place of safety."

"Motion seconded," said Mrs Hardcastle.

Even had I wanted to jump out and take the bust, I had lost the opportunity. I could not extricate myself rapidly from my awkward position. I heard the scraping of chairs before I struggled to get down, and they either did not hear the crash or it merely made them expedite their getaway from the scene.

It took me half a minute to get out and get my shoes back on. Of course, the widows had taken the bronze head with them. Arthur should still be waiting outside, and I was sure the lad would be able to tell me where they had gone. Then, the chase would be on.

My self-satisfaction lasted roughly ten paces out of the front door.

Chapter 21: The Black Widow

I was going down the driveway at a trot when a shadow fell across me and I heard an odd noise like a sack of coal being thrown to the ground.

I turned and found myself facing a dark, horrifying presence, no more than six feet away.

If I was to be truthful about what I actually saw at the time, my description would be a virtual blank. I have a vague impression of a dark thing, with enormous wings stretching out on either side. Minus the wings, it seemed roughly the size and shape of a man, but what confused me for a long moment was that I was looking for its face and found none. After that, I had no chance to notice anything at all.

From that description you might conclude it was like a dark angel, and that would be quite wrong.

With the benefit of subsequent information, and details which I did not spot at the time, I can give you enough information to satisfy a police blotter: what I would have seen, had I more time and attention.

If you took a lobster without a head, made it the size of a person, set the articulated body upright, and lengthened two of the legs so it could stand, you would have the trunk. Add the wings of a pterodactyl, like the ones in Crystal Palace Park, and you would be along the right lines. Its limbs were not like lobster legs, or anything else that grows on this Earth, and it had a lot of them, of different shapes and sizes. Where it should have had a head there was a sort of flattened, fleshy lump, with long feelers, like trembling whips, sprouting from it.

Natural creatures either have internal skeletons, as humans do, or external skeletons, like beetles and crustacea. This thing,

I believe, was something of a hybrid, with a tough but flexible exterior supported by complex interior structures. The wings were not leathery, as you might expect. In Pa's butcher's shop, I learned about every type of muscle, tendon and sinew found in living things, but the only thing I can compare with those wings would be a pliable, rubbery form of horn or hoof. The span of them was at least twice its height, maybe three or four times.

I instinctively dropped into a fighting stance. You always keep your eyes on the face of an opponent, reading their moves and seeing their body shift with peripheral vision. This thing had nothing that could be called a face, no eyes, or ears, not even a mouth that I could distinguish. I barely had a second before it attacked.

It half-leapt, half-flew at me.

Everything went black.

I was paralysed and suffocating.

The thing had enfolded me in its wings, wrapping them around me tighter than cabbage leaves. My arms were pinned, the air was being forced out of my lungs, and I was blinded.

The 'bear hug' is a wrestling move made famous, and some say invented by, the great George Hackenschmidt. Also known as the 'Russian Bear' or just 'the Hack,' he is a world-famous wrestler, a world champion, and these days an author, too. Hackenschmidt writes books on physical culture and, among other things, invented the bench press. They say he speaks five languages fluently.

The Hack is, of course, noted for his impressive upper body development. I had the honour of seeing him once, at an event at the Crystal Palace. He is truly formidable and you can see why the bear hug is his signature move. He locks his arms around his opponent, lifts them off the ground and forces the air out of their lungs until they submit or succumb.

Hugs are not permitted in professional boxing. Clinches must be light and not obstruct the arms. I have used bear hugs myself on obstreperous types when acting as a doorman, with satisfactory results, as the subject is restrained and subdued without undue damage. But I had never been subjected to one myself, and this one came as a shock.

I believe I am entitled to credit myself with more mettle than most when it comes to violent encounters with other-worldly beings, simply due to repeated experience. If this had been my first combat, it would undoubtedly have been my last. I would not necessarily have had a heart attack, as Mrs Travis must have done in the same situation. Not did I quickly pass out from lack of air so I could be dragged out of a window, like Mr Parrish, but with my oxygen supply rapidly dwindling, I had mere seconds to act.

At first I tried to force my way out by main strength. I could muster far more physical power than either of the other two previous victims, perhaps far more than this creature had ever encountered, but I was gripped tight in the black, unyielding wings that held me like a mechanical press. The thing was phenomenally strong.

If I had happened to have a sharp knife in my hand, I might have had a go at cutting my way out. But my penknife, with its six different blades, was in my coat pocket, and as inaccessible as if it had been on the moon. In any case, as it later occurred to me, wings that could resist the forces of flight would be resistant to ripping and tearing, and I would probably have asphyxiated before I could cut through it.

One wing partly covered my face. I did not think to bite it, but it would have been like biting bone.

I flexed my chest, my knees, my shoulders, remembering advice about how to escape being tied up, feeling for any place where it might be about to give way. Of course there was none, and now stars were swimming before my eyes.

My situation was actually quite simple. I could not move my head, neck, shoulders or arms, and my hands and torso had very limited play. I could not even cry out for help in my air-deprived state. I did not know any magic spells; even if I had, I doubt I could have spoken even the shortest.

Unlike the Hack, this thing was relatively small, not much more than five feet tall, and although its wings were extremely powerful its limbs may have been less so. It had not completed the full bear hug manoeuvre by lifting me off my feet.

There was one move I could make, and I made it, throwing myself forward with what might I could muster. It tried to resist, but we toppled over at more or less the angle I had aimed at, and I came down on top of it. I must have outweighed it two or three to one. A human might have sustained damage from that, and would certainly have had the wind knocked out of them, but the thing was hard and unyielding.

The stars in my eyes were getting bigger, joining up, and now there was a rushing in my ears. The referee was counting down the seconds to the knockout.

Using what play I could work up, I succeeded in rolling over and continued with the energy of a maniac. I was trying to loosen it, or find a nail or some other object on the ground which might pierce and damage my assailant, distracting it.

Thump, thump, thump we rolled over. It could not stop me, but I could not get free. Each time the blow felt less substantial, as though the world was drifting away and I was being carried off by the all-enveloping roaring sound.

I knew how just futile my struggle was, how ridiculous, a man trussed up with no chance of breaking the bonds that held him. But my old Army boxing instructor, Sergeant Eaglesfield, had always drilled it into me that, however hopeless the contest, you should never, ever, give up until the bell goes.

"Give them all you've got!" he ordered. It was imperative to put up a decent fight. For one thing, honour demanded it. For another, your fortunes might suddenly change, and a lucky blow might change the fight.

Then, the ground disappeared beneath me entirely, and for a crazed moment I thought we must have rolled off a cliff. Then, I thought it must just be me, falling off into oblivion.

The shock of cold water barely registered.

I really did pass out, but it must have been only for a few seconds, because suddenly I found myself in the midst of flapping sprays of water. It was like being attacked by a flock of swans. The battering stopped with a whoosh and a sting of spray.

I might have drowned, but for the fact that the water in the ornamental pond was barely knee deep. Instinct was strong enough for me to lift myself on hands and knees to draw a deep breath. I half-crawled, half-staggered, stumbling over the edge of the pond, shaking my head and just breathing, breathing as the world rushed back around me.

The thing was gone. The water level in the pond had fallen six inches, and the whole area was drenched as though a depth-charge had been detonated. I turned around and around, stupidly, still dazed by lack of air, as I worked out that I was alone.

Whatever it was, it had a strong aversion to being immersed in water. Maybe it would have drowned before I did, or maybe it had some other vulnerability. Odd, given crustacea are water creatures, but clearly this was no true crustacean.

"Mr Stubbs! Mr Stubbs! Are you alright?"

Arthur, looking terrified, stood twenty yards away.

"I believe I am," I said, cautiously feeling my ribs.

While being crushed, I had had an awful sensation of collapse, of my rib cage crumpling in on itself, but there was nothing worse than bruising and some abrasions on the back of my neck. Surprisingly, the storm glass was perfectly intact, though my watch was thoroughly soaked and would require repair.

"It was killing you!" he said, and looked up into the sky, this way and that. "What- what- was it?"

I was dripping wet and starting to feel the cold. There was no chance of catching up with Mrs Bridges and the rest of them.

"An alien creature, likely bred on Earth," I said, peeling off my sodden jacket. I needed some dry clothes. "Distantly related to lichen, I believe. Fetch my hat, over there, would you?"

It was an ignominious end to my attempted burglary, but I was alive and intact, and, after getting home and having a hot bath, I was ready to count my blessings along with my bruises. Tomorrow was another day.

There was some psychological effect though, and that evening I was still more than a little shell-shocked. I had told Sally, but nobody else, of my brush with death, but that encounter kept replaying itself in my head while I was trying to concentrate on other things. Which was why what should have been an eventful dinner was something of an anticlimax.

Sally and I were dining with my Ma and Pa, and my brother. Pa had brought some prime Welsh lamb—"Scottish beef, Welsh lamb and English pork" was a motto he lived by—and we had a cheerful time of it. The conversation was mainly Ma and Sally talking about past weddings, with only occasional interjections from us men folk.

Afterwards, Pa and my brother and I decamped to the living room to discuss the latest sporting news, chiefly football and boxing, leaving the women in the kitchen with the washing-up.

I had forgotten that this was the occasion when Sally had planned to tell Ma about her past. If I had remembered, I would have spent the whole time on edge, listening out for the sound of a dropped plate or a cry of horror. Instead, the chat from the kitchen seemed to drop in volume, and washing up seemed to take longer than usual.

When Sally came through with a post-dinner pot of tea, she was smiling, though I could see from her red eyes she had been crying. Ma, too, unusually, showed signs of tears wiped away.

"You take good care of Sally now," my mother adjured me as we were leaving, as though it were necessary. "That poor girl has been through a lot and she needs a good husband."

"I plan to be one," I said.

"You will be," she said, and suddenly started sniffling, and hugged me in a way which somehow did not at all recall the last embrace I had been in.

"Women and weddings, eh?" said Pa, catching my eye over her shoulder. "Sentimental creatures, they are."

When Ma released me he took her into his arms and held her. I felt a sudden pang of sentimentality myself. To belong to a family, to have the warmth of human contact, the joy of a meal together, and the contrast with cold bronze heads and alien creatures, showed everyday life in a new light. Sometimes we do not appreciate these things until we are faced with the threat of losing them.

Hand-in-hand, I walked Sally back to her lodgings. After the conversation with Ma, she was full of plans for our wedding, but I was all too aware of the dangers, yet to be faced, that lay between me and that happy day.

Chapter 22: On the Links

A slight mist clung to the well-tended grounds of the North Surrey Golf course. The grand, white-painted club house would not open for another hour and I was looking for someone to direct me to the first tee when a short, gnomish man with a golf bag slung over his shoulder hailed me.

"Stubbs, is it?" he asked cheerily. "You're not exactly dressed, but the club turns a blind eye to Mr. Bailey's friends. Tee's just down the path here. Name's Hale, I'm Mr. Bailey's caddy today. New to the game?"

"Very new."

I was not a complete stranger to golf. When I was working for Latham and Rowe there had been a midsummer picnic and we had all been bussed out to a place in Surrey where we ate sandwiches and cold roast chicken and played an abbreviated version called 'pitch and putt'. Mainly, I suspect, it was a chance for the partners and senior staff to show off their golfing prowess, and to see which of the juniors showed the right sort of skills. Needless to say, I was not among the select few to be congratulated on their prowess.

"Don't worry," Hale said with a wink. "It's not whether you win or lose, it's the taking part that counts."

That was not a sentiment which many boxers might find themselves sympathising with, but this Hale seemed like a canny chap.

Bailey was correctly attired for the game in tweeds and plus fours. Looking very much at home at the tee, he was practicing his swing with such diligence he hardly noticed my approach.

"Good morning, Stubbs," he said, with a glance at the clubhouse clock. "Punctual as usual. I thought we could play a few holes."

He looked down the fairway and narrowed his eyes as though trying to read a signboard on the green. I felt my patience being tested but there was no sense in my being needlessly antagonistic.

"I don't see why not," I said. "As long as we can talk while we're about it."

"Jolly good!"

He made another practise swing then positioned himself carelessly beside a ball which had been teed up, rearranged his posture, straightened his shoulders, then thwacked the ball down the fairway. We watched it disappear into the distance.

"Good drive, sir," said Hale. "Just about twenty yards short of the green, I should say."

"Thank you," said Bailey modestly.

I had asked to see Mrs Bridges, but Bailey, acting as gatekeeper, had interposed himself and arranged this meeting instead.

I could have objected. The golf was a pointless charade, and two minutes of conversation would give me the information I wanted. But Bailey did not want to do things that way. So I played along. I would let him lord it over me, give him the illusion of being in control.

"Now then, let's see how you do, Mr Stubbs," said the caddy. "Best I take your coat and hat first, eh?"

I exchanged these items for a golf club, and practised swinging in imitation of Bailey, while Hale teed up a ball on the grass surface smooth as a billiard table.

"Legs the same width apart as your shoulders," advised Hale. "Front heel lined up with the ball. Arms in a V-shape. Hold the club like you'd hold your girl—not too tight, but tight enough to stop her getting away."

My swing connected and the ball sailed in roughly the right direction, landing short of the green, bouncing on it and ending up on the other side.

Bailey pursed his lips, but Hale seemed satisfied.

"It'll do," he said, taking the club from my hands, and the three of us set off after it.

"I was sorry to hear that Mrs Bridges is indisposed," I said.

"When do you think she might be able to see me?"

Bailey blew out his cheeks as though such a thing was beyond any man's knowing.

"She is exhausted. She is not seeing any visitors today," he said. "Not admitting anyone to the house, in fact. She's practically had the house shuttered."

From his tone, I gathered that the exclusion applied to him and he was none too happy about it.

"Has she taken ill?"

"It is Mrs Bridges' way of saying she wants to shut the world out for a while. She has behaved in this manner before. Mainly fatigue, I should say, and unaccustomed emotional charge." Bailey sounded like a Harley Street man discussing a patient. "She had a bit of excitement yesterday. There was an emergency committee meeting. I'm afraid your investigation is making waves."

"Mrs Bridges expected as much at the start, as I recall."

"Yes, well, that's all very well when she has one of her little caprices," he said, swinging his club like a walking stick as we went. "But it is my responsibility to keep her whims under control. I'm concerned."

"I can see how you might be," I said. "Seeing as how all of Mrs Bridges' fortune is invested in the Widows Society."

I might have added that this meant all of his income derived from it, and that he would not be enjoying a morning's leisure here while a million others were crammed in trains jolting towards the office without the Society. But that might have been a little too much on the nose.

"I have always doubted there was anything substantive to be investigated," he said. "Has anything changed?"

I allowed myself a short laugh. A few murders, assaults on my person, an evil German doctor and his outlandish human experiments and the ancient other-worldly being that lay behind it all...none of which I was inclined to share.

Seeing that I was not about to give any further answer, and that we were approaching his ball, he returned to the game.

"Five iron, please."

He stood next to it for some time, adjusting his stance and

grip, before hitting the ball confidently towards the pin. It bounced and rolled, ending up no more than ten feet from the hole. He handed his club to Hale with a self-satisfied air.

"I'll need you to tell me anything relevant to Mrs Bridges' estate," he said, as though the shot had given him some authority. "This investigation is under my purview."

"My investigation is into the Society," I said. "I report informally to Mrs Bridges, but only informally. And not to you."

Hale, standing behind Bailey, was smirking, but turned away from me.

Bailey was forever shut out from the inner workings of the Society, something which must have irked him greatly and which I am sure Mrs Bridges baited him with at every opportunity.

"Even so—"

"There is a brass bust of the Greek goddess Athena which stands in the Society's head office," I went on. "I imagine you know it."

Bailey was not going to be caught out looking ignorant. Even if he was rarely allowed into their offices, he knew everything about them that could be gleaned from the outside.

"The figurehead of the Society. Mrs Bridges looked after it for years until she retired from an executive role and passed it to Mrs Kennedy. Ugly thing, but apparently it has great symbolic value to the Society."

"It does," I said. "And I am presently trying to establish its whereabouts."

Bailey scowled. He was on the outside, and he knew it. He affected indifference.

"Why, has it been stolen?"

"It is no longer in the Society's offices," I said. "I believe one of the committee members took it for safekeeping. Would that be Mrs Bridges?"

"Take your stroke," he said, gesturing at my ball.

Hale bent over to look, pulled a face and then selected a club for me. The ground fell away after the green so I had to hit it uphill.

"Just a nice little chip shot," said Hale.

I could hardly be bothered, but the competitive instinct dies hard in any sportsman, even when it's just a matter of knocking a ball about on a lawn. I gave it my best go. Too hard, of course, and it ended up right on the far edge of the green, only slightly closer to the hole than before.

"When Mrs Bridges returned she did not bring anything of that size with her," said Bailey. "Nor did her driver mention any luggage."

He might have been lying. He might well have been lying, if he thought there was any advantage in it for him. But it would be as easy for him to tell the truth, and he wanted me to keep clear of Mrs Bridges.

"Thank you," I said. "That is all I needed to know."

"Look here Stubbs, what's this all about?"

He did not seize me by my lapels, but from his rising colour he looked like wanted to.

What this was about was that Bailey was a parasite, one who had attached himself and gorged on Mrs Bridges' wealth for years. But he had been outcompeted by another parasite, one which was even more successful at preying on widows and taking advantage of their weaknesses.

"It's about a world which you have never experienced, Mr Bailey. One which exists beneath and beyond this comfortable pleasure dome of yours, a world of strange and relentless forces more powerful than you could dream, able to snuff out your world at a moment's notice," I said. "For the time being I would urge you to make sure that Mrs Bridges is safe. She has reason to be afraid. Do not allow any visitors to see her."

For a moment Bailey was lost for words.

"Now, I will deputise Hale here to play the rest of the round in my place," I said. "I'm sure he'll give you a better game than I can."

"I can't—" Hale started, but I was in no mood to be detained further. I was, you might say, richly fed up with Bailey's little games.

"Now I will leave you to your golfing and go about my business. Good morning to you both."

It was not the most inspiring of exits. But I felt I had earned it, and I enjoyed hearing Hale's short laugh and Bailey's if-that's-how-you-want-it harumph.

That was the last I ever saw of Bailey.

Chapter 23: Driven Away

I walked up the driveway towards the Widows Society, past the croquet lawn and towards the ornamental pond which had saved my life. A white limousine sped towards me from the house, forcing me to step smartly out of the way.

Mrs Kennedy was in the back. She did not seem to notice me, did not turn her head as she passed. I raced after the car, catching up once it stopped at the end of the drive to turn onto the main road.

"Mrs Kennedy! I need to talk to you."

Her eyes were closed and she looked unconscious. I tried to open the door, but it was locked from the inside.

"Wake up! You're in danger!"

The driver, who had been intent on pulling out into the busy road, looked around when I tried to open the door. I saw the deep inverted 'V' of scars across his face. His mouth moved, but I did not hear what he said. He put his foot down and the car jerked forward suddenly.

Instinctively I grabbed on to a wing mirror. With the older, smaller cars of a few years ago, you could stop them more easily, but this was a powerful, modern machine. The wing mirror came away in my hand and the limousine accelerated away onto the main road, forcing a cyclist to swerve.

The car accelerated away so fast there would be no chance of catching it on foot. A man in a chauffeur's uniform arrived, panting, beside me, and glanced down at the wing mirror in my hand. Two maids had emerged from the house behind him and were looking on.

"Who's driving?" he demanded, looking after the departing limousine. "Nobody else is supposed to touch the car."

"I fear Mrs Kennedy is being abducted," I said. "Is there another car?"

"What? No." He was understandably confused, looking from the car to me, and back. "Are you the police?"

"Unfortunately not," I said. "Come with me. I'll explain on the way to the station."

En route to the police station, I explained to the chauffeur what I had seen and obtained his patchy account of what had transpired. He had been in the kitchen with the maids. They heard a visitor arrive, and depart again a few minutes later, and had thought nothing of it until they heard the car engine start up. Alerted, the chauffeur had looked out of the window to see the car he should be driving on the move.

At the police station, I fretted while an old man discussed a burglary with the desk sergeant. At least the delay gave me an opportunity to come up with some sort of story.

Before I could open my mouth, the desk sergeant held up a finger, bidding me to hold on while he read some paperwork that had just been put in front of him. The police had radios, they could put a message out and stop that car, but I was already beginning to think we were too late.

I told the desk sergeant I had seen the car being driven by a scarred man I knew was not the driver, and who I knew to be a member of a criminal gang, and had tried to stop it. The chauffeur backed up my story, making it sound as though he was as much in the know as me.

"You know all this for certain, do you?" said the old sergeant, his eyes narrowing.

"Yes sir," I said. "He was one of a gang involved in illegal boxing matches at the old fire station."

"I see," he said. He might have recognised me; my face is not exactly unknown to the local constabulary, nor my reputation. Even if he did not, it would not take a Holmesian leap of deduction to connect me with the boxing fraternity. "What you're really saying here is, you admit to criminal damage of an automobile, and you do not approve of Mrs Kennedy's choice of driver."

"Excuse me," said the chauffeur. "Under the terms of my

employment, nobody else is permitted to drive that car—not even Mrs Kennedy, even if she could. It's a white Bentley and as of now you should consider it stolen."

He reeled off the licence number. The sergeant looked at the two of us doubtfully, considering the significant points of law, the credibility of the witnesses and the stakes involved.

"We don't normally take reports of stolen property unless from the property-owner," he said. "But under the circumstances I'll be taking statements from the both of you under caution."

"The circumstances?"

"It seems," he said, rearranging the notes on the desk in front of him, "that in the last few minutes we have had a report of a fatal road traffic accident involving a motor vehicle corresponding to the description you provided."

Both of us were speechless.

He picked up a pad of report forms and a pen.

"Name and occupation?"

I gave as brief, detailed and truthful an account as I could manage of my encounter, adding that it could be verified by the presence of the wing mirror which must still be where I left it on the driveway.

"This accident," I said. "Can you tell me...?"

"No further details of the incident are being released to press or the public at this juncture," he said. "They will be released by the usual channels and you'll read all about in in due course." He put the report form to one side and leaned forward. "Off the record, the lady was driving and ran into a tree at speed. Broken neck, died instantly."

Deaths on the road are all too common. Even at twenty miles per hour an impact can be fatal, and many modern cars go much faster than that.

"At least, that is what we are being told," he said laconically, taking up the statements we had just given. "The situation may of course change."

"No, no, no," said the chauffeur. "It can't be. She never drove! Didn't know how, never had a lesson. And Stubbs said he saw a man driving..."

"Excuse me," said a woman queuing behind us.

The desk sergeant waved us away and moved on to the next case.

"A put-up job, you think," I said to the chauffeur. "Murder made to look like an accident."

I wanted to find out more about how such a thing might have been engineered, but he was in no state to discuss details.

"It must be, there's no other explanation," he said. "But who—why? And what's going to happen to me?"

I could not answer any of his questions. I had a good few of my own, and they centred on Dr Vengler.

At around the same time, events were unfolding at Mrs Bridges' house, which it will be convenient to describe here even though I did not learn of them until afterwards,

After his golfing, Mr Bailey had returned to be with Mrs Bridges. At some point in the afternoon there was a commotion at the front door, with two visitors insisting on seeing Mrs Bridges, and the butler standing his ground. The visitors, two big, powerful men, became violent and had easily overpowered the butler.

At this point Bailey, forewarned that there might be trouble, instructed the housekeeper to phone for the police while he armed himself with a poker and rallied the male servants. There was a brief fracas in which the kitchen boy sustained a broken collarbone, and Bailey and a footman suffered several minor injuries. The defenders, though outmatched, were making a good showing until one of the intruders pulled out a revolver, and that ended the struggle.

But by this time a housemaid, following Bailey's orders, had shut and bolted the big oak door leading from the entrance hall.

The housekeeper shouted that the police were on their way. The intruder threatened to shoot Bailey unless he ordered the servants to open the door. Bailey refused, and was hit about the face, sustaining a broken cheekbone and losing some teeth. He still refused to order the maid to open the door. Whether she would even have done so is another matter, but Bailey stood his ground.

The intruders went out and tried to get in through the side door and then the kitchen door, but these too had also been secured. Thwarted, the intruders ran off to a waiting motor car.

My respect for Bailey greatly increased when I heard about his courageous action.

The newspapers reported it as a crude attempt at robbery, but I knew—as Mrs Bridges did—what they were really after was Mrs Bridges herself. Without Bailey I doubt she would have survived. Others, however, were not so lucky, and things were proceeding rapidly.

Chapter 24: The Fate of Dr Vengler

I returned to the office to pick up young Arthur before heading to Vengler's warehouse, but he surprised me with news.

"Mr. Stubbs, Mrs Hardcastle's gone!" he said, jumping up.

I had dispatched him to see Mrs Hardcastle and Mrs Smith, with letters to be placed directly in the hand of the addressee if at all possible. I had not placed a great deal of faith in his ability to get past the servants, but it was worth the effort.

Even though he had not been able to see either of them, he had definite intelligence of Mrs Hardcastle's absence. The words came out in a rush at first without pauses for punctuation, but he soon calmed down and reported like the stalwart agent he wanted to be.

"At my arrival, I observed a commotion in the household. At first there was no response to my knocking, but listening at the door I heard a woman saying, 'I don't know, I didn't see her.'

"The door was opened by a manservant who was not wearing a tie. He saw the envelope in my hand and that I was not a regular messenger, and asked me, rather eagerly, if I had any news. When I told him my message was important and for Mrs Hardcastle alone, he let out a sort of wild laugh.

"At that point, the woman came to the door behind him. She looked like a housekeeper and she had a sort of Manchester accent.

"'Is this about where she's gone?' she asked.

"When I told her that I was not at liberty to divulge any information, she threw up her hands.

"'Are you having us on?' demanded the manservant, taking my shoulder.

"'No sir,' I said. I did not like the way he was holding on to me, and he had a fierce look in his eye.

"'Look here, sonny,' he said, 'I know you're just doing your job, but you've got to help us out. Madam has departed, and a load of her jewels with her. If you know anything about it, anything at all, you'd better tell us—or you'll be talking to the coppers next.'

"I did not know what to say, Mr. Stubbs, but I remember what you always say about not lying to people.

"'My message says that she may be in danger and needs to contact Mr. Stubbs at once,' I said.

"The two of them looked at each other like this confirmed their worst fears.

"'Hell fire,' said the woman. 'We're done for.'

"'She's not here and we don't know where she is or when she'll be back,' said the manservant. 'So you'd better hop it.' And that was all I could gather."

He finished his report with a little bow, still breathless.

"Good work, lad!" I said, and I meant it.

"Thank you."

It was one thing for their mistress to go off unexpectedly without telling them, but what would really have worried the servants were those jewels. A disappearing lady is one thing, but when extremely valuable items disappear at the same time, there will always be a suspicion of robbery and violence. If Mrs. Hardcastle turned up again, all would be well and good, but if she really had done a flit and intended to disappear completely, her servants would be dropped right into a suspected murder case.

There was some ambiguity over whether Mrs. Hardcastle departed under her own steam. She might have been lured out on a false pretext, but why would she then take her valuables?

"No luck with Mrs. Smith, I take it?"

"No answer at the door," replied Arthur. "I tried to see in the garage, but it was dark and I couldn't tell if the car was there, so I posted the letter through the box."

Mrs Smith might have been away for the day, in hiding like Mrs Bridges, may have fled like Mrs Hardcastle—or been murdered like Mrs Kennedy.

Looking at Arthur's fresh, young complexion, I suddenly thought what madness it was to involve a thirteen-year-old in a murder case. I should send him home at once. The problem was, he might take it on himself to launch his own investigation. He had picked up enough about surveillance and trailing to think he could start following me about. This was still a grand adventure, and to him danger just meant excitement.

For the first time, I began to feel rather old. I was responsible for keeping young Arthur safe, and the best way to do that was to make sure he stayed where I could keep an eye on him, away from risk.

"It seems Mrs Kennedy has been murdered," I said.

"Who did it?" Arthur asked, eyes wide.

"A boxer in Dr Vengler's employ," I said.

Given the tight rein Vengler kept over his men, it was unthinkable that the man was acting independently.

If Miss Frey's theory was at all correct, the head was sending out messages over the radio waves. Vengler had a wireless set...

Vengler likely had little idea who or what he was working for. His desire to learn more and be on the inside would take him far beyond what most men would ever consider. But even he might draw the line at working for something so inhuman as that bronze head—or might at least be willing to negotiate with TDS.

Vengler stuck me as a man very much open to negotiation if the price was right. TDS could probably give him access to the sort of knowledge he craved, assuming they had not already decided he needed to die a fiery death.

"You're coming with me," I told young Arthur. "Your job is to act as lookout man."

He set his jaw in an imitation of a cinematic tough guy. He had been excited when I explained we were going to the warehouse-cum-boxing-gymnasium that was Dr Vengler's headquarters, likely in anticipation of seeing the horribly-marked boxers close up, if not meeting the sinister German doctor. The thrill evaporated as I made clear that he would not be going in.

"Looking out for what?" he asked.

"Anything of significance," I said. "Mainly though, you will be looking out for my safe return."

He looked nonplussed at that, so I went on.

"You have your wristwatch? Good. Note the time I go in, and if I'm not back out after twenty minutes—or if there is a violent commotion from within—you beat a retreat and go tell your father what the situation is, posthaste."

I was not at all sure what reception I could expect from Vengler. He probably knew that I knew about Mrs Kennedy's murder by automobile accident, but the fact I was on my own and not leading a squad of police would engender some confidence.

It seemed to me that Vengler was mercenary by nature and had no particular attachment to the Society, and had more than hinted that he would work just as happily for another employer. He knew I was not employed by the Society and would not see me as an enemy.

On the other hand, he was entirely ruthless and had not survived this long with his questionable activities before, during and after the war without a strong streak of self-preservation. He would be as happy working for a bronze head as for the Kaiser. I might rapidly switch from potential ally to a convenient supply of spare human body parts for whatever surgical experimentation he had planned.

Caution was therefore required. I slipped knuckle dusters into my jacket pockets where I could easily get them. A little preparation can be a lifesaver. I intended to make it clear before I entered the place that my location was known and my absence would draw a quick reaction.

"My life may depend on you," I said, patting Arthur on the shoulder. "I believe you have earned this trust."

"Thanks, Mr. Stubbs," he said, visibly swelling. "You can rely on me."

We paused as we came to the turning for the warehouses.

"You stay back here," I said. "But, hello, there's pigeons on the roof."

"What does that mean?"

"Nothing, probably," I said. "Now, you stay here and blend into the background."

"Easy," he said, taking a rubber ball from his pocket. He checked his watch, then proceeded to bounce the ball against a wall and catch it, just as any boy at a loose end might do.

As the well-worn saying has it, it was not just quiet, it was too quiet. Add to that the fact that I found the back door of the warehouse ajar by a couple of finger widths, and it was a worrying scene. I suspected I had come too late. I would find the place completely deserted and cleared out, stripped to the walls, and Vengler and his merry band of misfit pugilists departed for parts unknown.

As I stood on the threshold, I could see I was wrong in almost every particular.

The gymnasium was still present, along with the camp beds and other accoutrements of the indoor campsite for ex-soldiers, but there was nobody to be seen and no sound of human activity.

"Hello!" I called "Hello? Dr Vengler? Is anybody at home?"

My voice echoed back at me from the walls.

Entering quietly, not wishing to make a sound, almost on tiptoe, I noticed definite signs of a struggle.

That might be a strange thing to say in a boxing gym, where fighting is the order of the day, but that fighting is contained within strict limits. A broken three-legged stool looked as though it had been flung across the room. One wall was dented, as if someone had been thrown against it with great force. A trail of blood spatters led to the plywood cubicle which housed Dr Vengler's office.

"Hello?" I repeated, moving forward cautiously.

Violence has a particular smell, something given out by the sweat glands at times of crisis. I was smelling it now.

Leaning to one side for the best view, I gingerly pushed the door open to peer into Vengler's office.

He was lying in his desk chair, draped over it rather than sitting in it, and before I even stepped into the room I knew he was dead. The human head can take a great deal of punishment, but the brutal injuries he had suffered would have killed Vengler several times over. He had been struck in the front and side of the head multiple times, leaving visible impact marks.

Vengler's glasses lay nearby, trampled underfoot. There was

no sign of a murder weapon, though I judged a weighty blunt instrument had been employed.

It is important not to disturb the scene of a crime, and in particular not to touch the body. For one thing, this may destroy vital clues. For another, it might accidentally contaminate the scene and incriminate the leaver. As I had no business being there, I was especially eager not to leave any trace of my presence.

I looked about as best I could without getting close. Blood was liberally spattered around the walls, most of it behind Vengler, so I assume his assailant was striking from in front.

The desk was similarly decorated with blood, with the exception of a small area in front of the doctor. It looked like some paperwork which had lain there had been removed from the desk after the killing. A pen lay in one corner, leaking a trail of blue ink. Perhaps the doctor had been in the act of writing when he was murdered.

The racks of medicines were flecked with droplets of blood. Some were missing, with a large gap in the otherwise tidy arrangements where several of the bottles or jars had been removed. The radio set had also gone.

It was easy enough to picture a situation where Vengler eventually over-reached himself and pushed his boxers—his patients, his experiments, however he saw them—too far. It was not just a question of one of them snapping. As I had seen, Vengler maintained tight enough discipline that anyone who stepped out of line would be restrained by the others. They all needed to stay in his good books or face a horrifying degradation of their physical state when they were denied treatment.

Vengler had been confident that the boxers were not knowledgeable enough to survive without him, but whoever had taken those bottles had known what they were doing. I guessed that person had led the uprising against the tyrannical doctor.

Stepping out again, I noted that the kit bags, which previously hung on pegs, were all gone, along with every sort of personal possession. The men had withdrawn in good order, and, I suspected, as a group: a group under new leadership.

I backtracked, still stealthy as a cat. Leaving the place, I headed to the neighbouring warehouse where the watchman, Timmy, had been so helpful before. It seemed he was not in, as there was no answer to my knock, but as I turned to go, I heard the hatch above the door slide back.

"Hello, Mr. Lantern," he said shyly.

"Hello Timmy. I've just been next door," I said. "There's nobody in. Have they all gone somewhere?"

"If there's nobody in…they must have all gone," he said.

"When did they go?"

"Yesterday, just after elevenses," he said. "There was lots of noise. Cars and vans coming and going. And now it's quiet. Some always stayed, before, but now they've all gone. I think they've gone for good. I didn't like them much anyway."

"Did you hear a woman's voice?" I asked. He shook his head. "I wonder where they all went?"

I tapped my chin in a show of thoughtfulness.

"The doctor has another big place," he said. "Maybe they went there."

"Where's that?"

"I don't know. They cover my eyes in the car," he said, scratching his head. "The doctor gives me chocolate money when I go to do jobs there. I suppose he won't do that anymore now he's gone—I wasn't supposed to tell you that."

"Don't worry, Timmy, you haven't told me anything," I said, "but thank you anyway for your time."

As I left I tipped him a sixpence, which he took with great delight.

"The birds have flown the coop," I told young Arthur, who was still throwing and catching his ball. "And Dr Vengler is no more."

"What?" he said, looking at the warehouse.

"Murder most foul. Now, come on, you're not to get involved in that sort of thing."

"That's two more murders," he said, "that we know about. Mrs Kennedy and Dr Vengler, on top of Mr Parrish and Mrs Travis. And we don't know about Mrs Hardcastle."

I had a feeling that the count was likely to rise.

Chapter 25: Miss de Vere's End Game

The obvious explanation for events was that Mrs Smith, Mrs Hardcastle or both had been duped into doing the bronze head's bidding. There was also an outside chance that this was the work of TDS.

I did not want to be at cross-purposes with Miss de Vere. It also seemed too late for me to take action. Whatever was going to be done had already been enacted. The best I could do would be to find more bodies, and I had already had enough of that.

I went to make a telephone call to Miss de Vere's answering service. Then, I returned to the office to write up a brief report for her and put my notes and brain in order. Those boxers must be hiding out somewhere. They might have checked into a hotel. Mrs Hardcastle certainly had the money.

I sent Arthur out for the afternoon paper to see what details had been released of Mrs Kennedy's death. He came back all excited.

"Mr Stubbs, there's been another murder!" he said, waving the newspaper.

The paper carried a couple of short paragraphs about Mrs Kennedy. It gave her age and address, and said she had apparently been driving at speed, dying instantly in the collision. It described her role at the Society and made no mention of suspicious circumstances. As with Mr Parrish, anyone who wanted to view her death as a possible suicide would be free to do so.

But the story which Arthur drew my attention to ran to two full columns, with the promise of more to come.

FAMOUS ACTRESS STRANGLED TO DEATH IN NORWOOD ran the headline.

"The chauffeur killed her," said Arthur, before I could begin to read.

Mrs Smith was dead, as was Marks, her chauffeur. The man who had glowered hotly at me when I met Mrs Smith to escort her to the boxing. The man who had, in a jealous fury, attacked me outside the high-level station at Crystal Palace.

The story was mainly a recapitulation of Mrs Smith's acting career and mentions of her co-stars, some of whom were now quite famous.

"It doesn't say it in the paper, but the chauffeur strangled her and then hanged himself."

"How do you know that?" I asked.

"It's what the men round the newspaper stand were saying. They say he left a note. The two of them were having a passionate love affair."

Arthur coloured a little as he said this. Violent murder was grist to his mill, but romance was embarrassing. He would get over it with age.

"That may be no more than idle speculation," I said, reading that Marks had boxed in his youth, and had been arrested for assault on a number of occasions, but not charged. An anonymous source said he had fancied himself as 'a tough guy.'

The piece did not mention Mrs Smith's role in the Widows Society, though it did mention the whirlwind and faintly scandalous romance which led to her getting married, and her husband's distinguished war record.

It was the sort of story the papers loved: glamour, violence and the rich and powerful ending badly. A beautiful actress having an affair with a rough character, too; all they needed was to find he had some connection with organised crime, and a mistress on the side, and the thing would be complete.

"She was beautiful, too," Arthur added. "They had magazine pictures pinned up at the news stand."

"That's all of them accounted for except for Mrs Hardcastle," I said. By this time I had heard about the intruders who had been driven away after trying to see Mrs Bridges.

"And the warehouse burned down!" Arthur said. "There's a story about that too. 'Unexplained fire'—who did that?"

The minions of TDS, no doubt, tidying up after me. The other minions, I should say. Eerily enough, as soon I thought this, there was a rap at the door, none too polite. It announced a uniformed messenger boy with a telegram. He stood at attention, ignoring Arthur, while I read it.

Miss de Vere, my TDS contact, required my presence immediately.

I tipped the messenger the minimum necessary to prevent a sarcastic remark and reached for my hat.

"You guard the fort," I told Arthur. "I'm going to get instructions from headquarters."

I found the place easily enough after a bus journey and a bit of walking. A fine townhouse, built in the same grandiose era as the Society's building, for a time when people had big families and a lot of servants.

A short woman in a dark uniform, with something Slavic about her appearance, opened the heavy front door. She regarded me critically for a moment without saying a word, but stood back and let me come in before closing the door again with a boom.

"Good afternoon," I said, removing my hat. "My name is—"

She held up a hand to silence me, pointed up the carpeted staircase, and made a shooing gesture. Her expression was not the one of a servant greeting a welcome guest. It was as though I were a necessary but irritating tradesman: a plumber called to see to an unpleasant smell, perhaps.

"I'm sorry—" I started again, and she repeated the gesture.

Whether she was unable to speak or unwilling, I never found out. She turned and disappeared down an empty hall, leaving me to find my own way.

The house was as grand inside as out, high-ceilinged, with polished oak panels and bannisters, and long stained-glass windows over the stairs. One of the great houses built shortly after Mrs Bridges moved to the area, the mansions planted to claim all the best views. It had a peculiarly deserted feel, as though it had not been inhabited for a long time. The quietness seemed to go beyond simple absence of noise.

Perhaps it was just that all the sound from the outside world was muffled. I stopped, and it was true. I could not hear a thing from the street, even though there was a busy road not fifty yards away.

The one thing I could hear was a gramophone playing, some American jazz song I did not recognise. I followed the music through the echoing halls, to a half-open door that led to a darkened room.

The song ended at the exact second I stepped in.

"Miss de Vere?" I called tentatively, not wanting to intrude.

"Come in, Stubbs," came the voice from within.

The room was not quite dark. Blinds over the skylights admitted enough light for me to make out Miss de Vere in nothing but a white shift, lying on an enormous bed of white linen, her head propped up on two pillows. There were cotton pads over her eyes. She might have been the life model for a Victorian print entitled "Mother is tired."

I had the unsettling idea her eyes were wide open under those pads, the unblinking glass eyes of a doll that, however superficially perfect, fails to be quite human.

"Are you ill?" I asked, ready to leave.

"Sit down," she instructed. "No, I'm not. I have a long evening ahead and I need rest."

I noted boxes and shopping bags with the names of fashionable London shops, an elaborate gown hanging from a wardrobe. The dressing table was crowded with pots of makeup, vials of perfume and the rest of the feminine armoury.

A side table held a selection of liqueurs and two upturned glasses next to a gramophone and a wooden rack of records. If Miss de Vere was not preparing for a seduction that evening, I was a poor judge of settings.

This was a show. Whether I was supposed to be overawed by her ethereal, untouchable beauty, or abashed by being set so far below her that my presence was not worth opening her eyes for, I could not say.

I seated myself in one of a pair of white armchairs facing the bed. She was lying very still, just her lips moving. It was as though the body had been put into a trance, and a spirit was speaking through it. I noticed she was still wearing her narrow diamond bracelet, which I believed was an occult talisman of some sort. She was not quite as defenceless as she wished to appear.

"I didn't know you had a house here," I said, to fill the gap in conversation.

"The man who owns it is dead," she said. "Nobody knows yet, so we're borrowing it."

Her face was almost expressionless, but there was a smile somewhere in her voice. I knew that the man whose house it had been must have been an enemy. The only surprise was that the place had not been burned down. Maybe they would do that when they were finished with it. I did not doubt that the warehouse with Vengler's remains was already on fire.

"Very convenient, I'm sure," I said. "You wanted to see me, I understand. I assume you've read my reports."

"And very fascinating they are, as always," she said. "Though you don't draw too many conclusions."

"Hardly my place. I'm probably the least-informed person you could speak to on these matters."

"I'm interested in what you think. Tell me what you've deduced."

"Well," I said, turning my hat over and over in my hands. "If you want to hear a load of guesswork...there's this bronze head, which has been in this part of the world at least since the days of Paracelsus. It came with the Romanies; maybe it was with the Knights Templar before that. It can communicate, after a fashion, and it has become the sort of patron idol of the Widows Society. With its advice, they have thrived. I assume it has knowledge not known to others. It plays a long game, and it is expert at playing to each person's particular wants."

As Dr Evans had said, even the slightest evolutionary advantage made a big difference in the long run. Slowly at first, then with increasing momentum, the Society had become a mighty financial engine.

"And what is it really?"

"Something, I would guess, not of this world. The outer shell may have been made by human hands, but what lies inside came from somewhere else."

You never know for sure what is inside a tin can without opening it.

"For a man who has seen so many alien beings, you're very coy when it comes to talking about them, Stubbs."

Her body was still supine on the bed, but I had the feeling Miss de Vere was pacing up and down the room, regarding me.

"Forgive me, I don't often discuss my cases in those terms," I said. "But yes, I believe what is inside may have arrived 'from outer space' as they say, in the form of a shooting star. And it is some kind of fungus."

She did not reply immediately. I did not feel like filling the silence again, so it grew between us in a way that would once have greatly unsettled me. I was getting used to conversational tactics intended to keep me on the wrong foot.

"To put you in the picture," she said, "that thing is the seed of your black widow. Call it an interstellar spore pod. An intelligent one. Of course, it's a threat and we plan to neutralise it and the whole organisation."

"If you say so," I said, inspecting my hat. "My investigation has not gone deeply at this stage, but all the activities of the Widows Society itself appear to be harmless, if not actually benevolent. Mainly they are advancing the field of mineral extraction, and also of surgery."

"Huh." She put a lot of expression into that one syllable. There was contempt, disgust and more in there.

Her diamond bracelet seemed to emit a prismatic glitter.

A small landscape hung on the wall next to me. It started to glow with its own light. A night scene, that I took to be an African savannah or somewhere equally exotic, under a crescent moon and a mass of stars in the velvet sky.

"The mining is a front," said Miss de Vere, and the picture moved, buildings growing in the foreground with lights in their windows, more lights shining on cleared dirt and pit machinery. Winding gear marked it as a mining camp. "A way for them to get deep into the Earth and figure out how it works, how tectonic plates drive volcanoes. They can already predict eruptions, next they will be able to trigger them."

The landscape burst soundlessly, everything blown into dust

in an instant. After a second, there was nothing there except the stars and moon, and, drifting outwards, a series of tiny motes above a blasted landscape that was just one huge crater.

"Their life cycle," she said. "A spore pod lands on a new world, makes walking fungi, fungi make more spores. Then they blow up the world like a big puffball to spread the spore pods, and the cycle goes around."

The picture settled down again to a tropical night landscape. The first time I had seen that sort of display, I was overawed. Since then, I had seen more serious demonstrations of supernatural power. Even the most ignorant country bumpkin, who might be bowled over the first time they see moving pictures, soon becomes accustomed.

There is a reason why conjurors never repeat the same trick twice to an audience.

Her message, though, made some sense. Giant volcanoes might not destroy the world, but they would leave it in quite a mess. They say the skies were so darkened by the eruption of Krakatoa that there was no summer the next year, and widespread crop failures. I thought of the piece of Mars, blasted into space, that had ended up in a glass display case.

"Only on a world with volcanoes," I said.

"There are other ways to blow things up," she said. "I'm simplifying here, if you hadn't guessed. There are others of its type that it communicates with by radio."

"And the medical part?" I said. "Dr Vengler and palingenesis. They couldn't grow into that flying thing without his help. They needed him for the symbiosis, like lichen with fungi and algae."

I could not remember everything the doctor had said, but I did not doubt that, with a few hints whispered over the radio, and a pinch of spores brought by Mrs Travis, he had been able to start the process. Maybe, if Miss Frey had started years ago and listened for cryptic messages in German, she might have heard something more.

"Not symbiosis, parasitism," she corrected. "Anything they say about helping us is a lie. Remember that. Vengler helped infect a host so they could grow."

"So, the medical work is so they could grow black widows,"

I said. "And incidentally create a loyal army. The mining is amassing a fortune, but it is also so they can spread spores into space, destroying the world in the process."

"And it's time to stop them."

Spoken like a sentence of death. Which of course it was. I waited for the next part.

"How's this for size, Stubbs? Mrs Smith and Mrs Kennedy are gone. Mrs Bridges is old. Maybe she'll just die from shame when this gets out. Maybe she'll work with us. Mrs Hardcastle is on the lam. I guess she's in charge of Vengler's freaks—for now. That won't last. We'll get her if they don't. So, the four ladies are out of the picture. Nobody but them knew a thing. That leaves the way clear for us to take over the Widows Society."

"This was your idea all along," I said. "That's why you sent me in to stir things up, because you knew it would end this way."

Mrs Bridges had implied that the Society and TDS had been at a standoff for generations. Miss De Vere must have known all about the head and its activities for many years. I had not found out anything new; she just wanted to know how much I had deduced.

"I'll give you a minute to figure out why," she said.

"Radio sets," I said. "Mining drills with tungsten carbide drill bits. Global steamship travel. Atomic energy. The threat of blowing up the world becomes real."

"Smart guy figured it out all by himself," she mocked. "They've been waiting a long time for humans to get this far. Now they are ready for the final stage."

TDS must have known decades ago this would eventuate—maybe centuries. They had waited until now. Waited, perhaps, for the knowledge they would be able to siphon off, for the riches the Widows Society had been piling up for them to steal. Surely they could have tackled the bronze head any time they felt like it, but, for their own purposes, they had allowed things to go on this long.

"What do you need me to do?" I asked.

"Two things. One, burn out the nest where the fungus has been growing. Two, bring back the head. Don't worry about

Vengler's gang, they'll be taken care of. You'll probably read about it in the papers. I'm talking to a man tonight."

Maybe her poise was all an act, maybe this was business as usual. Moving pieces around in another minor skirmish in their mission to keep the world clean.

"I will need some more detail," I said.

"There's an envelope on the side table. Don't open it until you're going to do the job. You'll need to find the place Vengler used for his medical procedures; you will know the fungus when you see it, burn it all. After that...find the head and bring it back. That's all."

"Very well," I said.

"You don't bring much to the party, do you?"

I was not familiar with this Americanism, but I could tell my unresponsiveness was irritating her. I suspected she was used to men who were more forthcoming, more eager to please. My lack of interest about and enthusiasm for her cause was grating.

"I'm a boxer," I said. "You may judge me by my record."

I did not add that she and her associates had been nowhere to be seen, had appeared terrified during the last major case when I had been undercover at the asylum, and that I had tackled a major threat without her assistance.

For all their supposed omniscience, I was not greatly impressed by Miss de Vere's organisation.

She sighed.

"When we first met, I thought I could make something of you. I thought you had potential, but you're just another two-bit heavy, a hoodlum with half an education. So, yeah, that will be all. Good luck saving humanity. I don't think we're going to meet again, Stubbs."

"You just never know though," I said, standing up. "Even if you think you do, you don't."

That was one of the differences between us. I never tried to bluff or make out I knew more than I did, but doing so was her entire act.

TDS might be a huge, secret organisation, keepers of ancient wisdom wielding occult powers. But it might be a small group of people with a few clever tricks stolen from other groups, who rely on the illusion of strength for their influence, like the teacher who gives their class the impression of omniscience by staying one chapter ahead in the textbook.

I took the thick envelope from the side table.

"Put the record on again on your way out. Goodbye Stubbs."

I wound up the gramophone and replaced the needle at the start of the record without a stutter, despite the dim light. My hands were perfectly steady. The speaker emitted a slight hissing, like a singer clearing their throat.

"Au revoir, Miss de Vere," I said.

The music started up before I left the room, and continued as the maid escorted me all the way along the hallway and down the stairs. I noticed a calling card had been left on the side table: a Mrs Beaumont.

That would be Mrs Kennedy's assistant. Heir apparent to running the business side of the Widows Society. That made sense,

The maid closed the door behind me, the music was gone and I was back outside in the world.

Chapter 26: Elemental Fire

Where would Dr Vengler have carried out his work? From Sally's account he did his abortions at an old clinic or hospital, and while the women who went there were blindfolded, they had some idea of the neighbourhood. Timmy had said he carried out work for Vengler at a 'big building,' which I believed to be the same location.

That could be a myriad of buildings, but there might be an easy way of finding the right one. I looked into the municipal records, to discover who owned or rented the warehouse Vengler used, and, as I had suspected, this proved to be one of the army of companies Mrs Kennedy had set up for the Widows Society. A quick cross check had revealed that the same company managed a number of other properties, most of which were yielding rent. One, however, had been left vacant, unlet and undeveloped. It was not like someone as meticulous over every farthing as Mrs Kennedy to leave a potentially profitable site lying idle, and there had to be a reason for it. The address turned out to be a former hospital, located conveniently on the number sixty-eight bus route.

That, I felt, was a good day's work, and left me time for a stroll to contemplate matters and marshal my thoughts before the evening's mission.

The packing room next door was dark and deserted when Sally arrived in my office after her shift. Arthur gave up his seat for her and retrieved a stool from next door for himself, and the three of us gathered around my desk.

Sally had been doubtful about involving the boy, but went along with my thinking that he was safer when he was at least notionally under my command. She did not often give way to me. Our marriage would not be one where the husband made all of the decisions and it might not all be plain sailing. Assuming, of course, we both made it to the wedding day.

"This is a dangerous situation," I said, for Sally's benefit as well as Arthur's. "Some extra pairs of eyes might make the difference."

The envelope in front of me was the size of a normal business letter, with an object inside which, judging by the feel, might have been a fountain-pen, and a second object, slightly smaller.

My name was written on the front in fancy calligraphic script, like a wedding invitation. It also had tiny inscriptions on the corners and across the flap. Examining these with a magnifying glass, I had concluded they were written in a form of Enochian, a script used by magicians. It might have been for show, more likely it had some function in preventing the letter from being tampered with.

"It could be a booby trap," said Arthur.

"I do not believe that relations with Miss de Vere have degenerated that far just yet," I said.

"She needs Harry to do her dirty work," said Sally. "That one doesn't like doing the difficult jobs herself—she might break a fingernail."

Previous experience suggested that, as a field operative, Miss de Vere was not a success. I did not doubt that the task has been delegated to me because it was difficult, dangerous or required physical exertion.

Miss de Vere had trusted me with an occult fire weapon once before, in the Stafford case. In that instance, she had provided me with a small lozenge which acted like a firebomb. When thrown against a target it had immolated him, or rather it, almost at once.

"Go on, Harry, open it for goodness' sake and put us out of our suspense," said Sally.

I slit the envelope with a letter opener. It contained a single sheet of folded paper and two small objects. One resembled a miniscule cylindrical ink bottle, the other was a short stick of dark, waxy material.

The paper was crowded with several paragraphs of

instructions, with detailed illustrations of each. All was written in the same beautiful, calligraphic hand.

"What's in the bottle?" asked Arthur.

"Don't open it before you've read the instructions," said Sally, as if this was the sort of thing only a foolish male would do.

"I've never seen anything like this before," I said, taking up the stick, "but I daresay Paracelsus knew all about it."

"That's greasepaint, or something like it," Sally said. "The little bottle has funny writing on it, too. She takes her magic seriously, that one. It must have taken ages to write those squiggles."

The first step, according to the letter, was to protect myself. Following the instructions closely, and with Sally's assistance, I used the greasepaint to draw bracelets around my wrists, each one a double line that joined back on itself, with an added triangle. That, I recalled, was the alchemical symbol for fire. The stuff was peculiar: it felt cold going on and stayed cool afterwards. The marks it left were vivid, blacker than black. Arthur watched in fascination.

Then, I had to undo my cuff buttons to draw a curved line on each forearm.

I continued the application, pulling up my trouser legs to draw anklets around my legs and lines up my shins. I loosened my collar and, with help, completed a triple necklace.

I opened my shirt further and pulled up my vest so Sally could copy a diagram of a kind of pentacle over my heart, with a triangle at each corner. The greasepaint stick was disappearing fast. We had already used more than half of it.

An elaborate spiderweb pattern on my right palm, with lines running up my fingers and thumb terminating in more triangles, and a different, blocky pattern on the back of my left hand completed the set. Goodness knows how I would have managed it without Sally's help, though Arthur was also keen to assist.

I remembered Captain Cross with the three interlocking stars tattooed across his wrist, put there by a shaman during one of his many foreign adventures. He always claimed that the stars tingled to warn him of danger.

"At the Convent, they used to talk about being girded in the armour of God," said Sally. "I suppose this is girding you in some sort of magical armour. I don't mind whose so long as it works."

"Amen to that," I said.

The greasepaint stick had melted away faster as I completed the job and was now down to the size of a pea. We compared my markings to the diagrams in the letter and found a good match. Getting things exactly right is a matter of vital importance in occult matters. As with wiring up a radio, you have to get everything in the right place or none of it works. Or, worse, it blows the fuse under the stairs and leaves you in the dark—or electrocutes you.

"'Do not unstop the vial until you reach the innermost heart of the infestation,'" said Sally, reading from the instructions. "'Direct the elemental fire therefrom with your hands into every corner and crevice and spare none. Do not allow the flame to surround you, nor breathe the vapours, nor look too deep into its light.'"

Arthur looked puzzled and Sally questioning. I was in charge, and it was up to me to instil confidence in the troops.

"To be clear, there are alien creatures—I have seen one, and so has Arthur—and Miss de Vere recommends this as the best weapon to tackle them. Her organisation may have long experience in such matters, and they certainly command occult powers."

"I don't trust Miss de Vere one bit," said Sally.

"My enemy's enemy is my friend," piped up Arthur.

"Between the devil and the deep blue sea," she said. "They're bad, but that black widow thing was worse. I'd rather they fought it out without anyone else being in the middle."

I did not need to tell her that TDS recruited their foot soldiers from the local population. That was me, and if I did not exactly espouse their cause wholeheartedly, I was willing to throw my lot in with them against alien invaders any day of the week.

"This is my job," I said.

"What about smoke though?" Sally asked. "It doesn't say

there's protection for that, it just says not to breathe it."

I had thought of that. I held up a canvas bag and showed her the gas mask I had acquired earlier.

"I believe this will suffice," I said. "Now, if there are no more questions, we had better catch the bus."

I had to be careful not to touch anything with my right hand for fear of smudging the greasepaint, so could only use my left, but was conscious of the odd pattern showing on the back of my hand on the bus. Luckily, I am used to getting funny looks, and people always look away when I turn to face them.

The building was formerly a Victorian charitable institution, an early hospital now moved to other and more modern, hygienic quarters. The dark brick had turned black with city soot, and the place had a brooding aspect to it. A tall chimney thrust into the sky, and it struck me that this might be a convenient entrance and exit for something with wings.

The place was locked and shuttered, windows boarded up. A big sign saying CLOSED UNTIL FURTHER NOTICE was prominent above the front door, which was secured with a chain and padlock.

If there was any activity inside, the occupants were laying low. Initially, I had suspected Vengler's crew might be there, but it seemed they had quartered themselves elsewhere.

I positioned Arthur near the front, and told him to keep an eye out for anyone coming or going, and to give a whistle at any sign of trouble. Then I walked around the back with Sally and gave her similar instructions.

"Stay lucky," she said, and we kissed. I did not hug her, again because of the greasepaint.

I did not trust myself to say anything else. If I tried to say anything sentimental my words would only be choked off. Instead, without looking back, but still feeling her kiss on my lips, I advanced towards my objective.

The side door was much less formidable than the front, and could not be seen from the street. I tried the handle. It was not locked.

The place had the hollow sound of a building that is not just without people, but long abandoned. Somehow the human warmth and life drain away from such places, and they become something less animate and more hostile without the glow of humanity to keep them alive.

I stopped every few steps to listen for changes in the quality of the silence. A motor bus passed outside and the silence rolled back. The hallway had the grime and debris of long abandonment. Broken window panes, bird droppings, little drifts of dry leaves where the wind had taken them: the early signs of a building crumbling to ruin beneath the gentle, persistent touch of nature.

But it was not all like that. One white-tiled room had clean zinc work surfaces, two basins with running water and an operating table. There were powerful electric overhead lights with bulbs still in them, and a cupboard full of surgical instruments.

Then I head the footsteps. They echoed against the bare walls.

One man, taking no trouble to be quiet.

I had been expecting some sort of guardian, and this, evidently, was he.

I stood in the open to one side of the operating table.

"Who's there?" he called ahead of him. "I can hear you moving about. Timmy, is that you?"

He sounded Scottish, his 'you' coming out as 'ye'.

"I'm in here," I said.

A man in blue overalls peered through the door. I would have put him at a middleweight, in no great physical condition, the hair under his battered cap shot through with grey. He was holding a broom in front of him indecisively, not sure whether it was supposed to be a weapon. He raised it slightly when he saw me.

"What are you doing in here?" he demanded.

He was entitled to be suspicious and hostile under the circumstances. I played it friendly.

"I'm looking around," I said. "I'm an insurance investigator. Harry Stubbs."

I reached very carefully into one pocket and drew out a card. He did not attempt to take it.

"How did you get in? Nobody told me anything about it."

"The door was unlocked," I said. "They didn't tell you because they didn't know I was coming. Tell me, are you aware of what this building is used for?"

"I'm just the janitor here, man," he said, leaning on the broom. "I couldn't tell you anything about, about—about anything here. But you'll get yourself into trouble breaking in like that."

"I did not break in. Who's going to give me trouble?"

"Not me! I didn't mean that. But, you know, with the polis. I mean…" he trailed off uncomfortably.

I stayed quite still, not wanting to alarm him in any way. This was a fish I had to reel in gently rather than fighting.

"He's a German, you know, the man who uses this place. A doctor, of sorts. You know what sort?"

"I wouldnae know, I just try to keep the place from falling apart. Replace the odd broken window, sweep up, keep the rats down."

"I'm sure you do," I said. I made a show of looking him up and down. "Carrying out a perfectly legitimate occupation. I'm sure you've got no connection with any illegal activities. Even if you do seem to be the only person on the premises."

"You've no right to be in here," he said, making another sally. "You're not the law. I ought to…"

He grasped the air with one hand, not sure of just what he 'ought to.'

"I don't want to get you into trouble," I said. "In fact, it seems to me that things would be very much easier for the both of us if I did not see you and you didn't see me." I paused a second to let that sink in. "No complications that way, you see? Nobody has to talk to the law."

He brushed idly at the ground in front of him a couple of times.

"No names, no pack drill, eh?" he said.

I decided to push further. If he was complicit, it was not a willing complicity, and he might be brought round to helping.

"Did you ever see a woman all in black coming and going? Strange sort of woman, all veiled?"

"My eyes aren't so good without my glasses," he said, sweeping faster. "I never see anything."

"Maybe you hear things though. Like strange noises, when nobody else is supposed to be in the place?"

"Big old places like this, they always make strange noises, you ken?" he said, but he could not hide his bad conscience. I left a silence for it to win him over.

"I bet you'd sleep easier if someone else looked around, made sure the place was...safe."

He looked up sharply at that.

"I don't know what goes on in the basement," he said in a low voice. "I don't want to know. It's strictly off limits."

"Understood."

He rallied, asserted himself again.

"But if I come back in fifteen minutes and I find a someone's here who shouldn't be, I'm thinking I'll be calling the polis!"

He waved his arm in what I first thought was a dismissal. Then I saw he was pointing down the hall to a flight of steps going down.

Fungus thrives in the dark and damp, not up here where it would be exposed to daylight.

STRICTLY NO ADMITTANCE said the sign on the basement door. The janitor had not swept the steps down here though, and from the marks in the accumulated dust and dirt I could make out footprints, some newer, some older.

The door was a massive thing, the sort placed to prevent fire from spreading. I listened at it and heard nothing.

Moving carefully and without hurrying, I donned the gas mask and made sure it was a good airtight fit. Peering through the circular eyepieces and with the rubber mask around my face, I felt like a deep-sea diver about to enter the sub-aquatic realm. My breathing was strangely amplified.

I opened the door, stepping back as it swung open. As it did so, I took out the vial and made ready to open it.

The space beyond was not utterly dark, as I had expected. Diffuse shafts from hidden skylights covered with leaves shed a faint radiance which suggested the shape of the room.

My nose detected the mould before I saw it. Even with a

gasmask on I had a strong whiff of something ripe and earthy. There was a base layer of horse manure, and lots of it, but something stronger too. The floors, walls and even the ceiling were covered in dark stuff, which at its thinnest was no more than a layer of paint, but in places, especially the corners, grew into a thick encrustation. Towards the middle of the room, where it seemed older and better established, enormous bulbous shapes like wasps' nests grew out of the ceiling and floor. Great fins projected from the walls, all at perfect right angles, their edges wet and shiny. Other shapes suggested cauliflowers or giant marrows.

These must be fungal growth. In terms of their structure and appearance they were nothing like earthly fungi. I had an idea that the different structures might correspond to different parts of a huge body. Dr Evans might have been fascinated.

I uncorked the vial, holding it out and stepping back.

A puff of white vapour, two feet across, like stage smoke but more solid, emerged and formed into a sphere, swirling as though confined in a glass globe.

As I stood gaping, something in the cloud popped or snapped and it ignited, becoming a ball of dull fire. It developed a bright orange glow, flowing and expanding like ink drops in water, with a furnace-like heat I could feel on my face though the glass discs of the mask.

I automatically raised a hand against that heat, and the fire wafted away from my hand as though driven by an invisible wind.

I lowered my hand, and the fire remained in place, a luminous expanding cloud. I experimentally raised my left hand, the symbols towards the fire, and long tendrils of flame extended back towards me, tugging the rest of it like a tethered balloon.

Direct the released elemental fire therefrom with your hands, the instructions said.

I caught movement in the corner of my eye, and something misshapen was pulling itself free from a mass of material in the corner, like a man crawling out of a sand heap. Except this was no man, even in this light, even seen through the misty lenses.

By the number of limbs and the shape of the body, it was not remotely human.

The thing raised itself up and unfurled enormous wings, lurching toward me, the ceiling too low for it to take off.

Without really thinking I gestured towards it, and the fire stretched out like a striking snake, colliding with the fungus thing. The fire stuck and crawled over it, and the creature burned fiercely, shrivelling and busting apart into a shower of flaming flakes within seconds, with a series of popping and crackling sounds.

I sensed movement in another part of the room, rustling merging with the growing gas-flame roar of the fire. Backing away, I alternately drew floating, fiery blobs towards me and projected them out to wherever I sensed movement, rolling and sweeping fire into every corner of the room.

The fire had expanded in all directions, and half my effort was spent just fending it off from attacking me. There was not too much smoke, but I was glad for the gas mask. As it was, I was breathing the mix of fumes and fungal steam.

Scorch marks were appearing on my jacket and trousers, but I did not feel a thing. The wasp nests withered and crumbled into burning fragments, the fins blazing briefly before disintegrating. Whatever the elemental fire was, it ripped apart everything it contacted almost explosively, like a joyous child opening presents.

I flipped gobbets of fire upwards to cover the stalactites on the ceiling, bowled fireballs ahead of me, waving my arms like a mad conductor directing a symphony of destruction. I was backing away towards the door trying to leave myself a clear path.

The whole world seemed to be shimmering with heat haze, and flame covered every surface, the whole basement an endless inferno.

I turned and saw something almost at my feet. An elongated thing was crawling through the fire, dragging itself on several sets of elbows. After a moment I saw that it was already burning, and that it was not crawling towards me but past me. When it was almost near enough to touch, and I had a clear impression of a giant crayfish, the fire suddenly ate through its carapace at several joints, all at once, and it collapsed. The flesh erupted like rags soaked in petrol, and the sections of carapace fell away like burning cardboard.

A curtain of fire blocked my way to the door. I scrabbled and punched the air to wave it aside, then plunged forward, barged though the door and slammed it behind me. I ripped off the gas mask and took several gulps of air. At some point I seemed to have stopped breathing, and the cold, clean air was tremendously reviving.

Behind me, the weird roaring of the blaze was still rising in pitch, but before I really had time to register, the crescendo was fading again, as though every last scrap of flammable material was being consumed.

Maybe Miss de Vere could simply have told me to get a box of matches and a can of petrol and they would have been as good. Maybe elemental fire has some uniquely destructive power. Or maybe TDS, like the army, have their standard operating procedure and were reluctant to change, even though the world can now offer flamethrowers and incendiary bombs. If they had been doing this for centuries with previous fungal lairs, why risk changing now?

In any case, the job was done.

The floor underneath me felt strange as I made my way back. That was because the soles of my shoes had been mostly burned away. One knee poked through a hole in my trouser leg, and my jacket and shirt were ruined. My body, though, was entirely undamaged, with not so much as a singed hair.

"Harry! You're burned!"

Sally ran up and embraced me as though I were the survivor of a horrible conflagration.

"Not so much as a blister," I said. "The patent fireproofing worked a treat."

"But look," she said, leading me back and pointing at the tall chimney with a trembling hand. A torrent of grey smoke gushed upwards, but diminishing as we watched, merging into the heavy pall now hanging over the hospital.

"That'll soon disperse," I said, knowing how such unnatural

things quickly fade to nothingness.

"There were things coming out of the chimney in the smoke," she said. "Flying things. Several of them, almost too fast to see."

"They're gone now," I said. We walked around to the front, where Arthur was staring gape-mouthed at the chimney and the now dissipating smoke in the darkening sky. From his look, I knew he, too, had seen the flying creatures.

"That's all sorted," I said. "Someone else will deal with the fliers. There's just one more job I need to tackle before this is over."

Chapter 27: The Tower

"I assume something interesting is happening," said Miss Frey as I approached her, both of us pretending to browse the library shelves. Arthur had been assigned to trail Miss Frey's aunt, a few aisles away, and would give a signal, coughing three times if she moved in our direction.

Getting Miss Frey to the library that morning had required only a minimum of subterfuge. It was not her day for a visit, but a note slipped under the window in the back parlour by my young assistant had prompted her to suddenly express interest in getting a book on astronomy. The back parlour was Miss Frey's unofficial reading room, and this had proved a reliable way of getting messages to her.

"I need your help with this," I said, displaying the storm glass.

The storm glass was a glass cylinder about the size of a cigar tube, filled with clear liquid, stoppered at one end and sealed with green wax. It was a type of supernatural warning device. Just as the more conventional storm glass signalled changes in the weather, this one was sensitive to otherworldly forces.

"What does it detect, exactly?" asked Miss Frey, holding it up to the light.

"I don't know if anyone can answer that," I said. "I certainly can't. It came into my hands via a man called Gillespy. He died in an insane asylum and took a great, you might say an unhealthy, interest in these things. I have no idea where he obtained it."

"The sigil on the end is Enochian," she said. "So it must have been made in a wizard's workshop."

I suspected it had not been anything so grandly romantic, but Miss Frey is young. Maybe Gillespy made it himself, according to formulae he came across. The point was that it worked.

"It responds to unseen forces," I said. "The strength of the effect is proportional to the proximity. A faint threat produces a faint sign in the glass; a powerful one will fill it with strange shapes."

"I'd like to see that."

"Not really you wouldn't. The point being that it does not give any idea as to direction, but it does say something about the strength, or rather the combination of strength and distance."

"Aha, aha," she said, looking at me with a twinkle in her eyes. "I believe you are about to ask me a question about trilateration, Mr Stubbs."

"Some time ago, when I was listening to that radio broadcast, my friend said it was possible for the GPO to locate transmitters with special apparatus, which was really nothing much more than a type of radio. I was thinking that the threat is also transmitting another kind of invisible signal, and this glass is a receiver."

"Want to use the glass to locate it?"

"Exactly so," I said. "I would attempt trial and error. The glass will tell me if I'm getting warmer or colder, but I can't help but feel there must be a cleverer way to go about it—and that you might know what that is."

"Trilateration," she said with a smirk.

"I don't have the benefit of a private education. Can you explain that to me as if speaking to a ten-year-old?"

"Triangulation uses the intersection of three different angles to find a location. Trilateration does the same thing using distances. In this case it is slightly more complicated because we do not have a distance reading at all. What you can do, though, is find three points where the signal is equally strong, and plot them on the map as a triangle. The origin of the signal will be at the centre of the triangle formed by the three points."

When she wanted to be, Miss Frey could be quite lucid.

"That all seems eminently practicable," I said. "Assuming one knows how to find the centre of a triangle, which I rather imagine you do?"

"Drawing the medians," she said. "Let's find the geometry section and I'll show you. You'll need a measuring ruler for this. What you do is to find the midpoint of each of the sides, and draw a line between of the vertices of the triangle with the midpoint of the opposite sides. These connecting lines are the three medians. Where they meet is the centroid. Here."

We had moved from the science section to mathematics, and she pulled out a textbook.

"'Elementary Euclidean Geometry,'" I read.

"Elementary indeed, my dear Stubbs," she said, with a peal of laughter that had people looking disapprovingly up from their books. "Sorry."

It was a simple enough technique, although I would never have figured it out for myself. I had saved myself a deal of trouble by getting some help, even if it was from a fifteen-year-old girl. Paracelsus, who said you could get wisdom from everyone if you were not too proud to ask, was a wise man.

"Thank you," I said. "You have been an important cog in a big machine."

"I don't want to be a cog—can I be a counterweight? Or a flywheel? Though being a cog is still better than being a bridesmaid."

"Don't worry, you will be paid out for your bridesmaiding," I said. "And all your other good work."

"What is it you are trilaterating?"

There was no point in being excessively coy, given how much she already knew and her powers of deduction.

"A being from another world, which has designs on ours," I said.

"Do be careful!"

In theory, the head—and Mrs Hardcastle, and Vengler's entourage, with a black widow or two along for good measure— could have been anywhere by now. If they were abroad, then I would be letting Miss de Vere know she needed another operative with relevant experience. If they were by some chance still in the area it would be something of a mixed blessing; I would just as soon bow out of the case, feeling that I had done a pretty decent job of burning out the fungal infestation. On the other hand, nobody wants to leave a case unfinished.

Mr Hoade did not seem to be about, and on inquiring I

found that he was on indefinite sick leave. I left my best wishes if he should be in touch.

I left the library, with the book on geometry, and took a series of bus trips around the area, all the while keeping an eye on the shapes that formed and melted in the storm glass, which waxed and waned during the journey. Back in the office, I plotted my findings on a street map. I could not be exactly sure, but the 'centroid' seemed to be located somewhere in a small corner of South Norwood, close to the railway station.

Pretty close, also, to the old fire station, which currently lay empty between bookings as a venue for boxing and other entertainments.

One thing I was clear on was that there was no reason to put Arthur at risk in a situation where there might be gunplay.

"You will hold the fort," I told him. "You are here in case we get any message from Miss de Vere or other sources."

"Can't I at least wait outside again?"

"No you may not," I said. "If you want to get anywhere in this business, you need to obey orders. Clear?"

"Perfectly clear, Mr Stubbs," he grumbled. "I'll just stay here and read, and miss seeing all the exciting bits."

"There will be plenty of excitement for you later, when you're old enough."

He opened a book sullenly. After we left, I waited a minute outside just to check he was not going to follow us, but the lad, though resentful, was obedient as always.

Sally and I made our way to the fire station and completed a wide circuit of the streets around it, just another couple out for an evening stroll together.

Miss de Vere had warned me against trying to take on all of the boxers, not that I needed warning. I already knew Vengler's men were armed from the raid on Mrs Bridges' house, but even had they not been, I was not about to take on a dozen or more of them. This would be an act of burglary. If the head was under armed guard and I could not get to it, again I would tell Miss de Vere that she needed another man for the job. But if she believed it was possible for me to retrieve it, I assumed she had good grounds.

The place looked empty at first, but there were lights on and we saw figures moving inside. A figure draped in black stood at an upper window—veiled, so likely one of the black widows rather than Mrs Hardcastle.

As we passed by on the other side of the street, two heavyset men in long coats, hats pulled down over their faces, came out of the front door. Someone else closed it behind them. The two men headed off, purposefully. Maybe they had just been sent out to buy groceries, but I doubted it.

All the entrances at ground level would be well guarded but our circuit revealed an alternative: almost invisible against the dark brickwork, a metal maintenance ladder was bolted to the outside of the building. It led up the old fire station tower. The ladder stopped twelve feet short of the ground, but the roof of a lean-to would afford access, and getting up there would only require something like a dustbin to stand on. There were a couple of those just around the corner.

All a would-be burglar needed was a bit of gumption and a head for heights. Briggs would not have had the slightest difficulty.

I have never been a great one for high places. I would not describe myself as phobic, but I prefer to stay back from cliff edges and other unprotected drops. You, who have never felt quite the pull of gravity that I have, might feel quite secure in such places, never fearing that ground will crumble or guard rails give way under your weight. Without my bulk, you may never have hit the deck quite as hard as I have. As I have observed previously, an ant can survive a long drop, an elephant cannot—and I am more towards the elephant end of things.

This may be mere rationalisation. Everyone likes to justify their fears. I do not have a phobia though; I can and do scale heights whenever it is strictly necessary.

I felt my palms sweating.

"How are you at climbing, Harry?" Sally asked.

"Me and my brother used to race each other up trees like a couple of monkeys," I said.

I had not done any climbing since the army assault course, but I was in decent enough shape.

"You're not as light as you were then," she said. "And that ladder looks rusty."

I could tell she was having visions of a bolt giving way, the whole ladder coming away from the wall and me crashing to the ground. I was having similar visions myself.

"I'll take it slow and easy," I said. "Any sign of trouble and I go into reverse gear, and we find another way."

It was not in Sally's nature to let me go without an argument, but she nodded silently.

"If there's any difficulty, I'll throw the head out" I said. "You grab it and run, don't wait for me. You know Miss de Vere's telephone number."

She nodded again. It was an awful thing to think of Sally having to contact Miss de Vere after anything happened to me, but there were bigger matters at stake.

"Good luck, Harry. You knock 'em all flat."

We savoured the briefest of kisses. There would be time for more of that later.

I pulled on my gloves and set out at a brisk pace, across the street to the old fire station. Turning down the side alley, I moved a dustbin and ascended easily to the top of the lean-to. It was further to the ladder than I had thought, but I hauled myself up smartly and soon had my feet on the rungs.

The iron ladder was a little unsteady, and the rungs left rust on my gloves, but the corrosion was superficial—or so I hoped.

On the sixth step, the whole thing gave out a mighty creak as though it was feeling my weight for the first time. From the look of it, nobody had used the ladder for many years, and the ironwork was feeling its age.

I moved up one rung at a time, alternately moving my right hand and left foot, then left hand and right foot to join them, making sure I was securely supported each time. It was slow and deliberate, but it was safe. No reason to kill myself in a climbing accident just because I was rushing. I had, I told myself, all the time in the world. Maybe I could have scaled the thing in one minute, in a hurry, but no reason not to take three minutes and make sure I made it to the top.

Big flakes of rust were coming off with each rung now, and

the steps had more the feel of soft wood than solid metal. The higher up, the more exposed it had been to the weather.

It also struck me that the people inside the building must have been aware of this ladder. Did they think the gap between the ladder and the ground would stop intrusion by this route? Or had they made it secure at the top? I could not count on the head, or Vengler's squad, all being fools.

I glanced down, to see the dizzying spectacle of fragments of rust showering down below, disappearing from sight. I was not much more than thirty feet from the ground, but it felt like three hundred. The temptation to hurry and get it over with was strong, but that was the way to catastrophe. The ladder would not take the shaking of rapid movement.

From this distance I could see people walking along the high street. It was exhilarating, slightly unnerving, to get a birds-eye views of familiar places. I could make out the expanse of the cemetery, and the library, and the tracks leading to West Norwood Railway Station.

I took the ladder faster now, still with the care to ensure that each step was firm before moving on the next. At one point, a pigeon flew past, which would have made me jump had I not been clinging on so tight.

At length, I made it to the top.

The hatch into the tower opened the first time without difficultly. It had not been secured from the inside.

"Meredith," I said to myself, "we're in."

Chapter 28: Angel of Death

I was at the top floor of the old fire station, and I assumed the ground floor was where all the muscle would be, defending the entrances. Up should be the headquarters; literally, in fact, where the head I sought was quartered.

I tiptoed down a short hallway, ignoring a door marked 'Service,' towards another marked 'Control,' from which came sounds of human activity: papers being moved.

I had been hoping that, as in the Widows Society, there would be an empty meeting room with the bust prominently on display, ready to give advice or perhaps commands via Mrs Hardcastle. If I did encounter anyone, surprise meant I would get the jump on them, overpower them, and intimidate them into showing me where the head was. I had brought rope to tie up such a person, as well as a bag for the head when I found it.

I waited patiently at the door, listening to papers shuffling, small objects being moved about on a wooden surface, footsteps. There was no conversation or other indication that more than one person was present. I slipped on my knuckle dusters, quietly opened the door, and stepped in.

The room was almost bare, furnished only with a couple of tables and folding wooden chairs. Cables snaked around the outside of the wall, leading to the large wooden cabinet of Vengler's radio set. On one side were gold bars, a fortune in precious metal stacked like so many children's building blocks.

This looked very like the HQ I had hoped for. The head was not on display and there was only one occupant, a man with his back to me, leaning over some papers on the table, examining something with great attention.

He was wearing a sleeveless tunic, and the muscles would

have identified him as one of Vengler's squad of boxers even if the scarring across one shoulder had not identified him to me as Patrick Brady, the one I had seen boxing in blue trunks that first night.

I was more than a little relieved that it was not another one of the widow-things. I might have difficulty taking one on in a straight fight. Vengler's enhanced fighters were not a simple prospect, but I reckoned I would be a match for any one of them on his own, especially catching him by surprise.

I stepped into the room silently, but he somehow sensed me. He straightened up and turned around.

Where his head should have been the bronze bust of Athena faced me.

The bronze head had been grafted directly onto the boxer's neck, with fresh bandages covering the join between flesh and metal. Dr Vengler's great surgical expertise, and the magical healing elixir which promoted nerve growth, must have been stretched to their utmost.

The Hound of Mons, the transplantation of living brain from one body to another, had been an achievement bordering on the miraculous, albeit a grotesque and horrid one worthy of Baron Frankenstein. This work, the connection between an alien thing and a human body, must have been a degree more difficult.

If it was an achievement for the doctor, it was an apotheosis for the alien thing that now faced me. After countless millennia as a mere inanimate object, it had entered a new phase of existence as a living, active being. No longer confined to advising others, it was able to carry out actions for itself. No wonder TDS wanted to act now.

Vengler had not lived to enjoy his success. Once the thing had gained control of a human body, I guessed it had used its new power to eliminate him immediately. Maybe Vengler had been a threat, knowing too much about its origins and vulnerabilities. Maybe, given the doctor's instinct for survival, he might have tried blackmail, and threatened to expose it. Or maybe the thing was just cautious and preferred to tidy up loose ends. I did not imagine killing a human would have been a great ordeal for it.

"You're through, Prudence," I told it, acting as though I had been expecting just this encounter. "Or maybe I should call you Belphegor. The party is over. Your whole scheme has been uncovered—the mines, the volcanoes, the whole business. We have the place surrounded. You may as well come quietly and it'll be that much easier for you."

It was the speech the hero always made at the end of a detective serial. Spoken out loud, it sounded ridiculous.

The bronze face was impassive. Then, the thing moved, stepping over to a side table where three holstered revolvers lay nestled together. I moved just as quickly, kicking over the table and sending the weapons flying.

Without hesitating it raised its fists and faced me in a crouch.

"Harry Stubbs."

The voice, that sexless, almost mechanical voice, was coming from the radio set. It was trying to distract me. I resisted the temptation to turn around but remained focused on my opponent.

"We do not need to fight," it said.

"Are you surrendering then?"

For answer it came forward to throw a right. We exchanged a flurry of punches and I found myself in the fight of my life.

It seemed impossible that something which had only recently gained a human body should have any knowledge of boxing, or any other physical activity. I would have expected that, like a human baby, it would take months to learn to control its new body. But the thing boxed like an absolute professional, and moreover a pro from Vengler's stable, with the same quick, restless footwork. In fact, it boxed exactly like Patrick Brady.

Wherever all those hours of training had gone, whatever part of the nervous system those trained reflexes and muscle memory took up, whether they were baked into the muscle and bone or somewhere in the spinal cord, the thing had all of Brady's skill.

He fought pretty much according to Marquess of Queensbury rules, I guess because that was the way Brady had been drilled to box. That might give me an edge.

On the other hand my opponent had not only an overdeveloped musculature but also what you might call an iron jaw. Blows to the head, which are the most common sort, and certainly the most likely to win a fight, were right out of the question. The only way to win would be by the serious and repeated administration of body blows of the most punishing sort, hoping that in the meantime I did not sustain too much damage myself.

I weaved, backed off. Plenty of room here, plenty of space to work in. There were a few obstacles to watch out for, trailing wires and the like, but I was keeping my wits about me.

Body blows are aimed at the ribs, the liver and the stomach, and with knuckle dusters my punches were cruelly powerful. Blows weaken a boxer, and after a while he will struggle to move, defend himself, and even to breathe properly. He did not react like a normal boxer though, and while the head might have been aware of the damage inflicted, it did not seem to be feeling any actual pain.

It, on the other hand, was concentrating on shots aimed at my jaw and face, going for the knockout. He certainly had the punch for it.

Worse, as the fight progressed, he brought his guard lower and lower. He might have been a flesh automaton, but he was well-trained enough to adjust his fighting style when he saw I was not hitting at his head.

The odds were piling up against me. Wearing him down little by little was not going to work, not when I faced being brought down every time we traded punches. I needed a change of tactics.

The revolvers on the floor were out of the question. It would take much too long to get one out of its holster, find the safety catch, cock and fire it. But there were other potential weapons.

Our circling had positioned me next to the gold bars. I grabbed one and threw it at my opponent.

Or at least, I tried to. I should have paid more attention when I learned that a standard gold bar weighs four hundred Troy ounces. Though no larger than a house brick, in regular units that's more than twenty-seven pounds. The ingot thudded to the ground barely halfway between us.

I threw a chair next, but it was too light, and my opponent batted it away into a corner as if it had been a ball of paper.

We circled, engaged again, drew away again. His style was professional: not a mad rush of blows, but a calculated series of exchanges, each time trying for that final blow.

Time stopped a moment, then resumed—the momentary blackout that told me an uppercut had landed. I shook my head, and it watched me, not pressing the attack but assessing the results. It was used to working on very long time spans indeed, and learning, but the damned thing was horribly good at this activity.

It occurred to me that I might only have few minutes more to live, that these might be the last seconds of my life.

Oddly enough, with that thought, it was as though a great weight had been lifted off me. All worries and concerns melted away, like smoke in a strong breeze, leaving behind: Harry Stubbs, boxer.

I might have been a second-rate investigator, but I was a first-rate boxer—better than this metal-headed monstrosity, by a long chalk.

I was a fighter. This was what I was born for.

I did not just move, I danced. Lifted by the music of the fight, I dodged, I swerved, I jabbed. I was like water flowing off rocks, like a breeze blowing through a forest, smooth, effortless.

I was having a wonderful time. If I was going to die, I would have my hour of glory first, and land more punches than I ever had before. I would use everything I had.

I have never been one for trying to rile opponents, but it could not do any harm, and I had few other options.

"I ain't scared of you," I said. "I've fought tougher, and stranger, than you. I've taken on the minions of Nyarlathotep, two at a time. I've beaten one of those things from the Antarctic. I've been in the ring with mutant things that don't have a name, and dead things that kept walking—and I've seen them all off."

The radio crackled to life.

"Stubbs, your enemies are our enemies. We are as opposed to those Antarctic beings and the others as you" it said. "We are willing to negotiate an alliance with TDS."

"They don't want to be friends," I told it.

By now, I knew that anyone who trusted this thing was a fool. In this moment, it was just trying to wrong-foot me, but whatever deal it did make, it would break. Like the devil it was, it would always devour those it was pretending to help.

He packed a solid punch, and his reactions were all set on a hair trigger. With training, he might really have been a contender—although that head ruled out any career in the ring.

"We can teach you so much," it said.

"We'll get it all anyway. That's why they let you spin your little schemes, so they could reap the benefits. Vengler's elixir, they'll get that. All your knowledge about mining and geology that's been used, they'll get that too."

I was talking well above my station, but the point was that it sounded good, as though there had been a plan all along. Not just a haphazard effort in which yours truly lurched from one mystery to another, trying to make sense of things.

"You were tricked," I said. "When you saw me get involved, you panicked and had your moth man kill Mrs Travis. If you had just sat tight and kept mum, you might have made it.

"Mrs Bridges had her doubts about you for years. Did you offer Mrs Bridges immortality to keep her on your side?" I recalled her fascination with the glass case full of stuffed animals and their frozen, eternal existence. Had she been given the chance to become a brain in a tin can too?

I went in with a straight right, but this time it surprised me with a counterpunch that had me seeing stars again. Again though, it was slow to follow up, as though it took time to digest the results and formulate a new battle plan.

The clock was ticking down. We were getting to the close of the final round, and Harry Stubbs was going to lose on points at this rate. I needed a winning conclusion.

I had never used the Chinese punch in anger. I do not know the correct term for it, only that it was taught me by Mr Yang, who was a master at it. It focuses your energy, not just the gross physical momentum of the arm but more esoteric forces that are channelled by the human mind and body. This is the blow that can break through a wooden board with one punch—or kill a man.

Mr Yang may be able to deliver several blows in succession, but my skill is limited to one punch—and that had better end the fight, because the effort leaves me giddy and weakened.

And winding up for it was agonisingly slow.

Never having used it in a fight, I was unsure how easily I could deploy a punch which took so much deliberate concentration. It would be telegraphed well in advance, and there was no reason to expect it would be harder to dodge or deflect than any other. It might break the opponent's hand or wrist in the process, but that was going to be little consolation to me.

I had only one shot, and it was all or nothing, so I might as well raise the stakes as high as they would go.

We closed again, but I kept my guard up, fended off its punches, and gave it a good solid kick in the knee with my hobnailed shoe.

The leg did not go from under it, but, as I stepped back, I could see it was struggling to move. The brain in that bronze head might not feel any pain, but the body below was struggling to respond against the agony radiating out from that knee.

As it struggled, I held my breath and focused inwardly, visualising my life-energy as a steam boiler building up pressure. Then, as he came forward to take advantage of my quiescence, I unleashed as precise a straight right as I have in my life.

It was a pure and beautiful thing that straight right. If you could preserve a punch, I would have it framed in my living room.

I might have aimed at the body, but my fear was the punch would run into its defence and, maybe break a forearm and throw the thing backwards without inflicting serious damage.

Instead the blow was aimed squarely at that gleaming metal head, and it connected like a hammer striking a bell.

What happens when an irresistible force hits an invulnerable object?

That head was robust enough to withstand the depths of space, to survive the impact of asteroid, to crash into the Earth hard enough to leave a crater. I was under no illusion that I would be able to dent it, let alone damage it, not with all the energy I could muster.

My reasoning was that the head was maybe not anchored as securely to the body as it would be with a human. Lacking suitable attachment points, it would be secured with tendon and gristle. Dr Vengler's main concern was the nerve connections which would allow the head full control of the body and receive its sensory inputs. Something that was good enough to survive the thousand shocks mortal bodies experience day to day would have been his goal, not something that could withstand a sledgehammer.

The bronze head ripped loose from the shoulders in a shower of blood and bandages, flying halfway across the room.

The body took one step back, and for a ghastly moment I thought it might continue on its own. Given the boxing ability, some of the brain function must have been included there. But, after a fraction of a second, it crumpled, knees, hips and torso all going at once, and hit the floor as a corpse. Only a little blood leaked from the neck stump as the body of Patrick Brady died for the final time.

I took a minute to gather myself. My fist smarted a bit, but, incredibly, nothing was broken.

"And that's you back where you started," I remarked to the head, lying on its side.

A gunshot rang out somewhere in the building below me, followed by several more. I stuffed the head into the canvas sack I had brought.

"Mr Stubbs," came the voice from the radio again, "As I told you—"

I swung the bagged head in a wide overhand arc to smash the radio set with a satisfying burst of wooden fragments. That might make it harder to communicate with its minions.

The papers on the desk had the letterheads of shipping firms, and there were timetables and sea route maps. Collecting them might have given some idea of what the thing had planned, but that was not my job. I also contemplated grabbing one of those gold bars, but another fusillade from downstairs had me leaving the room in a hurry.

Back out the service hatch and onto the ladder, I spied Sally across the street, and heard a commotion inside the fire station.

I placed one foot down on the next rung, and another, and started to descend the creaking ladder, slightly disconcerted by the weight of the head swinging in its bag.

I heard a fluttering above me and looked up to see a flurry of pigeons taking off from the roof. Had I startled them, or had something else?

I looked down, looked back at the roof, then then moved down another step, and another, and another, and looked up again.

"Harry!" Sally's voice came up from far below. "Look out!"

I did not see it until it hit me. What saved me was pure instinct; the human need to cling to something substantial when in danger had me holding on to the ladder for dear life. I was hit by a flurry of blows from both sides in quick succession, not punches, but more like the effect of being flicked with a wet towel—a large, heavy towel, wielded with some force.

I crouched and ducked my head, while both hands gripped on to the ladder for dear life.

As soon as the attack had started, it was over. It had come within an ace of sending me plummeting to the ground, but without complete surprise it had failed.

Something flapped heavily past. I looked around, but could not make any sense of what I saw. It seemed to me that something like a tattered old umbrella had blown past.

Sally shrieked from below, another warning. I did not catch the words if there were any.

The thing landed on a ledge in the stonework ten feet away, and I saw it properly for the first time. This was when I got a first good look at the blackish surface that looked like horn or leather, the segmented body, too many limbs and whip-like feelers—and no face.

It launched itself into the air and flew at me. I let go with one hand to fend it off. It grabbed hold of my arm and, flapping and kicking off the wall, it tried to drag me off the ladder.

If anyone had looked up at the tower that moment, what

would they have seen? A man waving a ragged black flag? A figure partly enclosed in a dark sheet? Certainly nobody would have guessed I was struggling for my life against a thing from another world.

It gave a series of tugs, each of which threatened to dislodge me, while I tried alternately to free my arm, to hit the thing, or to bash it against the side of the tower. If I had been carrying a twenty-pound gold bar I should certainly have overbalanced and fallen. The ladder creaked alarmingly and I felt it shift, but it held firm. The struggle was ineffectual on both sides.

"Get off him!" shouted Sally, and something clanged off the rungs below me.

The thing may have been startled, because it let go and sprang free with a beat of those massive wings, then wheeled in the air and dived to the ground.

We cannot know what goes through the mind of a creature from another world. Its ways of thinking and motivations must be quite alien to our own. It was as constrained by tactics as I was. There are only so many ways to play chess, and I suspect even the most advanced intellect would still play much like a human.

Its flight was not as agile as a bird's, but I reckoned it could, for example, try landing on the rungs below me and pulling me down. Instead, perhaps frustrated by my resistance, or in a bid to get me to loosen my grip, it had settled on a different target altogether.

"No!" I shouted as it plunged towards Sally.

I caught a glimpse of her horrified face before it blotted out my view of her.

Sally is not by any means petite, not is she a frail, fainting creature. She works a shift in the pickle factory, hefting trays of pickle jars from one stack to the next as well as the next woman. Compared to me, though, she was much easier prey. I recalled the crushing force with which it had wrapped me in its wings. I had been able to withstand that with no more than some bruising, but it might squeeze the life out of Sally, her ribs shattering in that powerful grip like an eggshell.

I had always known there was a risk that I would not make

it to our wedding day. It never occurred to me that Sally was also at risk.

The two of them were facing each other. Sally has learned a thing or two about protection in her time, and had taken one of the most basic measures, putting a lamppost between her and the assailant. I descended as fast as I could.

It took a shuffling step towards her. She backed around the lamppost, staying in its lee.

I wanted to shout to her to run, but that would be fatal. It would take to the air and bear down on her before she got twenty paces. At present, she was in the only safe place in sight.

The thing was slower than her on its feet, but not that slow, dodging one way and then the other.

I was descending the ladder as fast as I could, ignoring the noises it made. This was why I did not see properly what happened next.

The thing leapt at Sally, although due to the proximity of the lamppost it could not enfold her in its wings. It grabbed at her with its arms, as you might call them, to pull her to it.

I have never taught Sally anything about the art of self-defence. It is my view that, in such a situation, fighting back is futile. The best self-defence of all is to run away; the second best is to call for help, which is likely to scare off an attacker. Teaching people to hit back may cause overconfidence and encourage to try to fight when they should be running.

For women in particular, I always say the best approach is to kick your assailant between the legs and run for it. Though in the heat of the moment this may be more difficult than it sounds, and women's shoes are not suited to either kicking or running.

Sally has watched me sparring in the gym many times, and if I had not taught her anything directly she had picked up plenty and knew a cross from an uppercut. As it grabbed at her, Sally punched it.

As her knuckles struck, there was a flash of light and a detonation like a thunderbolt.

It was more like a gigantic high-voltage short circuit or a lightning bolt than a gunpowder explosion—and I speak as a survivor of all three—and the blast threw both Sally and the creature backwards.

I reached the bottom of the ladder, lowered myself and dropped down, landing heavily on the grass, feeling the shock of impact in my feet, knees and ankles.

Sally and the creature were both dazed. The thing gathered itself from something like a kneeling position to a crouch, and I swung the bronze head in its canvas bag hard, knocking the thing down, and then again and again.

The force of that blow from a solid object would have knocked out any human, but the thing was moving, albeit sluggishly. I suspected that was due to the thunderbolt rather than my actions, and that hitting it was futile.

Dropping the bag, I moved in to grapple, seizing on to the misshapen lump it had in place of a head. I reasoned that, like a human neck, this would have only limited articulation, and I wrenched it around violently in a way that would have broken a man's neck.

It clawed at my back, and the wings wrapped suddenly round my waist. I wrenched harder on the head, and harder still, and then I was turning and turning without any resistance, going around and around as though to unscrew the thing. I half expected the head to come away. It stayed attached, but dark gooey stuff leaked out from around its base.

The thing had stopped struggling. I unpeeled the wings from around me and let it fall free.

"Harry!"

Sally and I fell into each other's embrace, then I held her at arm's length.

I was aware of more shooting in the building beside us.

"Are you hurt?" I asked.

"My hand's numb," she said, flapping it about. "But I'm not hurt. But you—"

"I'm fine," I said, not knowing whether or not it was true. Maybe I had jarred a few things, and I could feel blood trickling down my back from where I had been clawed, but nothing that was going to slow me down for the time being. "Let me see."

It was only when I saw her hand that I realised. The ring, the engagement ring I had given her, the one set with that strange five-pointed stone from the Antarctic. That green stone, brought back by the Shackleton expedition and made by an ancient alien race, had produced the blast.

"Ooh," said Sally, opening and closing her left hand. "It's all pins and needles."

"Good punch," I said.

The stone, like other devices produced by the polar aliens, had a protective function against their enemies, as I had found during the Stafford case. The flying things were clearly also enemies of the polar breed, and the stone was able to repel them.

Looking back, I wonder whether I had been needed in the fight at all. The stone may have already struck the fatal blow, and it might have already been dying when I waded in. In any case, my view is that you cannot be too sure of these things. It is the mark of an amateur not to finish off an opponent and bring the fight to a conclusion at the earliest possible opportunity.

"Oi, you!"

Two police constables were standing at the end of the alley.

"Come out from there, this building is being cordoned off."

Sally and I were allowed out, and found that the area around the fire station was being roped off by the police, with sign boards announcing 'DANGER—MILITARY EXERCISE AREA—NO ENTRY'.

There were a couple of three-ton army lorries pulled up, and men in khaki wearing gas masks and carrying rifles were running about, taking up firing positions.

"What's all this about?" I asked.

"Military exercise is what it says," said the constable. "You two had better wait here a minute, if you don't mind."

A last shot rang out, and then the firing ceased.

"What for?" I asked, wondering what sort of trouble we might be in.

I was answered a minute later, when a man in the uniform of a major—but without any regimental insignia—approached us.

"These persons were—," started the constable, but the Major cut him off.

"I'll take it from here, Constable," he said. "You chaps secure the perimeter."

"Very good sir."

The Major glanced at us, and the alley, and noted the metal ladder. His lips pursed. This was an exit route his reconnaissance had failed to identify, and had not been sealed off properly. Without me, Prudence might have shot a couple of his men as they came up the stairs, then made its escape covered by the winged creature.

"Mr Stubbs, I presume," he said, extending a hand. "Major Harris, military intelligence. In charge of this, ah, special training exercise in modern urban warfare."

Two soldiers, still wearing gas masks, had entered the alley and now emerged with something slung between them, wrapped in canvas, which they slung unceremoniously into the back of a lorry.

"You were expecting to see me, Major?"

"We were briefed," he said, with a tight smile.

"You know what this is really about?" I asked.

"German spy ring led by the late Dr Vengler," said Harris, "who carried out some ghastly human experiments. Or, ah,— that's what we were told."

He raised an interrogative eyebrow.

"Something like that," I said.

More human-sized bundles were being loaded into trucks, along with crates piled with papers and other material. There seemed to be dozens of soldiers.

"Say no more," said Harris.

"Was there a woman in there?" I asked.

Soldiers were leading out captives now, big men with hessian bags over their heads, one of them with a bandaged shoulder.

"I mean," I said, "an actual woman, not…someone dressed as one."

"No," he said. "No actual woman. But if you're looking for Mrs Hardcastle, I have some bad news."

Mrs Hardcastle's body had been found on waste ground by the railway. She had been stabbed to death, her fingers broken where thieves had taken her rings. The assumption was that she had strayed into the wrong area, at the wrong time, and been attacked by robbers. So far as the world knew, that was the whole story.

After a short conversation with Major Harris, who noted, but did not ask to see, the head in the sack, Sally and I were released. We went back to the office to share the good news with young Arthur.

The situation at the office was ominous. The front door of the building had been broken down. I raced inside and up the stairs, and found my desk was on its side and the window open. At least there was no blood.

A library copy of Ivanhoe lay open on the floor where it had fallen.

"Is he here?" Sally called up from behind me.

My heart sank at the thought of having to tell Arthur Renville that his son was missing.

We quickly put the place to rights, finding no evidence of what had transpired, and with a heavy heart set off for the Electric Café.

"Mr Stubbs!"

I cannot express the feeling of joy I felt as young Arthur ran out from behind a corner. He looked completely unscathed.

I clapped a hand to my chest.

"What are you doing out here?" I demanded. "What happened?"

"Those men came!" he said. "The boxers. Five minutes after you left. They were banging on the front door, and I looked out and they were smashing it down!"

"What happened?"

"I remembered what you told me," he said. "About not getting into fights you couldn't win. So while they came in, I climbed out of the window and onto the tree there."

Arthur had previously commented that he thought he would be able to make the leap onto a convenient branch. I, of course, had forbidden any such dangerous messing around, but luckily his tree-climbing skills were as good as he thought.

"I couldn't get down so I hid behind the leaves," he went on. "I watched them through the windows. They threw the furniture about and left. They were shouting your name."

I was not sure whether the men would have returned to the fire station and been caught up in the general action there, or whether they might still be roaming about, looking for me at my other haunts. I now assume it was the former, because I never saw them again.

"You did well," I said.

"I was a bit scared," he admitted. "But I stayed hidden."

"Good thinking."

"I wrote down their descriptions right afterwards, like you said I should. What they were wearing and everything. And I saw the 'V' ever their eyes," he added excitedly, mimicking the inverted-shape with his fingers. "'V' for Vengler! And what I overhead them saying, but it was mainly 'where is he?' and things like that. But…I didn't stay in the office, because I thought they might come back, so I just hid over there until I saw you."

"Well done, lad," I said, patting him on the shoulder. "You did a good day's work there."

"What about you?" he asked. "Is the oracle in the bag? Can I see?"

I allowed him a peek at it, without really thinking.

"Why is it covered in blood?" he asked.

"You are going to have to learn not to ask so many questions," I said. "From now on, this is a story about German spies, a mad scientist and medical experiments, and nothing else."

"But that widow with the veil—"

"German spies," I said.

He looked puzzled and frustrated, but after a second his face settled. He was one of us now, one of those on the inside and in the know. Maybe that was better than having a good story for his friends—though he would have that too.

"German spies," he said, relishing the sound if it now. "A spy ring in London working for Hindenburg."

"You father will be proud of you," I said.

Epilogue: Church Bells

I am adding this hurried postscript simply to record that our wedding day did finally arrive—and passed in a flash.

It was not, by any stretch, a splendid affair. It was Sally's second marriage, and she preferred not to have too much fuss made about it, but both of us enjoyed every second.

The whole thing is a blur to me. One moment Ma was checking that my buttonhole was straight and admiring the fit of my rented morning coat, the next I was in the church, listening to the wedding march as Sally came down the aisle—and didn't she look wonderful—the next we were both giggling like children during the vows. Then it was the reception and the speeches and talking to one set of people after another, all happy and cheerful and excited, and the dancing, the next thing I knew it was late at night and the taxi was waiting to convey us to our hotel.

It was only a small affair, but even the minimum number of guests still made quite a throng. My brother and his wife, obligatory uncles and aunts, plus three cousins I had grown up with but not seen for years and their husbands and wives, a few friends from childhood who were now drinking companions and a few from the boxing ring, and of course my fellow lodgers, Thompson and Barnes, and my landlady.

I had to invite some people from my more recent career. Of course there was Captain Cross and his lady wife, Charlie Baxter the plumber, Captain Hall and his wife, Donny Bear who had been my driver on occasion with a lady friend, and Elsie Granger with her fiancé, Smith. Dr Blake was there of course, and surprised me by bringing the medium Elizabeth Belhaven as his escort.

Sadly absent was Mr Hoade, who, Smith informed me, was as well as might be expected. He had been admitted to the asylum on a precautionary basis due to his family's worries, but the prospects for his recovering his mental equilibrium seemed decent. I said to pass on my best regards.

There were an equal number on Sally's side, more than I could keep track of. I still do not know who half of them were. Her little boy and his cousins were no better behaved as you might expect for children of that age, but nobody minds a bit of running about and shouting at a wedding.

Sally had suggested using makeup to cover my facial bruising, but I was more embarrassed by the thought of makeup. Of course, everyone joked about it, but nobody seemed the slightest bit surprised. As the wedding photographs are black and white, bruising would not show up on them anyway. Arthur Renville was, of course, Best Man. I knew he would expect first refusal, given our long association, but I was delighted he could find time in his busy schedule not only to attend but to give a showstopper of a speech, relating several comical incidents going right back to my youngest days.

Sally's brother-in-law, Lucas, stood in for her late father, and I should have known that, with his vicaring experience, he would know how to speak well and hold an audience. His speech was not as funny as Arthur's, but did include some amusing anecdotes about Sally's girlhood, gleaned from her sister.

So many details of the day are lost to me. I do remember one moment, at the wedding breakfast, grinning across at Sally, and seeing the crates of real champagne in the corner, next to the table with the towering cake, and all the flower arrangements on the tables and every other available surface, and thinking how amazing and wonderful it all was. There were a pile of wedding presents to be opened too, making it feel even more like Christmas.

I can report Miss Frey did a sterling job as bridesmaid. She looked decidedly uncomfortable when all dressed up, but carried out her role as dutifully as Sally could have wished. I had been expecting her aunt to come as chaperone, but instead she brought Claudia Oldham—all in black, of course—and the two of them spent most of the time chatting with Dr Blake and his medium friend.

Arthur Renville Junior was also present, wearing a morning coat as though he had been born to it, mingling with the grown-ups, silently pretending to be Ronald Coleman with a glass of bubbly in hand. In the evening, he danced—once—with Miss Frey, after Sally told her it was expected. I believe his father put him up to it, by way of broadening young Arthur's life experience and giving him something more to boast about to his schoolmates. I cannot see the two of them being friends.

If I heard the joke about meeting my match once, I must have heard it ten times, and it was funnier every time. The same with the line about Sally being a knockout, which she certainly was.

Afterwards at the hotel we read through the stack of telegrams, some from absent friends and family, many from my old army mates, but others too. My old employers, Latham and Rowe, sent one, and so did the brothers Wu. And, a surprise, there was one from my old partner, Skinner, of all people, still evidently alive and in one piece, telling me what a terrible mistake it was to get married but wishing us both every happiness nonetheless.

And a telegram from Mr Bailey, on Mrs Bridges' behalf, with the usual best wishes for the future et cetera, and thanks for my good service. Despite the recent shocks, maybe she might make her centenary after all.

More sinisterly, there was one from 'my employers' at TDS wishing me all the best. I had half expected Miss de Vere to make a dramatic entrance to the church, like some evil fairy godmother. Evidently she was satisfied with sniping from a distance.

Anyway, I think I have spent enough time getting this all down on paper. Sally and I are setting off on honeymoon. We will be catching the train from Liverpool Street shortly—both our first experience of First-Class travel!—so I will just get this finished and sent off.

And whatever the future holds, Sally and I will face it

together, in what will be, I hope, what Dr Evans would call a truly symbiotic relationship.

Editor's Note

As usual, Harry Stubbs' narrative has stuck closely to established facts, but some notes are necessary.

While Paracelsus did visit the British Isles, no authenticated account of this journey has been found, and the travels described here must be considered apocryphal. If more of his lost writings are found and validated, the account may be confirmed.

On the other hand, Grim the Collier of Croydon, and the many associated works which are related by Hoade, are much as described. The author of the original remains unknown. Any connection with 'Baphomet', the head supposedly worshipped by the Knights Templar, remains speculative.

The West Norwood Fire Station has, since, falling out its original use, been employed for a number of purposes. These include, reputedly, illegal boxing matches.

The Hound of Mons is a well-established piece of trench folklore. It was popularised in a 1919 book by Captain L.F. Newhouse, who asserts that the medical experiments were carried out by one Dr Hochmuller. No supporting evidence has been found that such surgery is even possible, or that a doctor of that name ever existed.

The winged, partially fungal alien creature corresponds with a type known as Mi-Go described in H.P. Lovecraft's The Whisperer in Darkness (1931), a fictionalised account of events in New England. But, as with HPL's other works, this is no longer taken seriously by educated people.

-WB

About the Author

David Hambling is a journalist and author who has lived in Norwood, South London since 2000. He writes about science and technology for New Scientist magazine, The Economist, WIRED, Popular Mechanics, and writes a science column for Fortean Times ("the magazine of unexplained phenomena"). In addition to non-fiction books, his "Shadows From Norwood" project seeks to bring HP Lovecraft's Cthulhu Mythos to South London, via the Harry Stubbs novels and a number of short stories.

Visit the Shadows from Norwood Facebook page :

https://www.facebook.com/ShadowsFromNorwood

...for links, photographs, interactive map and more about the Harry Stubbs Adventures series

Curious about other Crossroad Press books?
Stop by our site:
http://crossroadpress.com
We offer quality writing
in digital, audio, and print formats.